I0732807

PRAISE FOR FREYA BARKER

Freya Barker writes a mean romance, I tell you! A REAL romance, with real characters and real conflict.

~Author M. Lynne Cunning

I've said it before and I'll say it again and again, Freya Barker is one of the BEST storytellers out there.

~Turning Pages At MidnightBook Blog

God, Freya Barker gets me every time I read one of her books. She's a master at creating a beautiful story that you lose yourself in the moment you start reading.

~Britt Red Hatter Book Blog

Freya Barker has woven a delicate balance of honest emotions and well-formed characters into a tale that is as unique as it is gripping.

~Ginger Scott, bestselling young and new adult author and Goodreads Choice Awards finalist

Such a truly beautiful story! The writing is gorgeous, the scenery is beautiful...

~Author Tia Louise

From Dust by Freya Barker is one of those special books. One of those whose plotline and characters remain with you for days after you finished it.

~Jeri's Book Attic

No amount of words could describe how this story made me feel, I think this is one I will remember forever, absolutely freaking awesome is not even close to how I felt about it.

~Lilian's Book Blog

Still Air was insightful, eye-opening, and I paused numerous times to think about my relationships with my own children. Anytime a book can evoke a myriad of emotions while teaching life lessons you'll continue to carry with you, it's a 5-star read.

~ Bestselling Author CP Smith

In my opinion, there is nothing better than a Freya Barker book. With her final installment in her Portland, ME series, Still Air, she does not disappoint. From start to finish I was completely captivated by Pam, Dino, and the entire Portland family.

~ Author RB Hilliard

The one thing you can always be sure of with Freya's writing is that it will pull on ALL of your emotions; it's expressive, meaningful, sarcastic, so very true to life, real, hard-hitting and heartbreaking at times and, as is the case with this series especially, the story is at points raw, painful and occasionally fugly BUT it is also sweet, hopeful, uplifting, humorous and heart-warming.

~ Book Loving Pixies

ALSO BY FREYA BARKER

Cedar Tree Series:

Slim To None
Hundred To One
Against Me
Clean Lines
Upper Hand
Like Arrows
Head Start

Portland, Me, Novels:

From Dust
Cruel Water
Through Fire
Still Air

Snapshot Series:

Shutter Speed
Freeze Frame
Ideal Image
Picture Perfect (Coming Soon!)

Northern Lights Collection:

A Change Of Tide
A Change Of View
A Change Of Pace

Rock Point Series:

KEEPING 6

La Plata County FBI
ROCK POINT SERIES 2

CABIN 12

FREYA BARKER

Cover Design:
RE&D - Margreet Asselbergs

Editing:
Karen Hrdlicka

Proofing:
Joanne Thompson

Interior Design: CP Smith

ISBN: 978-1-988733-10-4

DEDICATION

To the team of brilliant, strong women guiding my way in this book world: Karen, Joanne, and Stephanie.

Three forces of nature who have the ability to lift me when I get down on myself, are not afraid to correct me when I am losing my way, and don't hesitate to keep me humble when I fly too high.

Three individuals much more savvy and smart than I can ever hope to be, dedicated to making me better than I am.

Three beloved stars on my firmament.

CABIN 12

CHAPTER 1

BELLA

"Can you believe this?"

I squint to see through the windshield of our rig. Thick wet snowflakes obscure our vision as they hit and slide down the glass in a sheet of slush.

Mother Nature in the Colorado Rockies sometimes surprises us with erratic weather. In this case; a snowstorm in early May.

No, I cannot believe this shit.

Even yesterday, I was out and about in shirtsleeves, but sometime overnight this cold front settled in, and I had to wear a jacket going into work this morning. It wasn't snowing then, but it sure as shit is now.

"Days like this I wish I was back in New Mexico, where at least the weather is predictable," I share with Ryan Patterson, my partner.

An EMT, he drives the ambulance, while I usually

man the back of the rig. For years, I worked as an EMT in Farmington and finally went back to get my paramedic certification. When I moved to Durango, almost a year ago, I was lucky enough to get hired on as a paramedic through Mercy Hospital right off the bat, and have been teamed up with Ryan from day one.

He's a good guy, a little older, maybe mid-forties, with a couple of kids and a sweet wife. I'm happy to be matched up with a married man. It sets clear boundaries from the get-go, something I needed after maneuvering the blurred lines of a workplace romance. No chance of that with a good-hearted, family-oriented man like Ryan. He treats me like a sister. Not quite like my brother, Damian, who is protective to the point of overbearing, and doesn't trust me to look after myself, let alone others. Ryan actually respects me. He has no problem letting me take the lead on calls, and has faith in my abilities, as I do in his. Most men I know would feel called to take over, by mere gender distinction.

We make a good team.

Ryan pulls up behind a police cruiser at Joel's Bar on West 8th where we were dispatched. A single police officer is trying to disperse a small group of onlookers, crowding a man lying on the sidewalk. I quickly grab my trauma bag from the back and rush over to the prone man.

"What happened?" I ask the fresh-faced cop I've only seen around once or twice. Belker, or something.

"Slip and fall. Unresponsive," is the curt answer. I throw a quick glance at the young officer to see what his deal is, but he just looks nervous, keeping his eye on the crowd.

A low moan draws my attention back to the man on the ground. I'd guess he would be north of fifty, dressed in well-worn clothes not suited to our current weather, but I'm pretty sure he's beyond caring. The alcohol fumes rising up from him make me gag. I don't get any real response when I ask a few basic questions, so I quickly examine him on the spot as Ryan pulls up the stretcher.

"What've we got?" he asks, leaning in before he visibly recoils. "Other than inebriation," he adds quickly.

"Judging by the deformity of his left forearm, I'd venture to guess: fractured. Other than that, doesn't respond to simple questions so he may have hit his head. Let's stabilize him and take him in."

It takes us less than five minutes to get him secured on the stretcher and loaded up. In the meantime, another patrol car has shown up and I give a quick wave at the officers before climbing in the back of the ambulance.

I radio ahead, so the ER knows what to expect, and cringe when I hear the voice coming back at me. Dr. Scott Lipczyk, or LimpDick, as Ryan likes to call him.

"Get a saline IV going," he orders in that annoying drawl of his. "It'll save us time here. It's busy." Even just his voice makes my hair stand on end. The guy is a sleazeball.

"10-4," I quickly respond, effectively ending the call before I turn back to my patient.

He barely moves as I remove the strap pinning his arms to the board, so I can place the IV. Leaning over the gurney, I pull everything I need from the small storage shelves, when I feel a burn on my upper thigh. I rear back to find my patient grinning wildly, a switchblade in his good hand.

What the hell?

"Don't touch me," is about the only distinguishable thing coming from the man's mouth, as he struggles to free his legs from the stretcher. I immediately start pounding on the little window separating Ryan in the front of the ambulance, from us. I see him check his rearview mirror and nod. Right away I feel him put on the brakes. This isn't the first time he's had to give me a hand with an unruly patient.

I turn back to the man, who still struggles to get loose, with one arm strapped to his chest in a sling, and the other hand apparently unwilling to let go of the knife. He seems more terrified than angry. "Calm down," I coo, my voice steady and my hands up as I try to stay out of reach, with my back pressed against the side door. Not an easy feat in the confines of the ambulance. It takes just a minute for Ryan to round the rig and the door opens behind me.

By the time the two of us manage to get the knife away from him, and strap him back to the bed, the man is weeping.

"Jesus, Bella, he got you good."

I look down to see blood on my uniform pants, and suddenly I don't feel so good.

"Sit the fuck down." Ryan pushes me on the bench and starts rummaging through the shelves, coming back with a handful of dressing pads. "Keep pressure. We're a couple of blocks from Mercy. We'll get this guy and you looked after. Hold tight."

Before I have a chance to respond, I'm left alone with our patient, who is safely secured once again and looking at me with tortured eyes.

"It's okay. It'll be all right," I reassure him as calmly as I can, with my hands pressing down on the stack of pads covering the cut in my leg.

I'm still cooing at the distraught man when we pull into the ambulance bay at Mercy just minutes later.

"Let's go, Gomez," Ryan says, as he opens the door. "Can you stand?" He waves over a nurse with a wheelchair, and I realize he must've given the hospital a heads up.

Obediently, I sit down in the chair, but grab hold of Ryan's hand when he starts moving toward the back of the rig.

"Wait. Don't make a big fuss about this, please," I whisper, hoping the nurse can't hear me.

"What big fuss?"

"I mean do we need to notify the cops? Can't we just…"

Ryan bends down, his hands on the wheelchair's

arm rests and his big bulk hovering over me. "You know better," he says in a soft voice, but one that packs power. "I get why you'd ask, but I'm not willing to break rules and you shouldn't be either. Besides, they're already on their way." With that he straightens, turns, and walks to the back of the ambulance.

Damn. If the cops know, it means it won't be long before my brother—who is Special Agent in Charge at the La Plata County FBI field office here in town—gets wind of it. And he won't hesitate to barge in and try to force me to take a nice cushy inside job, instead of the one I'm doing. The one he thinks is too dangerous for me. Not for women in general, he's not that much of a misogynist, unless it comes to one of his sisters. Especially the baby sister, which would be yours truly.

Damian—dammit—his wedding is in ten days, and I'm supposed to be a bridesmaid for Kerry, his awesome wife-to-be. I frantically try to remember whether the thigh-high slit in the bridesmaid's dress is on the left or the right side. It's not gonna look pretty if the exposed leg is carved up. Shit.

Adding insult to injury, the attending ER doc, waiting for me in the cubicle I get wheeled into, is none other than Dr. LimpDick.

Fuck my life.

"If it isn't the beautiful Bella," he simpers, making me cringe. "Looks like I'll finally get you out of your pants."

My mouth falls open at the highly inappropriate

comment, and even the nurse, who luckily stayed, takes in a sharp breath.

"Just kidding," he quickly adds, realizing his mistake.

For months I've been evading his ever increasing come-ons. It's gotten to the point where I go out of my way to avoid him, since he clearly doesn't grasp the meaning of the word no. This man believes he is so irresistible, I'll eventually have to give in. What he doesn't know is that there isn't a fat chance in hell that will ever happen. Even if he weren't a blatant slick operator, I still wouldn't ever consider going out with him.

Not going that route again. I may make occasional mistakes, but never the same one twice. Not fucking likely.

I am tempted to ask for another doctor, but I noticed how busy it was when I was wheeled in. Every single cubicle looked to be occupied, and the brief glimpse I got of the waiting room wasn't much better. Besides, that kind of outright rejection would probably make occasionally working together even more difficult. I throw the nurse a look, silently imploring her to stick close, and from the slight nod of the older woman, I know she got my message.

Which is why I don't object when Scott helps me from the chair onto the bed and proceeds to cut off my already useless uniform pants.

The cut is bigger than I thought, close to five inches by the looks of it, but luckily not that deep. It is still bleeding, though. Thankfully quiet, he rinses the wound thoroughly before he starts placing careful stitches, only occasionally stroking his fingertips over my skin. The nurse, Brenda, sticks close by, until Scott is almost done and asks her to check on a patient for him while he finishes up.

I brace when she disappears through the curtains, an apologetic smile in my direction. I don't have to wait long for his hand to land just above my knee, as he leans into me.

"So when are we going to stop torturing ourselves, and you go out with me?"

"Look, Scott," I say, a little too loud, as I scoot further up the bed to escape his touch. "I hoped I'd made it clear to you I'm not interested. I don't date people I work with. Not ever." When he opens his mouth to protest, as he'd done before, I feel the need to go a step further. Something I'd avoided doing before, for the sake of our working relationship. "And even if I did; I'm sorry, but the answer would still be no."

The look on his face changes on a dime. From his smarmy smile, I'm now looking at flared nostrils and an angry scowl. The fingers of his hand dig into my skin so hard, I let out a yelp.

Suddenly the curtain is pulled open, and my initial relief at the interruption instantly evaporates when I see who's on the other side.

"Go, go, go, go!"

I swing the battering ram into the run-down bungalow's front door when I hear the order through my headset. We have surrounded what is supposed to be the hideout for one of the key players in a drug trafficking pipeline from Mexico to the East Coast. Close to two years of intensive investigation by a large number of agents across eight states, and with the involvement of Mexican authorities, coming down to carefully timed raids in a drive to eradicate one of the larger smuggling rings by the root. It's a given these guys won't go down easy.

The door cracks but holds, so I swing again; this time the doorpost splinters and the lock springs free. A well-aimed kick finishes the job and I drop the enforcer, about to make entry when a volley of rounds is fired from inside the house. With the shouting and chaos of a small army of law enforcement officers forcing their way inside, I can't quite get a bead on the direction of the fire. I step over the mangled door, a couple of guys behind me, with orders to clear the front two rooms of the house, but I don't get further than a couple of steps inside before a second volley knocks me off my feet.

"Officer down!" I hear yelling as I try to suck in air. Sliding down the wall in the hallway while the rest of the team surges forward, I realize they're talking about me.

There's a fucking elephant sitting on my chest and my lungs are burning.

Another volley of fire, this time from two different directions.

"Kitchen! Suspect down!"

The sudden quiet is disorienting after the high-octane pandemonium of seconds before, but I can hear the sound of footsteps coming this way.

"Let's get this fucking thing off," Dylan says, kneeling down in front of me as he pulls at the Velcro on my vest. He may be the youngest on our team, but Dylan Barnes is cool and collected under pressure. Someone I'm glad to have at my back. "He nailed you full in the chest."

Breathing becomes a little easier, although no less painful as I suck air into my lungs. Fuck, that's gonna leave a mark.

"Well, shit. Looks like he clipped your shoulder."

It's not the first time I've been shot, so I'm not surprised that it takes a minute for the pain to register as the adrenaline wears off.

"Load him up, take him to Mercy." I glance up to find Damian looking down at us.

"It's just a graze," I protest, trying to get to my feet, when I'm grabbed under my arms and hauled up.

"Bleeding nicely for just a graze, Jas. You're getting checked out."

Damian's expression clearly indicates he won't

take no for an answer, and since he's my boss—and my shoulder is starting to really fucking hurt—I don't argue this time.

"Barnes, get him seen to and get back here."

"Yes, sir," Dylan says to Damian's retreating back.

"Didn't get shot in the leg." I brush off the younger man when he tries to offer support.

"Ballbusters—the lot of you," he mutters, and he's not wrong. As the last to be recruited, he's still finding his place in the team, and it's our job not to make it too easy on him.

I don't argue when he opens the passenger door to one of our Explorers for me. I don't even make too big a fuss about him clipping my seat belt on. Truth is, my shoulder is killing me and I swear I cracked a few ribs, despite the bulletproof vest.

—

The ER is packed, but bullet wounds tend to draw immediate attention so I'm taken straight back. It doesn't take long for a doctor to come in and assess my wound.

"Bullet went straight through. I'm just gonna clean out any debris, put in a couple of stitches, and you're good to go."

The entire procedure takes no more than half an hour, before I'm left to wait for a few painkillers and a clean shirt to go home in. The one I was wearing is lying in pieces on the floor.

I lie back on the bed, closing my eyes briefly against the glare of the overhead lights, and listen to the constant hum of the emergency room. In the cubicle beside mine, I hear a man's voice, then the rustle of a curtain being drawn aside, and the sharp click of a woman's footsteps passing by. My ears try to focus on the low rumble of the same voice talking to someone else on the other side of the partition.

Then a woman's voice sounds; a lot clearer and I can hear every word. Recognition has me sit up straight in my bed, and I raise an eyebrow listening to her speak. There's an edge to her voice that raises the hackles on my neck, and when she lets out a sharp cry, I'm up and off the bed in a flash.

Ripping back the separating curtain, the sight of a hulking guy in scrubs pinning the painfully familiar woman to the hospital bed, has me seeing red. In two steps I have him by the scruff of his neck and pull him away from her; my boss's little sister, and the reason for a few too many sleepless nights.

Bella Gomez: curvy, lush-haired fireball, and general pain in my ass. A woman I met last year and have worked hard to avoid ever since. Other than the fact she is Damian's sister, she is the epitome of the kind of woman I'd prefer not to get myself burned on—a high-maintenance princess with sharp claws. She hadn't liked me any better than I did her. In fact, she made it clear I was no more than dirt under her designer heels the first time I introduced myself. Any attraction I may have felt to the luscious brunette, I quickly suppressed.

"What do you think you're—"

The guy had pulled himself up to his full height, which was still short of mine by a few inches, and puffed up his chest. One firm shove against his sternum has him suck up his pompous attitude.

"Get lost," I growl, glaring at him from under my frown.

"I'll call security," he sputters.

"Good. I'm sure they'll be thrilled to hear how you tried to force yourself on a patient."

"Jasper…" Bella's voice sounds from behind me, but I block her out. I'm too busy staring the asshole down.

The slimeball takes one last look at the bed, and me, before he almost runs out of here.

"Well, shit." This from the bed.

I swing around and take my first good look at her. Her legs are bare. A large bandage is covering her left thigh, which my eyes zoom in on.

"What the hell, Bella?"

"It's nothing," she says, trying to cover up with the sheet tucked under her, while shooting daggers at me. "Besides, you're a good one to talk. You look like you were run over by a tank and shot for good measure." She takes a thorough inventory of my bare torso, where even just the impact of the bullets on my Kevlar vest are showing up in vivid color.

"We're not talking about me."

"You may not be, but I am. Jesus, Jasper—were

you in a gunfight or something?"

Or something is right. I dig through my pocket to fish out my phone.

"What are you doing?" she swats at me as I'm scrolling through to find Damian's number. "Don't you be calling my brother, Jasper Greene!"

I grab her hand as it flies by again and hold on tight as I lean in.

"Then you'd better start talking," I threaten her without any compunction.

CHAPTER 2

BELLA

"Estás hermosa!"

A quick glance in the mirror shows my impatient mother sticking her head in the bathroom.

"Ma—give Kerry a break, will ya? We'll be out in a minute."

"Okay, I'll be right out here," Mom answers, leaving the damn door open a crack. I firmly pull it shut and return my focus on the bride.

I don't envy Kerry, coming into our family. We are an overwhelming bunch, my mother leading the pack. Damian had done a pretty good job holding Mom and my sisters off during the planning stages—a good thing, since my brother and his bride are going for a simple wedding, and that concept is not within my family's grasp—but the Gomez women swooped in two days ago to 'help' with preparations. Poor Kerry was about to call the whole thing off ten minutes ago, when my mother and oldest sister decided she needed a little 'fixing' and started fussing with her hair and makeup. She already looked perfect in her simple soft chiffon wedding dress and loosely gathered hair.

The moment she tried on that dress, it looked made for her: a fitted bodice with deep V-front, the back edged with lace that continued as wide straps sitting low on her shoulders, and the long skirt—a simple flare of chiffon. Both her best friend, Kim, and I told her she could stop looking.

When Mom got her first look at the dress this morning, she wanted to know where the sparkles were; that was the first time Kerry was almost in tears. This time, she actually burst out crying when my older sister, Gabriella, started pinning down the loose curls Kerry had wanted framing her face. She was dousing the poor girl in hairspray when she bolted and locked herself in the bathroom.

For the past ten minutes, I've been trying to restore her minimal makeup and relaxed hairdo, while simultaneously attempting to get her to stop crying, but the tears just keep coming.

"Ignore Ma," I say to her back, placing my hand on her shoulder. Her head is hanging low and her shoulders are shaking. I'm not sure I'm ever going to get her back together in time for the wedding. "Want me to get Kim?"

Kerry's maid of honor is trying to get her son to go down for a nap in the spare bedroom down the hall, while we finish getting ready. I'm already wearing my dove gray dress, similar in cut to Kerry's wedding dress, except instead of lace and chiffon, the bodice has fabric crisscrossing over the chest and gathered at the shoulders. Oh yeah, and there's the side slit in the skirt going to mid-thigh, luckily just hiding my newly acquired scar. That is, as long as I'm careful sitting down.

"No, leave her, I'll be fine," Kerry assures me.

"You sure? It's no problem."

"Positive." She turns around and I'm surprised to see her grin through her tears. "I'm a mess."

"I know, I'm so sorry." I grab a tissue and blot the tears under her eyes. "My family—"

"It's not your family. Well," she says, after a moment's hesitation. "It's not *all* your family. I was going to tell Damian tonight, but I'm afraid if I don't tell someone, I'll go nuts."

"What's wrong?" I'm instantly alerted. God I hope she's not sick—that would kill my brother.

"Not *wrong,* per se. I'm pretty sure it's a good thing. At least I hope it is." She nervously wrings her hands, a watery smile playing around her lips, and it dawns on me.

"Ohmigod! Really?"

"Shhhh," she admonishes me, her finger pressed to her lips. "Please, I don't want your mother announcing it to all the guests before I have a chance to inform the father. And don't you start crying—you'll ruin your makeup."

"He will be over the moon. I'm so happy for you," I sniffle, dabbing at my own eyes before folding her in a tight hug.

Twenty minutes later, I'm walking down the stairs in front of a blushing bride, both of us smiling around our happy secret, when I catch a pair of blue eyes in the group watching our descent.

Jasper.

I knew he would be here, since he's part of the wedding party, but I haven't seen him since he pulled Dr. LimpDick off me in the hospital ten days ago. He was absent at the rehearsal dinner last night, finishing up a case.

I'd convinced him I would handle Scott Lipczyk myself, and in return, he'd made me promise to tell my brother about the knife incident myself, or he would—right before a nurse came looking for him. I did tell my brother, albeit a slightly modified version of events—which already had him up in my face about career choices—but I hadn't really done anything to deal with Scott, other than avoid him. Dealing with his inappropriate advances would create exactly the kind of situation I'd been trying to avoid. Been there and wore the scarlet letter back in Farmington. Not something I'd care to repeat here.

With everyone's focus on Kerry behind me, I can feel his eyes glued to me as I self-consciously take the final steps, holding my skirt firmly in place. His gaze travels down the length of me, and I feel fully exposed when his eyes find my hand covering the scar peeking out. The moment my feet hit the hallway tiles, I turn my back and rush into the kitchen, needing a quick drink of water—and an escape.

Moot, as I discover seconds later, when he is waiting by the back door. I'd forgotten he's supposed to lead me down the garden path to where my brother is waiting by the edge of the Animas River to marry his bride.

The ceremony was lovely, and I swear I saw my brother surreptitiously brush away a tear. Something I will file away for future use, should I need some extra leverage.

Of course I was back on Jasper's arm, following the newly married couple back to the house, and just like the walk up the aisle, he was silent. A tad unsettling, since what little I know of him, he never seems at a loss for words. The silence felt ominous.

I'm reminded of that when I spot him coming out of the house, holding a beer bottle by the neck between two fingers, casually making his way over. I look for an escape but am weighed down by Kim's little boy, who I offered to watch while his parents dance under the strings of lights covering the roof of the rented canopy tent. Exhausted from the long day, Asher fell asleep on my lap in seconds, his warm cheek pressed against my cleavage. There's no way I can slink away with a sleeping toddler plastered to my boobs.

"Your scar is showing," he says, pulling out a chair and sitting down, his back to the dance floor.

"Shit." I try to reach around Asher to tug my dress into place, but part of my skirt is wedged underneath his little butt.

"Lift him up."

Fearing my family will make a scene if they see my injury, I do as he orders, but throw in a scathing look for good measure. A blush quickly replaces it, when I feel the surprisingly rough pads of his fingers brush the skin where my thick thighs are pressed together. My body responds immediately, and I'm suddenly grateful for the little boy on my lap, effectively hiding the evidence.

Damn that man. I mentally scold myself for responding to him the way I do. It's like it's genetically ingrained for me to be attracted to this type of guy. Handsome, charming, charismatic, and easily distracted by the next piece of fluff darting in front of his eyes. It's not healthy.

"Last thing I expected was to find you sitting here looking like some kind of modern-day Madonna with a child on your lap. I'd figured you'd be partying it up on the dance floor by now." His raspy voice draws me from my musings, and I'm not quite sure whether to be insulted or flattered right now.

"And I'm surprised you sat down to join me, I keep looking around to see where you might have left your flavor of the day."

Clearly I went with insulted, echoing back what I

choose to take as a negative characterization. His eyes go big in his head as he looks around him, appearing confused.

"Flavor of the day?"

"Your date? The tall blonde I saw you schmoozing with at dinner?"

Last thing I expected was the deep belly laugh escaping from his wide smile.

JASPER

That's funny, and not just because only someone of Bella's short stature would consider Kendra tall, but Neil would probably skin me alive if I just looked like I was coming on to his wife, Kendra.

Neil James is a fellow IT specialist, except for an independent agency our office has worked with on several occasions in the past. Fellow techie nerds, we've become friends over the years, so when he was held up on a case in Boulder and asked me to escort Kendra to the wedding, I didn't think twice. He and his wife have become family to me: something I haven't had much of in my life.

What's really amusing is the fact I wasn't the only one being evasive while keeping tabs on Bella. She clearly has been doing her own surveillance of my whereabouts today.

I'm about to tease her with that knowledge, when

a widely smiling Kimeo and her somewhat less expressive husband, Mal, walk up to the table. I'm struck at the similarities between the two women. From behind they could be twins; both sporting long silky brown hair, both rather short in stature, and both looking like absolute knockouts in those formfitting dresses, clinging to their respective lush curves. Mal is a lucky man, and from the way he handles Kim, he knows it too.

"Look at you," Kim comments, smiling at Bella. "I'm gonna call you the baby-whisperer. All day we couldn't get him to settle down, but five minutes on your lap and he's out like a light."

"Story of my life," Bella jokes, drawing a laugh from Kim, but a long hard stare from me.

"Here, let me take him." Mal bends down to scoop his son up in his arms. "We should be heading home. We have a bit of a drive."

"You're not staying at the hotel?" With people coming from out of town, I know Damian blocked off a bunch of rooms and cottages at the Apple Orchard Inn in Hermosa, only two minutes away, so folks don't have to drive home.

"As you have witnessed today, Asher is not a great sleeper anywhere other than in his own bed," Kim points out. "Trust me, the hour and a half drive will be well worth the good night's rest."

"Unless we can leave him with you." Mal grins at Bella.

"Normally, I'd be all over that," I'm surprised to

hear her say. "I love babies, but unfortunately I have an early shift tomorrow, so I have to be up and out the door by six thirty."

"Ouch. I'm guessing you won't make it too late either, then?"

"Too late for that," I contribute, looking at my watch. "It's almost midnight now."

"Then I'd better grab that dance with my pops before he collapses," Bella says, getting up. "I haven't had a chance yet. Too many women standing in line."

I'd noticed her father almost nonstop on the dance floor with just about every woman in attendance. The man knows how to dance, unlike yours truly, who was blessed with two left feet. I can hold a rhythm, that's not the issue, but don't ask me to make any complicated moves. It's not pretty.

I watch her head off in search of her father as I say goodbye to Mal and his family. I sit back to finish my beer, and as I'm taking the last tug, Bella is spinning around in her dad's arms, and an idea forms.

When the first strains of Eric Clapton's "Wonderful Tonight" stream from the large speakers beside the DJ I just bribed with a few bills, I walk up behind Bella, who is securely in her dad's arms. Mr. Gomez senior is as sharp as his son, since he's already wearing a grin when I approach and easily removes his hold on his daughter, spinning her to face me in the process.

"My legs are tired, *mi hija*. You need young legs to hold you up."

With that he walks off, leaving Bella momentarily

flustered enough for me to step into his spot, curving my arms around her. I ignore the fact her arms are still hanging limply by her side when I start my signature rhythmic swaying moves.

"Why?" Her softly uttered question is meant rhetorically, given that she is staring off toward the river as she reluctantly moves with me. Her hands come up to rest on my lapels, and aside from the fact you could drive a herd of buffalo between our bodies, she feels good in my arms. I feel inclined to answer her.

"Because I want to make up for whatever I have done to make you dislike me so much. Nothing more, nothing less." Those last words come out by rote, but as I'm saying them I know they're a lie.

Funny, isn't it? You have a firm picture of someone in your head, based on…nothing really. An impression based on an experience or comparison that has little to do with the person you're judging, but everything to do with *you.*

The truth is, if I hadn't assumed Bella was all cover—no content—I would probably have pursued her. The first crack in that mental image I had of her came when I saw her in that hospital bed, not a stitch of makeup, her hair pulled back in a utilitarian ponytail, and those damn sensible white cotton panties. The second came moments later when she begged me not to tell her brother some lunatic had carved her with a knife, because he would hound her until she gave up her job, and she loved her job. The third appeared when she pleaded with the cop, who came to take her statement, not to charge the drunk with assault, explaining her suspicion the man was suffering from hallucinations as a combined result of alcohol and PTSD. Of course a report had to be made, but she was so convincing, the officer listed reckless endangerment, as opposed to straight-up assault.

The whole hospital incident surprised me enough that she'd been on my mind these past days. And then earlier, when I watched her coming down those stairs, looking like fucking Venus de Milo, all curves and glowing skin, I'd already made up my mind.

But what really cemented it was watching her from a distance as she settled little Asher on her lap, and sang softly to the boy with her cheek to the top of his head, her eyes trained on the river, much like they are now. If longing had a look, this would be it.

Of course Bella wouldn't be Bella if she didn't come right back swinging.

"Puleeze. You haven't given me the impression I've been on *your* speed dial list, Jasper Greene. And besides, where is your date?" she asks, lashing out and doing it with a dramatic roll of her eyes I suddenly find cute instead of incredibly annoying.

"Touché. However, I have recently come to see the error of my ways when it comes to you, and my date is actually my friend Neil's wife, Kendra, whom I am escorting as a favor to her husband, who is held up on the other side of the state."

It's almost comical to see realization settle into

embarrassment on her face. She doesn't say anything, but she does slide her hands up to rest loosely on my shoulders. I'll take that as a win.

Still, when the song ends, she is off like a shot, mumbling something about needing to get home. If I didn't know any better, I'd say she was running from me. I head off after her—to make sure she's okay to drive home, or so I tell myself—when her father grabs my arm.

"She's a handful, that one. As fiery as she is beautiful. Growing up the youngest in a family of strong-willed people is not always easy. Everybody always knows everything better, does everything better. There isn't much you can claim as your own and whatever mistakes you ever make become your lifelong burden to carry." I don't tell him I wouldn't know, growing up in foster care, but I'll take his word for it and nod politely, not quite sure where he's going with this. "My baby, she picks a career that counters every expectation. My wife, she cried when Damian started working for the FBI, but she was laughing when Bella announced she wanted to be an EMT. She was mortified when she found out our girl was serious, but the damage was done. Ever since, our Bella has worked hard to prove she is good at what she does, but she never talks about it. Not with me, and not with anyone in our family. She's stubborn, my girl, but she deserves the best."

I'm not quite sure what message I just received, as I watch the older man walk away and get swallowed up by his family, but there was a warning in there somewhere.

Looking around, I can't find Bella anywhere, so I head inside where I bump into the bride splashing cold water on her face at the kitchen sink.

"Are you okay?"

She swivels around and grabs a towel to pat her face dry. "Fine, just a little hot from dancing. Where are you off to?"

"I'm looking for your sister-in-law, actually," I confess, and watch Kerry's eyes reach her hairline.

"Really? Well, she just darted out the front door to head home."

I'm already on the move before she stops talking, but I can hear her soft chuckle follow me. Outside, I find Bella digging through a ridiculously large purse she has perched on the hood of an equally ridiculously small car, cursing up a storm under her breath. I startle her when I walk up behind her, stick my hand in her purse, and come out with her keys firmly clasped in my hand.

"Jesus, you scared me."

"Sorry, I forgot to ask how your leg was." I realize how lame an excuse that is the moment it's out of my mouth.

"It's fine," she responds with a smirk, "given that I was just dancing with you."

"Right."

"How's your shoulder?" she counters. I inadvertently grab my left shoulder where, aside from the occasional pinch, my injury is healing just fine.

"Just about good as new." Determined to end the inane conversation that only seems to get more awkward, I change topic. "You sure you're okay to drive home?"

"I'm fine. I can take care of myself, but to put your mind at ease, I had two glasses of wine with dinner and only ice tea after." Her tone is still mildly annoyed, but her eyes look at me studiously, making me feel like a bug under the microscope.

"Well, good," I mutter, suddenly unsure what the fuck I'm doing here.

"Good," she echoes, unlocking her car door, which I hold open as she climbs behind the wheel.

Reluctantly I close the door for her, but when she starts the car, I follow my impulse to knock on the window. When she rolls it down, I bend over, stick my head inside, tag a hand in her thick hair, and kiss her surprised lips.

The taste of her is as sinful as her curves, and it takes an outside light, coming on over the garage doors, to alert me to the fact I'm standing in front of my boss's house, kissing the air from his baby sister's lips.

Abruptly I pull back, hitting my head on the fucking doorframe, and stupidly tap the roof of the car.

"Drive safe."

Turning around on my heel, I make my way back to the house, willing myself not to turn around and pull her from the car so I can kiss her properly.

I don't hear the car drive away until I have the front door open.

CHAPTER 3

BELLA

"So?" Kerry leans her elbows on the counter and props her head on her hands.

"So what?" I glance at her, my arms up to my elbows in flour, as I knead the dough for my pesto bread.

Today will be another invasion of my family, only a week after we were here last for the wedding. This time it's to send my brother and his wife off on their three-week Mediterranean honeymoon. They're starting off in Alicante, Spain, where they'll rent a car, travel up the coast, along the French Riviera, through Monaco, and into Italy. The plan is to end in Naples on the other side.

Personally, I could think of other things to do on my honeymoon than drive fifteen hundred miles or however the hell long that is, and soak up the culture. I'd probably find a spot on a beautiful beach, somewhere along the Riviera, where they serve drinks with umbrellas and park my ass in the sand for the duration. Confined in a car with my brother for three weeks is not my idea of a good time, but Kerry is over the moon at the prospect.

So we're having a party, and it is something worth celebrating I guess, because I can't remember a single time when Damian has gone away on a holiday. The send-off today was Ma's idea, not surprising, but she has no idea the reason my brother agreed so readily, is because he has his own agenda for this get-together.

I smile at the prospect. My mom is going to go ballistic, which is why this is actually a brilliant plan. Damian is no fool. He'll drop the bomb and hightail it out of town for three weeks tomorrow, giving my family—really just Ma and my sisters—a chance to calm down. Smart move.

Anyway, that's why I'm over at my brother's place on a Saturday morning, making my pesto bread, trying to ignore my sister-in-law.

"Well?" she prompts, and I briefly close my eyes. "I saw him go outside after you."

"He just wanted to make sure I was good to drive." I use the same excuse he gave me, but apparently Kerry's not buying it either.

"Right. And I guess you never cozied up with him on the dance floor either?"

"He was just being polite," I suggest, shaping the dough into two balls.

Kerry's derisive snort is loud, and I have to admit, the excuse sounds lame even to my own ears.

"Polite would've been dancing with your mother, but he only danced once, and that was with you."

"Look," I enforce, smacking a ball into one of the loaf pans. "You know I've never seen eye to eye with that man. He may be pretty to look at, but even if he were interested—which I'm sure he's not—there's not a chance in hell I'll let myself go down that rabbit hole again. I'm done with players, no matter how smooth his moves." Not to mention how soft his lips, but I'm leaving that bit of information out. I've been trying too hard to pretend that kiss never happened, I'm not about to share it with Kerry.

I fill the second pan and press down on the dough, when Kerry's hand reaches out and grabs my wrist.

"He's not like that. Jasper is a good man," she offers softly.

I don't even have a chance to respond when the front door slams open and the Gomez clan marches in, the house instantly filled with their loud voices. Kerry gives me a little knowing smile, and my arm a light squeeze, before turning to greet the family. I quickly throw a damp towel over the loaves for their final rise, wipe my hands, and steel myself before joining them.

<hr>

"Have you tried Papa's dessert wine?"

My sister, Chrissy, holds up a bottle for me. Christina is the second oldest in the family, after Gabriella. After her comes Damian, then Francesca, and finally me. Of all the women in the family, Chrissy is the most laid-back. That's not saying much, not in my family.

"I'll try some." I hold out my glass over the table, littered with the remnants of our dinner.

Also customary in my family is the sheer quantity of food for any gathering. Inevitably there are enough leftovers for everyone to enjoy another full meal the next night.

"Kerry? Would you like some?" Chrissy goes to pour some in Kerry's still pristine wine glass, but it is quickly covered with my brother's big hand.

"None for Kerry," he says, and a collective gasp of indignation can be heard.

Not from me; I'm smiling as I sit back in my chair and wait for the announcement I've been anticipating all night.

"Damian!" my mother exclaims, followed immediately by protests from the rest of the family.

I wink at Kerry, who wears a mild look of panic, but whose eyes are suspiciously shiny. A quick glance around the table finds my father quietly observing everyone, as he usually does, a gentle smile lifting his craggy face as his eyes land on his daughter-in-law. Very observant, my papa.

"Quiet!" Damian's booming voice instantly silences the acrimonious titter around the table, and all attention focuses on him when he gets up out of his chair. "I have an announcement to make." He lowers his eyes to Kerry, and the look of sheer adoration they share makes my heart ache. "We're going to have—"

"A baby?"

I'm sure they can hear my sister Gabby's screech back in Durango, and chuckle when Damian rolls his eyes to the sky in exasperation. In the chaos that ensues, my father's warm eyes find mine. This time the gentle smile is for me, and I hold on to his calm, a lone tear rolling down my cheek.

Later, when the family is getting ready to leave, Papa pulls me aside.

"Proud of you, *mi preciosa.* I don't know if I tell you enough. If it were up to your mother and sisters, they'd have you swept back home to Farmington, but you've thrived on your own. You've stuck your neck out, forged ahead to follow your dreams, instead staying safely in the family fold, and that fills me with pride." He holds me by my upper arms and gives me a little shake. "Don't let fear hold you back now."

I still have those words bouncing around my head when, ten minutes after the clan finally drives off, and I'm in the kitchen helping Kerry clean up, Damian suddenly barks out my name from the living room.

"What the fuck is this?" he asks, when I walk into the living room, Kerry on my tail. He's pointing at one of the pictures my family took at the wedding.

"What are you talking about?" Kerry leans over the back of the couch to get a good look. "That's

Asher on her lap.”

“Look at her goddamn leg,” he growls, his angry eyes never leaving mine.

“I didn’t know you got hurt. When did that happen?”

“That’s what I’d like to fucking know.”

“It’s nothing,” I start, perching on an armrest, intending to blow him off, but then Papa’s words come back to me, and I square my shoulders. “I had a patient with PTSD in the middle of hallucinations. I scared him, he thought he was defending himself.”

“Show me.”

“Damian, you can’t—”

“I want to see,” he grinds out between clenched teeth, cutting off his wife’s protests.

“It’s okay,” I assure her, figuring I’m in for a penny—in for a pound—and stick my leg out, lifting my dress to expose the scar.

“Jesus,” he hisses, taking a good long look. “Who is that son of a bitch? And why didn’t you call me?”

“It’s taken care of, Damian. I didn’t call you because I was trying to avoid a scene like this. You know these things happen. Besides, your right-hand man was right there looking after me.”

“What the hell—Jasper knew?” I realized my mistake the moment those words were out of my mouth. Last thing I wanted was for him to get in trouble over this.

“Leave him be. I asked him to keep it to himself.”

“He should’ve told me.” My brother is as stubborn

as the day is long. "And as for these things happening? They wouldn't fucking happen if you had the sense to pick a less risky job."

"Damian!" Kerry's admonishment is accompanied by a solid punch to his shoulder. "I can't believe you'd say that. That's misogyny at its worst! How dare you talk to your sister like that." Her sharp words clearly shock my brother, and his retort is meant to appease.

"She's my baby sister, it's my job to look out for her."

"Actually…" I interrupt their little spat on my account, "I stopped being a baby about thirty-six years ago, and looking out for me is *my* job—not yours."

Any gatherings with family are always exhausting, and this particular one leaves me feeling a little bruised. By the time I drive through Durango on my way home, I'm in dire need of some comfort. In my case that translates to food: unhealthy food.

I make the well-rehearsed turn into the McDonald's drive-thru and place my order. I'm almost ashamed to admit I recognize the shy smile of the kid at the window. The soft-spoken young man with his pock-marked face is like my dealer, the brown bag he hands me the fix I need to soothe my soul.

My favorite kind of drug—French fries.

JASPER

A quick glance at my watch tells me I stayed at the office much longer than I intended. It's easy to lose track of time when you're trolling the darknet for information on a possible security threat.

Last week, our office in Denver contacted me to give them a hand. Apparently there's been some online chatter, since the beginning of this year, suggesting major tourist destinations as possible ISIL targets, and I've been putting in extra hours, screening the net.

Tossing my reading glasses on the table, I run my hands over my face and through hair that could probably see a cut again soon. I'm beat. Sixteen hours a day, seven days a week on a diet of coffee and fast food, wears you down quick. And if that doesn't do it, lack of sleep will. The few hours a night when I'm actually in my apartment, and should be sleeping, are spent staring at the industrial ceiling.

I had plans to get some groceries, cook a proper meal, and spend the night watching something on Netflix to help my mind shut down so I could maybe sleep. Given that it's almost eleven at night—again— looks like that's not going to happen.

With a groan, I push myself up out of my chair, stretching my back as I do so. This shit is hell on my body too, and I haven't taken my bike out once since the snow melted. There was a time when I could go forty-eight hours nonstop, barely getting up from behind the computer to take a leak, but those days are gone. I'm feeling every one of my forty-one years after this week and am in dire need of exercise. This is underscored when I dive under my desk to unplug every single one of my computers—a habit I still haven't been able to shake, despite all the security walls I have put up—I swear my joints creak.

The sudden shrill ring of my phone, through the otherwise empty office, startles me and I shoot up without actually clearing my desk, banging my head, yet again.

"Greene," I snap, rubbing the bump on my head that never quite gets a chance to go down.

"You'd better have a fucking stellar reason why you wouldn't call me right a-*fucking*-way when my sister is in the damn hospital."

I'm tired, hungry, sore, and have a doozy of a headache forming, which is probably why I do something I rarely ever do.

Lose my cool.

"Last time I checked, your sister was a thirty-seven year old, grown-ass adult, who can stand on her own damn two feet! If she asks me to keep something to myself, I will fucking keep it to myself. You may try to run her life, but you sure as shit ain't gonna run mine. Now, I'd love chatting with you some more, but I've gotta get home: I haven't eaten since breakfast, haven't slept since sometime last week, my eyes are rolling out of their sockets, and I'm starting to look like Grizzly Adams on a bad day. Feel free to leave any work-related information in an email, but other than that, don't come pissing to me because your sister has to resort to secrecy to keep you off her damn back!" I take in a deep breath, expecting return fire, but the line is surprisingly silent. Good, 'cause I'm not quite done. "I'm going home to get some rest, so I can be ready to cover your sorry ass when you leave for your three-week vacation, and I suggest you do the same. And by the way—a good fucking evening to you too."

Now I'm done.

I end the call, turn the ringer off, and shove it in my pocket. My blood pressure is a little elevated, and I would normally work off any emotions on my computers, but I already shut those down. I take one last look around the office, momentarily tempted by the laptop I promised myself I'd leave behind. Still, I force myself to flick off the lights and pull the door shut behind me.

Looks like it'll be takeout again.

—

"Quarter Pounder with Cheese, a Southwest Grilled Chicken Salad, and a large ice tea, please."

Instead of my usual two Quarter Pounders, I order a single and the salad as a healthier concession to my recent lack of proper nutrition. Although, one has to wonder how 'healthy' those fast food versions of a salad really are. Definitely not something I'm going to concern myself with tonight. I'm too fucking tired.

I watch the kid—who looks like a much younger version of Ray Liotta, with the squinty eyes and acne-scarred skin—punch my order in on his screen and pull out my billfold to pay.

The place is deserted, and I sit down at a close by table to wait for my food, which always takes a couple of minutes this time of night. I should probably be worried I'm that familiar with McDonald's routines. I'd go somewhere else, if there were other places open this time of night between work and home.

Home is my one-bedroom apartment in the historic Jarvis building on the corner of Main. I'd much prefer a cabin on a mountain somewhere, but high-speed Internet can be a problem, and besides, this place is close to work, which means I usually just cycle in. Which reminds me, I need to get my bike out of storage. The weather has been nice enough since that last storm.

Just as I'm about to get up to see about my food, I notice a familiar candy-apple red Fiat 500 come out of the drive-thru. If my guess is right—and I'm betting it is, since there aren't that many people driving a dinky toy like that in the mountains—the woman who apparently raises my blood pressure, by mere mention of her name, will be behind the wheel. As the car passes by the window, I get a good look at the driver. It is Bella, and she looks like she's stuffing a fistful of fries in her mouth.

"Your order is ready to go." I turn around to grab my own meal from the kid behind the counter.

But when I head out to my car, I do it with a grin on my face.

CHAPTER 4

BELLA

"She's crashing!"

Fuck, I hate these calls.

A residential fire on the north side of town, in the early morning hours, resulted in a young girl—maybe five or so—pulled from an upstairs bedroom. By the time we got there, trucks from Fire and Rescue stations two and three were already on scene, battling what looked to be an out of control blaze. I'm not sure about the details, there was little time for that. We were notified there were two critical patients for immediate transport, so we weren't the only ones called out.

We weren't on the scene long, just barely enough to stabilize the little girl and load her up, while the other crew focused on the mother. The woman had managed to get a toddler and an infant to the safety of concerned neighbors, before apparently braving the spreading flames to pull the girl out.

You hear stories like this from time to time: people showing unimaginable courage and strength to save another. More often than not, it's when parents blindly risk their own lives to save their child.

The little girl had been stable before we took off. Badly burned and covered in soot, but she had a strong pulse and I managed to thread the five millimeter endotracheal tube through her rapidly narrowing airway.

Still she is crashing under my hands.

"Ryan! Step on it!" I call out over the din of the sirens, as I'm desperately trying to get the little girl's heart to restart.

I've lost patients in my care before. Sometimes their death is an inevitability even the most experienced hands or advanced equipment can't stave off. Sometimes you fight hard to keep them here, but they don't respond to anything you do. Those are hard. Those leave you with the nagging question if you did enough.

But I've never lost a child before, and this little girl will not be my first. It's not even a fucking option. Not after her mother went through a wall of fire to pull her out alive. Not on my watch.

I force my focus on counting compressions: …twenty-seven…twenty-eight…twenty-nine…thirty. Two quick breaths. One…two…

"Two minutes out!" Ryan yells over his shoulder.

"Hang in there."

—

Just two hours into my shift and I'm ready to call it done.

With the smell of smoke clinging to my uniform, I want to go down to the locker room for a quick rinse and change. I don't think I'll be able to make it through my day with that scent up my nose.

"I need a change," I tell Ryan. "I reek."

"Go, I'll finish up the paperwork," he offers. When I turn to walk away, he claps his hand on my shoulder and whispers in my ear, "You did everything you could, Bella."

I nod once, without turning around, and the moment he lifts his hand, I hurry down the hall. I manage to keep the tears at bay until I'm under the hot stream of water scouring the smell off my skin.

The girl's heart never started again. They worked on her for another thirty minutes before making the call. It was the sight of her father, who'd come rushing into the hospital straight from work just minutes after, which hit me hard. The burly man, still wearing tool belt and plaster dust that tagged him as construction worker, had crumbled to the floor upon hearing his daughter had died.

—

A steady stream of relatively minor calls helped get me through my shift, but as I close my locker after handing off our last patient of the day, the full weight of this morning's events settles back heavily on my shoulders.

"Let's go grab a drink," Ryan suggests. He's leaning against the wall outside the women's locker room, waiting for me.

It's on my lips to turn him down. For the past couple of years, I've avoided hanging out with people from work, and the last six months I was still living in Farmington I'd even started shying away from the few friends I'd maintained since high school. Any socializing these days is with my family; mainly Damian and Kerry. I wouldn't turn to my brother with this, it would only fuel his displeasure with my chosen profession. Kerry is the one I'd seek out, but they're traipsing around Europe for another two and a half weeks.

For a brief moment, I entertain the thought of calling Jasper, but quickly dismiss it. I haven't heard a damn thing from him since he stuck his head through my window and ambushed me with a kiss. I will not be that girl again, the one who runs after a man she knows better than to involve herself with.

"Sure," I therefore agree. God forbid I'm tempted to make stupid decisions when I'm this vulnerable. Going for a drink with Ryan is the safe choice.

I follow him to The Irish Embassy Pub on Main and West 9th, and luck out when a car pulls away from the curb, halfway down the block. I've been here only once before with my brother, which is how I know it's a favorite hangout for first responders. I probably would've preferred a quiet table in the corner of any other establishment, but Ryan insisted.

About halfway through my second—and final—glass of wine, I'm starting to see why.

I spent the past hour and a half talking about this morning's call, mostly with people who were there on the scene. Sharing experiences turns out to be therapeutic, especially when you discover you're not the only person who feels unwarranted responsibility for the outcome.

I'm actually chuckling at a joke from Bert, one of the older police officers I'm sitting next to at the bar, when someone comes barging in the door.

"Officer down!" the man calls out, and instantly you can hear a pin drop. "The parking lot of Whitewater Park."

Suddenly there's a cacophony of scraping chairs and a rush for the door by about a third of the crowd. After the door falls shut for the last time, the hum of conversation builds again as snippets of information starts filtering in. Even Bert, my neighbor, has his phone out and relays bits and pieces he picks up in a monotone voice.

Apparently a young couple pulling in at the park—for some private time at the river's edge, I'm sure—found an officer bleeding beside the open driver's side door of his cruiser and called 911. No one else was in the parking lot.

"Do they know who got shot?" I ask, knowing a few of the officers myself.

"Young kid, pretty new on the force. I barely know him," Bert, who didn't follow the stampede out the door, answers as he takes a long deep drink of his beer. "Name of Belker?"

Jesus. The same cop I almost tore a strip off for being rude the night I got knifed. Kind of a jittery guy, from what I remember.

"Dead?" I ask, not sure I even want to know the answer. I've already had my fill of death today.

"Still breathing when your guys got to him."

"Do you know what unit?"

"Dunno."

It doesn't really matter anyway, I'm pretty confident whoever showed up at the scene would be busting their asses to keep him alive.

"Are you heading to Mercy?" I ask, eyeing Bert who has aged at least fifteen years since ten minutes ago.

"I will in a bit."

Suddenly bone-tired, I abandon my half glass of wine and head over to where Ryan is talking on his cell.

"*I'm off,*" I whisper.

"Hang on," he tells whomever is on the line. My guess is his wife, like most families of first responders probably would've by now, she likely heard of the shooting through the grapevine. He presses the phone against his chest and turns to me. "If you give me a minute, I'll walk you outside."

"Nah—no need. I'm parked right outside," I brush him off. "See you tomorrow? Say hi to Beth."

With a half-hearted wave to a defeated-looking Bert at the bar, I head home, where I have a good book and half a bottle of wine waiting to keep me distracted.

I hope.

JASPER

For once I'm out of the office at a decent hour. If you can call eight thirty decent.

Early enough to cook a proper meal in any event.

Stopped at the traffic light to turn left, I hear sirens. A few seconds later, four or five police cars tear through the intersection, heading south. Curiosity almost has me switch to the right-hand lane to have a look, but a rumbling stomach has me stick to the left side. I'll check the scanner when I get home.

I turn it on first thing when I get in the door and try to get a handle on all the crackled chatter flooding my apartment. Pulling open the fridge, I'm hit with the distinct smell of something rotting in there. A steak I thought I'd pulled from the freezer just a couple of days ago has a slightly green sheen, and whatever vegetables I had in the crisper are now wrinkled and floating in a dark oozing soup. I'm in worse shape than I thought, I'm going to have to hit up the City Market before I can eat.

Just as I finish tying up the garbage bag that now holds two-thirds of my fridge contents, my phone rings.

"Are you listening to your scanner?" Dylan jumps in when I answer.

"Yes, but other than the ABP on an armed suspect in a black, older model Honda Civic missing a rear license plate, I can't make heads or tails of it. I saw a bunch of units go by, south on Highway 160."

"Cop got shot in Whitewater Park. First call came through maybe thirty minutes ago. It's been nonstop since then."

"You're shitting me. Bad?"

"Doesn't look great from the sounds of it. I'm thinking half the force will be in the waiting room at Mercy. Want me to call Blackfoot?"

I'm tempted to say yes, since Durango PD Operations Commander Keith Blackfoot and I do not exactly see eye to eye. I'm not a huge fan of his particular brand of humor, usually at someone else's expense, and nothing I've learned over the past few years of working in close proximity with the police department has been cause to sway my opinion. Still, since I'm in charge of the office with Damian on his honeymoon, I don't think I can pass this off.

"I'll take care of it. Could you give Luna a heads-up?"

"Okay. I'm gonna check in at Mercy. I have a few friends on the force."

"Keep me updated."

"Will do."

The moment Dylan hangs up, I try Blackfoot's number. I almost expected it to be busy, so quickly shoot off a text without guilt. The tone politely concerned, at least I hope it is, and an offer for any assistance the police department may need. That should do the trick.

I barely have a chance to stuff my phone back in my pocket when a return text comes through.

Thx, be in touch.

No longer in the mood to pretend I'm in any way, shape, or form domestic, I grab my keys and the garbage bag I'll toss in the dumpster, and head out the door to grab some Chinese food from May Palace down the block instead.

I'm just walking out of the restaurant with a quantity of food to tide over an average family, and a stomach growling with hunger, when I spot a familiar mane of shiny brown hair bouncing against a well-rounded ass across the street.

"Bella!"

She's just about to step off the curb behind her little red car, when she turns her head and spots me. Her car door is already open by the time I jog up to her.

"What are you doing here?" she asks tentatively.

I hold up my bag to show her. "Grabbing a bite. I live a block over. What about you?"

"I was just having an after-work drink with my partner on my way home. I should get going. Did you hear—"

"Look, there is—" We both start talking at the same time. "You first," I offer.

"Oh, I was just going to ask if you'd heard about the shooting."

"That's what I came over here for. I heard, and the shooter is still out there. Toting a gun and probably pumped up on adrenaline—I don't want you out on your own." I can tell from the eye roll, Bella is less than impressed.

"I'm going straight home. Wasn't exactly planning to wander around town." There's the attitude that works like a red flag on my otherwise laid-back demeanor.

"Need I remind you, your place is halfway up a mountain and fairly secluded?" And there I go, destroying what little goodwill I may have had left after kissing her and bailing.

"I'm perfectly well aware, since I've lived there for almost a year—as you seem to have forgotten."

"But we haven't had armed and dangerous suspects on the run from an entire police department on the hunt. My guess is the guy is in a hurry to get off the road, trying to find a place to lie low. Where better than in an empty house, halfway up a mountain road, mostly hidden from the road?”

“I’m not an idiot. I have a gun in my bedside table.”

“That won’t do you much good if the guy is already hiding out in your house. Or forcing you off the road before you get there, because he needs another vehicle.”

“I’m not an idiot,” she hisses, folding her arms under her ample chest, and I’m momentarily distracted. It doesn’t go unnoticed, and now she’s not only annoyed, she’s pissed.

Yup, I most definitely annihilated any remaining cordiality. Taking a deep breath, I try again, this time without the sarcasm. “Let me follow you home. I’ll do a quick check of your place, make sure your windows are secure, your gun is still where it’s supposed to be and properly loaded. It takes five minutes and then I’m outta your hair, and you can lock your doors behind me.” She tilts her head, clearly considering my words, so I give it an extra push. “You already got me into your brother’s bad book by keeping information from him, how do you think he’ll react if he finds out I didn’t make sure you got home okay?”

She looks a bit guilty as she shrugs her shoulders, and I know we’ve turned a corner.

“Fine,” is the reluctant response.

“Give me a ride to my truck, I’m parked behind the Jarvis.”

I don’t give her a chance to respond, and scoot around the car, where I open her passenger door and fold myself into the seat. From the corner of my eye, I see her slide behind the wheel, her lips pressed together. The moment I turn my head, just about the only part I can move, she bursts out laughing.

"Comfy?"

Smartass.

"Other than my knees bumping my chin and Dandan noodles leaking into my belly button? Just ducky, thanks."

BELLA

Okay, so I may have put up a fight, but I'm secretly relieved Jasper pushed hard to see me home.

The truth is, I was already doubting the wisdom of heading out alone, when I realized how deserted Main Street was as I walked out of The Irish. Normally, the old downtown area is bustling. Day and night. Especially now that we've hit more pleasant temperatures and the tourists have started flooding in. It even was busy earlier when we got there.

The eerie quiet was ominous, and I was hustling to get to my car, when I heard my name called. My initial response had been relief at seeing him, if I hadn't had a minute to steel myself as he ran over, I might actually have hugged him. I am that emotionally strung out. Luckily attitude comes natural to me, and I freely fling it around to hide my vulnerability.

But with Jasper twisted like a pretzel in my cute little ride, his Chinese food crushed somewhere between the tangle of his legs and his folded torso, I can't hold on to my bratty facade and burst out laughing.

I'm still laughing, tears running down my face, when I drop him by his more appropriately sized Dodge Ram. By the time I turn out of town onto the 160, his big gray truck right on my tail, I'm crying. From one minute to the next, I'm a sobbing mess. I have to wipe my eyes constantly to be able to see, because now that I've let loose, it looks like I can't stop.

I'm grateful I didn't drive myself into a ditch when I pull up in front of my little house, but I've barely had a chance to turn off the engine when my door is yanked open, and Jasper is in my face.

"What the hell is wrong with you? You're swaying all over the road, almost getting—" His mouth snaps shut when he notices my sorry state. "You're crying?"

I have it on my lips to give him a catty retort, but when I open my mouth all that comes out is another sob.

Apparently that's enough for Jasper, who pulls me out of the car and wraps me in a bear hug.

"I fucking hate crying," he mumbles in my hair.

"Sorry." My voice is muffled against his chest.

"Don't apologize," he whispers.

"*Okay.*"

At some point, my arms may have slipped around

his middle, because I'm reluctant to release my hold when he tries to disengage.

"Gonna have to let me go if I'm going to check out your place, Squirt."

CHAPTER 5

Bella

Squirt?

Last person to call me that was my brother, about twenty years ago, and he earned a karate kick to the gonads then. Never mind it was intended for his gut, which I didn't quite manage to reach. I'm short, I've known that my whole life, I was teased enough. I didn't need Damian to remind me of it in front of my then boyfriend, whose name I've long since forgotten. It was one of those things, like being tagged as the baby of the family, which grates on you when it's used dismissively.

It didn't sound that way coming from Jasper, and I'm not about to bruise his precious jewels; I'm too busy staring at his tight back end as he walks up to my door, dangling my keys in his hand.

I was told to wait in the car, which I didn't argue.

I just lived through my first winter here, and let me tell you, it is quiet here when there's a pack of snow sucking up any sounds. Yet the silence and solitude never felt as oppressive as it does tonight.

He slips in the front door, and I suddenly remember the disaster I left in my kitchen this morning, when I had to rush out of the house because I was late. I'd woken up with a craving for my mother's stuffed waffles and thought I'd have time. Given I'm a rather enthusiastic cook, I'm sure the waffle iron I left out on the counter is not the only thing wearing drips of congealed batter.

As I watch lights come on inside, I mentally go through every room, trying to remember if I left any other disasters. Not that there's anything I can do about it now. It's just a few minutes before Jasper steps onto my small porch and waves me over.

"All clear," he calls, and I grab my purse, get out of the car, and walk up to him. "Except maybe your kitchen. You might want to call a hazmat unit out for that."

"Whatever." I bite down a grin as I squeeze by him to get inside. I hear him following behind me, closing the door.

"You may want to clear your unmentionables from the kitchen before you invite them in, though."

My eyes shoot up and immediately find the pile of lacy underwear on the counter, beside the door to the small laundry room. I'd planned to hand-wash those this morning, when I got distracted by my mother's waffles, and forgot all about them when I rushed out. I move fast, snatching the pile off the counter and tossing it into the laundry room. Jasper's chuckle sounds behind me as I pull the door firmly shut.

"What are you doing?" I ask, when I turn around and see him wiping down the waffle iron with my dishrag.

"Cleaning this mess so we have room to sit down and eat."

I open my mouth to object, when a timely rumble reminds me I haven't had anything since this morning's waffles. All I have sloshing around is a whole lot of coffee and a glass and a half of wine.

"Are you sharing?" I ask instead, earning me a grin.

"I'll go grab the food." With an overhead lob, he tosses the rag in my sink and heads out to fetch the May Garden bag from his car.

—

"Whoa, this shit is spicy." I wave one hand in front of my mouth while the other reaches for my water glass.

"Mmmm…best Dandan noodles in town," Jasper mumbles around a mouthful.

I'm not sure how much Jasper normally eats, but the sheer volume of food he pulled from that crumpled bag was impressive. I still can't quite believe I'm sitting at my kitchen counter at nine thirty at night, having dinner with Jasper, of all people. He expertly handles the chopsticks that came in the bag, but I opted for a fork. Never quite mastered those things.

"It's good," I agree, shoving another bite in my mouth. "I grew up on mostly Mexican and Southwestern cooking. I like a little heat."

"I'll say."

I drop my fork and turn to him, my hackles immediately up.

"What does that mean exactly?"

Jasper shrugs casually, unmoved by my sharp tone, as he slowly turns his eyes on me. "Only that you're highly flammable. Fiery." I huff, trying for indignation.

"So I have a short fuse; I'm passionate, it's my Mexican genes."

That earns me a snort from Jasper. "I don't think it has much to do with that. You forget I know your brother."

"He's an anomaly in our family."

"And I met your father, he's a pretty cool customer."

"Yes, but the rest of us take after our mother," I point out.

He bumps his shoulder into mine, chuckling. "Your mom is from Texas, not Mexico."

"Whatever," I mutter around the piece of Kung Pao chicken I quickly shove in my mouth, annoyed. I can feel Jasper's eyes studying me as I chew.

"So what was with the tears earlier?"

I almost choke on a piece of chicken shooting

down the wrong hole. Jasper pats my back when I start coughing.

"It's nothing," I manage, when I'm able to breathe again.

"Can't be nothing. It's the first time I've ever seen you cry."

I roll my eyes, but he seems unimpressed; just keeps scrutinizing me with those baby blues.

"Fine," I eventually give in. "I lost a patient this morning."

"I'm sorry." The simple comforting gesture of putting his hand on my knee is enough to threaten tears again. He's right, I don't cry that much, not in front of others anyway. "Want to talk about it?"

"No, I don't want to talk about it," I snap, annoyed when I feel a tear slipping free.

Yet, not a minute later, I find myself spilling the entire story, from the moment the call came in, up to and including, the part where her father goes to his knees in the hospital hallway. By this time Jasper is gently stroking my back as I snatch up a napkin and dab at my wet cheeks.

"I don't normally—" I start to apologize for emoting all over him, when he cuts me off.

"I know, which only goes to show how much you needed to let that out. Tough call," he adds sympathetically.

"Yeah. And then the shooting. I just saw Belker on a call, not too long ago. He was jittery as a June bug."

"Belker, is that the cop who got shot?"

"He's just a baby, fresh from the academy."

JASPER

I bite my tongue not to let it slip that the guy didn't make it. After the day she's had, she'll have a hard enough time getting to sleep tonight, without me telling her about the message I received from Dylan while I was going through her house.

Bella stifles a yawn, as she gets up and starts clearing away the remnants of dinner. We made a good dent, but there's still some left.

"Let me put that in your fridge. You'll have enough dinner for tomorrow," I offer. I have a feeling I won't be home much in the days to come anyway. "It's just gonna spoil in mine," I quickly add when I see she's about to protest.

"In that case, thanks." The weary smile she gives me is sweet nonetheless, but then her expression turns serious as she puts her teeth in that plump bottom lip of hers. "And thanks for listening. That was…kind. I normally do okay processing through work stuff by myself, or sometimes I'll talk to Kerry, but…"

"She's on her honeymoon," I finish for her.

"Right. Besides, I don't know if I would've shared this call with her. Not now that she's…"

"Pregnant?" I complete her thoughts again. Her

eyes shoot to mine, surprised.

"You knew?"

"That's why they pay me the big bucks, for my superior powers of deduction." I grin when she rolls her eyes. "Actually, I tried to offer her wine twice at the wedding, which she refused, and then I caught her in the kitchen with her head under the tap when I went looking for you."

"Clever. I see not much gets by you," she pokes, smirking, but her eyes are weary when she looks at me. I bet I know what she's thinking about and it's time to air that little bit.

"I kissed you," I blurt out. "I promised myself I wouldn't—that I'd be buying myself a whole lot of trouble if I did—but I did it anyway." A pretty blush creeps up her neck and stains her cheeks a deep pink, which I mistake for bashfulness.

"So that's what you think of me? A whole lot of trouble?" she asks sharply, instantly setting me straight.

"Actually, your brother," I correct her. "He's my boss, and given the fact he won't be happy to find out I'm thinking of you like that, it could seriously impact our working relationship."

"Thinking of me like what?" She looks at me from under the thick fringe of her eyelashes. I grin and step into her space, putting one hand on her waist. With the other, I slide her thick hair off her shoulder before curving my fingers around her neck, forcing her to look up at me.

"Like I want to have my hands all over your curves, my mouth on your skin, exploring every inch of you," I confess, as her mouth falls open in a perfect little O.

"You don't even like me," she whispers.

"I like you fine, attitude and all. I've just tried to steer clear of you, for everyone's sake."

She seems to need a minute to think on that and lowers her gaze to the middle of my chest. I use the time to feel the soft skin of her cheek with a light brush of my thumb. I inhale deeply of her scent; something subtly floral, maybe her shampoo, when she raises her eyes back up.

"Yet you kissed me anyway."

"I did. Thought maybe if I could get it out of my system…" I let my voice trail off when her tongue pokes out for a quick lick along that bottom lip, distracting me momentarily. "It didn't. Quite the opposite, in fact. I've tried to drown myself in work, but clearly that's not working either, since I'm here, standing in your kitchen."

"So you are." I'm fascinated by the way her eyelids lower, her lips slightly part, and her head tilts to the side. Added to her sultry voice, there is no mistaking the invitation.

Fuck me, a saint would be tempted, and I never claimed to be one. Yet before I can lower my mouth to take her up on the invite, she stifles another yawn, and I firmly step back. She's clearly tired and vulnerable from the events of the day, it wouldn't be fair to take advantage of that. Granted, tomorrow her attitude will likely be back in full swing, and her silent offer may no longer be on the table, but maybe that's for the best.

"You need to get some sleep. You're swaying on your feet."

"I was just about to kick you out," she lies, enhancing her words with an exaggerated yawn. "I'm as worn out as a cucumber in a convent."

Three hours later, staring at my ceiling, I'm still chuckling.

-

Four hours after that, my phone wakes me up.

"Yeah?" I groan, not bothering to look who's calling.

"Morning, sunshine!" Dylan chuckles in my ear, much too chipper.

"What time is it?" I manage, rubbing the sleep from my eyes.

"Almost six thirty. Thought I'd give you a quick update before you head in."

"Give it to me from the top."

I swing my legs out of bed, pad over to the bathroom, and hit mute on my end of the call, so Dylan doesn't have to listen while I relieve myself.

"The cop's name was Christian Belker; new guy. He pulled over the black Civic with the missing license plate, and checked in with dispatch before exiting the cruiser. Looks like he barely made it out, when he got shot twice. He never even had a chance to unclip his sidearm. One bullet caught him in the shoulder and the second went in just above his ear. They figure he was about to close his door. He was all but gone when the first unit showed up. Autopsy scheduled first thing this morning. CBI was called in to process the scene. No shell casings found."

The CBI, Colorado Bureau of Investigation, has an office in Durango as well. They're frequently called in by either the sheriff's office or police department to assist, often to provide forensic support.

"Sounds more like an ambush. Targeted. Anything on the car or the perp?" I ask, unmuting the phone as I dry my hands.

"Perp is still out there somewhere, but the car matches the description of a vehicle reported stolen two days ago from behind the Walmart, just a couple of miles south of the park on South Camino Del Rio."

"What about a dash cam? His cruiser outfitted?"

"Apparently. They're tight-lipped about specifics though. I'll see what I can find out."

"You sleep at all?" I ask, Dylan's enthusiasm for the job often interferes with his self-preservation. Damian's sent him home more than once.

"Sure," he says easily, but I can hear the smile in his voice. "Pot calling kettle."

"Dude, you've got a kid. You've gotta learn to pace yourself, or you'll burn out." Dylan is the single parent of a seven-year old boy, and although I know his mom and stepdad help out quite a bit, I have no idea where he finds the energy. It's bound to run out one day. I have a feeling he is driven by something more than just his love for the job, but like most of us on the team, we're not always good at sharing that stuff, and not just because we're guys. Luna Roosberg, the only female agent on our team, is even more reserved than the rest of us. She's a kick-ass operative, and I'd trust her to have my back under any and all circumstances, but other than her name and the fact she cleans up fucking nice in a dress, I know virtually nothing about any life she has outside of the agency.

"I know. I really did sleep, I'm just up because I had to get Max up for school anyway," Dylan assures me.

"Fine, get him off to school and grab some more sleep. I'll head into the office shortly and don't want to see you there until noon, at the very earliest."

"But the autopsy—"

"I know. I was going to check in with Blackfoot anyway. I'm on it."

CHAPTER 6

JASPER

"What do you want, Greene?"

I stop just inside the door and raise both hands defensively.

Judging from the collection of half-empty coffee cups, food wrappers, the gaunt face, and hair sticking out every which way, I'd say our Detective Blackfoot has been going nonstop. This might explain the snarling attitude, accompanied with warning glare he shoots me.

"Just here to offer help, Blackfoot." When he looks at me suspiciously, I add, "We closed two cases this week so far, we've got some time on our hands. Not looking to step on any toes."

Keith rubs his face in his hands, before waving me in. "Close the fucking door, will ya?"

"Sorry about the loss of your officer," I offer,

when I sit down across from his desk, the door duly closed. His bloodshot eyes come up and there is no sign of the cocky player I had him pegged as. This is a man suffering under the weight of his responsibilities.

"Fucking kid. Just got off the phone with his father, a farmer in Crete, Nebraska. The man wants answers, and I have none to give him."

I make a sympathetic noise before asking him, "Run by me what you couldn't tell him. Fresh eyes, more resources."

He regards me for a second, then slides a folder across the desk before sitting back in his chair, and folding his arms behind his head. I flip open the folder to find autopsy photos and a detailed report on findings.

"You got this back already?"

"Coroner had him on the slab at six this morning. We needed those slugs."

"Nine millimeter," I confirm, scanning the report. "One entering the body at the left shoulder, cut a path through the joint and soft tissue and was found lodged in the clavicle. The other went in right above the ear and ricocheted inside the skull, instead of exiting." I look up at Keith. "Shooter must've been at a fair distance for those bullets not to go straight through."

"I figure," he answers. "Trajectory was upward at a moderate angle. I'm guessing the guy never got out of his car."

"Both distance and angle would indicate a pretty damn good shot."

"Slugs are with CBI, once they run some ballistics tests, I'm sending someone to check local shooting ranges."

"I can run the test results through our Federal database when you hear back. Dash cam tell you anything?"

"Fuck all. This wasn't a traffic stop gone bad," he suggests, turning to stare out his window. An assessment I'm already in agreement with.

"Doesn't sound like it. I understand he never unclipped his holster?"

His chair squeaks as he swivels back to face me. "I'd like to know where the fuck you got that information." I shrug, but stay silent. There's no point. "*Christ,*" he finally hisses, exasperated.

After that he seems to brush the chip off his shoulder and takes me through all he has, which isn't a whole fucking lot. Too many directions to go in and not enough leads. Without any witnesses, we have to make do with what we know; nine-millimeter slugs, and a stolen Honda Civic.

"Are you pegging him for local?" I ask. I figure with the car stolen in the Walmart parking lot, a couple of days prior to the shooting, the perp obviously hung around. So he's either local, or would've had a place to crash.

"Good possibility."

"Got anyone checking short-term rentals? Lodging?"

"Was about to."

"Why don't you let us take that on? Dylan is frothing at the bit to do something, and Luna is good at prying loose information." I can't help notice the way Keith's eyes sharpen at the mention of her name. If I usually don't see eye to eye with the detective, it's nothing compared to the animosity between those two. "Anything comes up, I'll let you know."

I interpret his sharp nod as agreement and take my leave.

Luna is way ahead of me. When I get back to the office, I find her and Dylan bent over a list of places she'd already compiled. I quickly update them before sending them off and picking up my phone. Three o'clock already. I feel the sudden urge to check up on Bella.

Not sure exactly what time her shift ends, I send her a text instead of calling and am surprised when I get an immediate response.

Me: Day going okay?
Bella: It's going. You?
Me: So so. You off?
Bella: No. Just at Mercy finishing paperwork on last run. THEN I'm off.
Me: Plans?
Bella: Pint of Ben&Jerry's Peanut Butter Cup ice cream, episode of Bloodlines, and sleep. In that order
Me: Need help?
Bella: Trust me, you don't want to come near

me when I'm holding Ben & Jerry's.

Chuckling, I'm about to send off a smart response when she sends another message.

Bella: Gotta run.

I quickly erase what I'd written before and instead shoot off a simple *Okay*. Somehow I get the feeling my, *Who says I'm after your ice cream?* is probably better left unsaid anyway.

BELLA

"Four vehicle pileup just south of Hermosa, Gomez. Multiple casualties. We're on."

I quickly shoot off a message to Jasper, tuck my phone in my pocket, and run outside after Ryan, who's already climbing behind the wheel of our rig.

Five minutes more and I would've been off to grab my ice cream from the Walmart down the road. Looks like my evening's plans are postponed indefinitely.

"What do you know?" I ask Ryan, belting myself in, as he flicks on the siren and tears out of the parking lot.

"Tractor trailer carrying natural stone lost half its load into oncoming traffic. Two vehicles buried under the stone, victims trapped. One other wedged under the back of the truck. It's a mess."

"Jesus."

"Yeah. They already have heavy equipment en route. We're one of three units dispatched, and a Life Flight helicopter is on standby."

"Gonna be a long night," I comment, already regretting passing on the muffin he offered me earlier in the hospital cafeteria. Looks like my stomach will have to do without sustenance, despite its current loud protests.

"Granola bars in the glove box, courtesy of my wife," Ryan says with a grin. "I swear, even after seventeen years of marriage, she's still afraid I'll wither away if she doesn't feed me."

"You could have bigger problems," I suggest, tearing the wrapper off and shoving a good-sized bite in my mouth.

"That I could."

We're mostly silent the rest of our drive, listening to radio updates and occasionally updating our ETA to the scene. We know we're close when all traffic comes to a halt. It takes some hair-raising maneuvering from Ryan to get our sizable rig around the gridlock; at times barely clinging on to the edge of the mountain. I'm not a great fan of heights on my best days, but looking out my window—seeing nothing but air beside me—has me hyperventilating with my eyes squeezed shut.

Already a Colorado State Patrol unit is redirecting traffic back the way they came, to make room for emergency vehicles. I can see why when we drive up to the scene. The entire width of the road is blocked off.

"Let's go see what we've got," Ryan says, already halfway out of the rig.

—

It takes two and a half hours before enough stone is cleared for us to get to the crushed cars.

Three deceased in the rear of the van, while the driver along with all three occupants in the other vehicle were pulled out alive, but barely. The most critical patient was airlifted, and the others were stabilized and loaded up.

I look out the small window in the back of the rig, to the devastation on the road, as Ryan drives off. It's a miracle anyone lived through that.

Our patient—a middle-aged woman with a crushed leg, and a variety of other injuries, including a nasty head injury that almost scalped her—starts coming to when we drive into the ambulance bay. It's at least another hour before we've handed over her care and filled out all necessary reports.

"I've got to head back to the ER," Ryan says, as we're coming out of our respective locker rooms. "Beth's mom fell down her basement stairs and was just brought in by ambulance. Beth's following behind with the kids in the car."

"Oh no. Is there something I can do?"

"Yes. Go home. You're swaying on your feet."

"You sure?"

Ryan tilts his head and looks at me mockingly. "Positive. Go home, get rest, we've had a heavy couple of days." That has to be the understatement of the year.

I wave, watching him climb up the stairs as I head outside. The small garden courtyard with waterfall on my way to the parking lot is empty, and for a moment, I'm tempted to enjoy the peace and quiet after another chaotic day, but I'm so tired, I'm afraid I'll fall asleep on one of the benches.

It's poorly lit on the far end where the employee parking is, and when I get to my car, I have to use my cell to find my keys in my bag. No sooner do I pull them triumphantly from my favorite Michael Kors tote, when they slip through my fingers and bounce off the pavement, under my car.

Exasperated, exhausted, and near tears from frustration, I let out a barely controlled cry, before going down on my knees. I don't even want to think about the shit I'm running my hand over in my efforts to find the damn keys, but I'm praying I still have some disinfectant wipes left in my car. Gross.

My torso is half stuck under the chassis when my fingers finally locate them. I'm just backing out when a scrape on the ground behind me has me freeze.

"A view straight from my fantasies."

At the sound of the familiar voice, I shoot straight up. Not a good idea, given that I'm still halfway under the car. I hit my head so hard that tears burn my eyes.

"*Fuck!*"

"I've imagined that a time or two as well."

I scurry out from under the car to find Dr. LimpDick hovering over me, a smirk on his smarmy face. I bat at his hand when he reaches to help me up.

By the time I scramble to my feet, my head pounding already, I've had it up to here and let my temper fly.

"That's it! I've had a long fucking day and I really don't need this. I've put up with your crap for the sake of keeping the peace at work, but I'm done. You—" I stab a pointy finger in his chest for emphasis, "— are a little hard of hearing, so I'll repeat again. I am *not* interested in you, will *never* be interested in you, but your inflated ego just won't fucking give up! Your come-ons and innuendos are not sexy—they revolt me. Leave me the fuck alone, or I'll be filing sexual harassment charges."

Had I been paying more attention to his reaction, I might've recognized the moment I pushed too far. As it is, from the rage I see in his eyes, I'm in a whole new world of trouble.

"Try me," he hisses between clenched teeth, sticking his face in mine. "I can promise you won't get very far. I suggest you check out the hospital's board of directors. I have friends in very fucking high places."

"Everything okay here?"

The glare from a flashlight momentarily blinds

me, as one of the hospital security guards comes walking toward us. Scott immediately turns around, stepping away to create some distance, and I blow out a relieved breath.

"Fine," the fine doctor responds, "just helping her find her keys."

I'm tempted to give my own version of events when the guard beams a bright smile—not at me—but at the man beside me.

"Ah, Dr. Lipczyk, I didn't recognize you."

"No worries, Hank. How's your wife?"

With them exchanging pleasantries, I quickly open my door and slide behind the wheel, starting the car. Both of the men automatically step out of the way, and I give them a little wave as I back out and take off. The shaking of my hands is making it hard to shift gears.

I'm not looking forward to coming home to my dark empty house. I don't want to go home, I need to settle down first. The lights of the Walmart parking lot beckon. With a surprising number of cars still in front of the store, there are sure to be people milling around inside; human contact plus a pint of Ben & Jerry's is what I need right now. It's a sad state of affairs if you stop at Walmart when you feel alone.

I park my car and am about to get out when my phone pings with the arrival of a message.

Jasper: Are you home?
Me: At Walmart.

Immediately the phone rings.

"Why are you at Walmart this time of night?" Jasper's voice, even clearly annoyed, is like a warm blanket. Safe and secure.

"Getting ice cream."

"Now?"

"Yes now." I'm getting a little annoyed myself. "I had the day from hell, just finished my shift, and I need ice cream. Something wrong with that?"

"Whoa, I thought your shift ended at three?"

"It almost did, but we got called out to a horrendous accident. Anyway, I'm too exhausted to explain."

"The tractor trailer up on Highway 550? Heard about that."

"That would be the one. Anyway, I'm beat, I want my ice cream, and then I just want to go home."

"Go," he says softly, the warm sound causing a lump to form in my throat. "Get your ice cream. I'll see you soon."

Feeling better than I did five minutes ago, I toss my phone in my tote and drag my ass into Walmart.

Ten minutes after that, I climb in my car—not one but two pints of Ben & Jerry's, and a bottle of Pinot Grigio richer—and drive home.

"What are you doing here?" I find myself asking once again, when I find Jasper sitting on my porch steps. I walk toward him as he slowly unfolds his long legs and stands up.

"Just want to make sure your place is secure," he answers with a shrug.

"You planning to do this every night?"

He shrugs again before holding out his hand for the keys. "The shooter could still be in the area, we don't know."

Right. With a pang of guilt, I realize I'd almost forgotten about that. I drop my keys in his hand, but this time when he opens the door, I follow him inside. Shooter or no shooter, I'm not about to let my Ben & Jerry's melt.

In the kitchen, I pop one pint in the fridge, and stick a spoon in the second one, while Jasper does the rounds of my house.

"All clear." He comes out of the short hallway to my bedroom a minute later, just as I've shoved my first spoon of ice cream in my mouth and am having something just shy of an orgasmic experience. "Good?" He grins as I try to swallow down the ice cream all at once, giving myself brain freeze.

"Mmmm. Want some?" I offer, more out of politeness than anything else. I don't *really* want to share a single bite.

Jasper just shakes his head, as suddenly his eyes narrow on my face.

"What the fuck is that?" he asks, pointing at the side of my face. He takes the tub from my hands, sets it on the counter, and steps in close—his fingers on my chin—tilting my head this way and that.

"What?"

"You're fucking bleeding. What happened?"

"I banged my head. Must've been harder than I

thought." My hand automatically reaches up to probe my scalp.

"Don't touch it, you'll just get dirt in it. Where's your first aid kit?"

I direct him to the vanity cupboard in the bathroom, realizing a little too late it's also where I store my tampons and pads. I could run after him and get the kit myself, but decide to shove another spoonful of Peanut Butter Cup ice cream in my mouth instead.

I'm still groaning in bliss when he walks back into the kitchen, shaking his head.

"Sit."

I obediently do as he says and quietly let him do his thing while I gorge myself.

"Ouch," I complain, when he almost rips out a clump of hair by the roots. "I like my hair where it is."

"You're distracting me," he accuses, clearly annoyed, although for the life of me I can't figure out why. I've been sitting still the entire time.

"I'm not doing a damn thing," I protest.

"Do you have to make those sounds when you eat?"

"I'm just enjoying my well-deserved treat, is there a law against that? Besides, why are you doing this all of a sudden?"

"Do what all of a sudden?"

"Looking out for me. Making sure I get in okay. Checking up on me during the day. In all the time we've known each other, you've never done anything like that. Now you're here for the second night in a row."

He steps into my field of vision, and I tilt back to look up into his face.

"Your brother—" he starts.

"I call bullshit," I counter, cutting him off. "You keep bringing up my brother when you need an excuse for either coming or leaving. What is it?"

For a long time he just looks down at me, clear conflict playing out behind his eyes, when finally his hands come up, cup my face, and he leans in for a kiss that has me clasp onto his wrists to stay upright. Holy shit, the man can kiss.

"I better go," he whispers against my lips, before pressing a final kiss to my forehead, and making for the door.

Shut down again.

I wake up feeling like death warmed over.

My stomach is sloshing with one and a half pint of Ben & Jerry's and the full bottle of Pinot Grigio I comforted myself with last night. I don't know which is worse, the nausea or the throbbing headache that has me see stars.

A ping indicates a message, and I slap my hand on the nightstand a few times until I find my phone.

Jasper: Hope you slept OK.

His abrupt departure last night still rattles me, and I'm not in the mood to entertain his mixed messages, so I type:

Fuck off.

I trust that's clear enough.

CHAPTER 7

JASPER

"Why is it I have to find out from my wife's friend what's going on back home?"

I grin when I hear Damian's voice on the line. It's been a shit week so far, with dick all to show for it. Other than the report of a burned out, black Honda found in a canyon off the 213 about twenty minutes south of town yesterday, that is. Two hikers ran across it when they followed a trail down into the canyon over the weekend. They made a report of a torched car, but somehow it was overlooked in the manhunt for the shooter. Yesterday a unit went to take a look and discovered the car matched the description of the shooter's vehicle. Hadn't been easy to get the damn thing out either, they called in CBI and it took them most of the day to hoist it out. The car is currently sitting in the forensics lab.

The only other piece of concrete evidence, a tire tread in the parking lot at the scene, which can be used to match the prints found at the top of the canyon to confirm this is the car, but that doesn't really get us any further.

"Maybe because you're on your honeymoon and should be focusing on your wife, and not on work?"

"A cop was shot, Jasper. That's a major incident."

"Well aware of that, and I've offered the PD our full support, but so far it's a single incident, with little else to show in terms of evidence. Besides, I thought you trusted me?"

"It's not about that," he backtracks.

"Like hell it's not. Trusting me is knowing that if we really needed you here, I would not hesitate for a second to call you in. So far, I've kept David abreast of everything. You have a little over a week left, just enjoy it."

"Fine. Just one thing," he concedes. "Can you see how Bella is doing? I don't like the idea of her alone, without anyone checking in from time to time."

I grimace; if only he knew how close the tabs are I've been keeping.

"Will do. Say hi to Kerry. I'll see you next week."

I put the phone down on my desk and try to focus back on the encrypted files up on my computer screen, when Luna walks in.

"Nothing," she announces when I look at her questioningly. "We've been knocking on doors for days, but no one knows anything or remembers seeing anything.”

“What about shooting ranges, gun shops?” I ask.

“Blackfoot’s been looking into those and I’m not about to ruffle his feathers,” she says, sitting down at her desk. “They’re ruffled enough as it is. You know, I’m thinking our guy is either local, or was passing through. This may have been an isolated incident.”

“I’d like to believe that, but what little we have points to someone who knew what he was doing. Not a random incident. Ballistics is suggesting he’s using a silencer, based on their findings, which explains why no one reported hearing shots fired. He left no shells at the scene. He scoped out a remote location to dump and destroy his car. Somehow he either got back to town, or hitched a ride into New Mexico. I doubt he walked back. That’s a fair distance. Someone has to have seen something.”

“We’d have to call on the public. Talk to the media.”

Luna voices what I’ve been suggesting to Blackfoot these past few days. So far he’s held off. He has his reasons. If the dead officer was a random victim, it’s highly probable the shooter is scanning media closely to glean any information on the investigation, it may even have been his motivation to kill—notoriety. If Officer Belker was specifically targeted, it would indicate a personal connection, and from what I understand, that is still being looked into. All good points, but it’s frustrating to sit and wait for information to filter in before any action can be taken.

"Have you had any luck?" Luna asks, opening up her laptop.

I shake my head. "Nope. Nothing popping up on social media."

I'm limited to general fishing expeditions for certain keywords that might relate to the shooting. Believe it or not, there are idiots out there who commit a crime and then boast about it on their social media accounts. Some even post pictures. I had a feeling this guy would not be that dumb.

It's a massive job filtering through all that information. I've limited myself to local IP addresses only, but that still is a substantial number of accounts to scan. Especially when you have no other information that can help you narrow it down.

The only good thing about the tedious work is that it's sucking up all my time. It's been a good distraction from Bella, whom I haven't seen or talked to since I walked out of her house last week. Actually, since she told me to fuck off via text the next morning.

A grin spreads over my lips at the memory. Little does she know that brand of attitude only cranks up my interest. And now her brother wants me to actively look in on her, giving me an excuse *and* permission.

For once, luck is on my side.

"I don't even wanna know," Luna says, scrutinizing me over the top of her screen with a look of distaste. "That kind of shit-eating grin only spells trouble."

She has no idea how true that statement is.

It's always a drag to transition from one shift to another the first few days. Especially going from day shift to nights.

After my late-night pity party last Thursday, I'd called in sick the next morning, and spent Friday hugging the toilet. I had a sneaky suspicion by afternoon, it wasn't just due to the hangover I'd given myself. The nausea and throbbing head were persistent, and I'd spiked a decent fever somewhere along the line as well.

I was miserable all weekend, unable to keep much of anything down. Monday was a little better, and yesterday I thought myself well enough to head back into work for our first night shift.

"Hey, I haven't seen you in a while," Joanne, one of the emergency room nurses comments when I step out of the shower. "New shift tonight?"

"Started yesterday," I share, grabbing another towel to wrap around my hair.

"I'm just starting tonight. Not looking forward to it," she complains, putting on her scrubs. "The first time since coming back from maternity leave that they have me on the night shift."

"I hear you," I offer sympathetically. Joanne is a nice girl, one of the first ones to introduce herself when I started here. "It always takes a few days to get into the routine."

"Ugh. Tell my little one that. She won't care her mommy has to sleep. I'm lucky my mom is close by to help out during the day."

"For sure."

I grab the blow-dryer from my locker to try and get the worst of the moisture out before tying it back.

"Here, want me to put it in a quick braid?" she asks, looking at my reflection in the mirror. "Now that I have a girl, I'll need the practice. I haven't had long hair myself since I was twelve."

"Have at it. Anything to speed things along. Ryan is waiting for me."

I close my eyes when she takes the brush from my hands and starts running it through my hair. My mom, or one of my sisters, would do this for me all the time growing up. It's comforting. Even though I don't really know Joanne well, the small gesture of kindness makes me wonder if it isn't time for me to be a little more socially active.

I haven't really allowed myself, since people I thought were my friends collectively turned on me back in Farmington. I have trouble trusting anymore. Another thing to thank my ex for.

The man not only cheated on me for the almost seven years we were together, but he did it with my friends, and he did it at work. Philip Presley was a physician at San Juan Medical Center when I was hired there. From day one, he made it clear he was interested. A few of the girls warned me, but I was so smitten, I didn't want to hear.

For four years out of our seven together, I was blissfully oblivious. Once the first seed of doubt was planted, it became quickly and painfully clear I was being played. Still, coming from a family where I felt like a black sheep already, I wasn't about to concede to what would be yet another failure in their eyes. So I tried to stick it out.

And that is what ultimately tainted me with his behavior, because at first I defended him against the accusations. That's what you do, right? You stand by your man? Yet at some point, the complaints of sexual misconduct became impossible to brush off.

Six months I lasted after he disappeared under the heat of the investigation into the allegations. I was hounded by the police, convinced I knew his whereabouts. I was harassed and later shunned by coworkers and former friends. And never once did I let my family in on what was going on.

Until I finally cracked under the pressure and had a nervous breakdown. Not the best time in my life, but I've come a ways since then—I'm rebuilding.

A new start here in Durango. New place, new job, but I'm sorely lacking in the new friends department, which is why maybe next time Joanne asks me along for a drink or a coffee after work, or asks me to come meet her new baby, I should really say yes.

"There, all done. Looks amazing, if I say so myself."

I look in the mirror to find she has twisted my hair into an intricate French braid that curves around my head and ends in a thick plait on my left shoulder.

"That's amazing. Much too fancy for work, I'm afraid it'll get messed up."

"Anytime you want to look pretty for a night out, just hit me up. Happy to help." I smile at the woman, touched by her kindness.

"I'd like that."

"Good. You look gorgeous. Just steer clear of our resident dirtbag; he sees you like this, he won't take no for an answer."

I don't bother telling her he's already made that perfectly clear.

"You're looking a little pale," Ryan notices when I climb into the back of our rig, where he's already restocking from our earlier call.

A young guy, early twenties, so hammered at nine at night he'd passed out at a backyard party, and they were unable to wake him. Alcohol, and God knows what drugs were in his system—according to his equally inebriated buddies—who at least had the sense to call for help. When we loaded him in the back, I rubbed my knuckles firmly over his sternum to rouse him, when the damn kid upchucked all over me and the inside of our rig.

Not the first time, and probably not the last either, but with a stomach still not quite back to normal, I almost returned the favor. Nothing a quick shower and change can't fix, but I wasn't looking forward to the prospect of scouring vomit off the walls and floors of the rig.

"You're a prince," I tell him, looking around the clean rig, where the smell of bleach overwhelms the last lingering traces of puke stink.

"Tell my wife that," he counters, giving me a long hard look. "You sure you're good to go?"

"Positive."

"All right, then go grab me another adult blood pressure cuff, just had to toss the other one."

Just as I climb back in a few minutes later, handing Ryan the fresh cuff, a call comes in.

"…Mercy 7-13, we have a 29B1, single vehicle, injuries unknown. College Drive, half a mile east of 9th."

Ryan looks at me, an eyebrow raised, and I nod. I'm ready.

"10-4," he responds, when we climb into the cab. I strap myself in, Ryan flicks on the lights, and we're off on our next call.

Traffic is light this late at night, especially once you get out of downtown. College Drive is not particularly well-lit, but we can see the flashing lights up ahead.

Ryan pulls in behind the cruiser, parked on the opposite side of the road, on the shoulder. I can see headlights reflecting off the tree line about ten yards down from the side of the road. Only the rear of the vehicle is visible sticking up in the brush.

"Take the flashlight," Ryan suggests. "I'll grab the kit and the backboard."

I grab the light wedged in a charger between our

seats and get out, flicking it on.

The first thing that strikes me is how quiet it is. Granted, it's past eleven on a weeknight, but still; you'd expect to hear some sounds. There's nothing, not even a rustle from the officer who is likely down by the wreck, and a chill runs down my back.

I round the cruiser and carefully step into the low brush leading to the trees below. My light is aimed at the crashed vehicle; not a smart move as I discover a moment later, when my foot slips and I land flat on my ass, sliding a few feet before I dig in my heels and come to a stop.

"Gomez!" Ryan yells from above. "You okay?"

I turn around and am about to holler back when the beam from my flashlight catches the outline of a leg. The leg is attached to a body, and I realize the reason I wasn't hearing anything is because the body belongs to the officer, and he doesn't look good.

"Officer down!" I yell up, fighting to keep the panic from my voice as I scramble the few feet uphill to get to the man's side. "Call it in. Officer down!"

"*Fuck!*" I hear him exclaim, but I don't pay any mind to anything else. I have a job to do.

I don't even register the sirens approaching, I'm too busy fighting what I already know is a losing battle The man under my hands was likely gone the moment the bullet entered his skull. Still, I work on him the best I can, as the force of my compressions on his chest have me sliding backward down the slope every so often.

I ignore Ryan repeating my name quietly, and I don't notice the crowd of uniforms gathering around me. All I care about is the man with whom I shared a drink and a laugh just one week ago at The Irish, who informed me during that conversation that he only had four more months to go until retirement.

"He's gone, honey," Ryan says, finally wrapping his arms around me from behind and pulling me off Bert. "There was absolutely nothing you could do."

JASPER

I'm already in bed, watching the late news, when I hear the call go out on my scanner. *Officer down.*

This time I don't hesitate, I'm dressed and jogging out the door in seconds. I call Dylan hands-free when I get in my truck.

"Yeah," I hear his sleepy voice.

"College Drive, another shooting. Meet me there."

"Fuck. I need to call someone for Max. Mom and Clint are away this week."

Shit. He mentioned it but I'd forgotten.

"Never mind, look after your boy. I'm calling Luna."

"Jas, keep me in the loop? I won't sleep."

"Sure thing." I smile to myself in understanding. The hungriest agent on our team, and his hands are tied. I'm sure he'll be up until he knows as much as we do, even if he can't be there.

"Luna, shooting at—" I start when she picks up the call.

"I heard, already on my way. Was about to call you," she snaps, before she adds, "Bella is at the scene."

My sense of urgency heightens ten-fold at that bit of news. I don't bother asking how and why she knows this, but I also don't question the validity of the information.

"Thanks. See you there."

There are at least eight or nine emergency vehicles on scene, one of which is blocking the road. I have to flash my badge a few times when yet another officer tries to block my way. The atmosphere is tense, which isn't a surprise, given that it seems clear someone is targeting cops.

I stop at the edge of the slope, where I find Luna standing a step behind Keith Blackfoot, watching a group of officers carry up an empty backboard. I immediately know this is a fatality.

"Who?" I ask softly. Keith doesn't even turn around, his eyes stay fixed on the prone body left below, a single officer standing guard.

"Bert Cummings. Fifty-two, a wife, two kids, a new grandbaby, and four months from retirement," he says, his voice raspy with emotion, and I watch with interest as Luna steps in and puts a hand on his back. He doesn't even seem to notice.

"Jesus."

"Yeah."

"No sign of the shooter?"

I get a sharp shake of his head before he expands. "EMTs who found him didn't see anyone. Damian's kid sister and her partner," he adds, indicating the two following the group of officers up. "I gather she knew Bert. Was still fruitlessly trying to revive him when I got here. Her partner had to pull her off."

I watch her partner support her as she takes the last steps to find level ground. Her face is gaunt and her eyes blank. She doesn't even notice me until I step in her path and take her in my arms.

"Not now, Jasper," she whispers against my chest, a plea in her voice. "I need to write up a report and wait for the coroner to get here. I have to do my job. Don't let me break down."

I'm not sure what I can do to prevent that, but I let her go all the same.

"Go. Write your report, finish your job, but I'll be waiting right here with you until the coroner shows."

CHAPTER 8

JASPER

"Car was reported stolen earlier today. Or by now, yesterday."

Luna walks up to where I'm standing, keeping an eye on the open rear of the ambulance where Bella is doing whatever she needs to do.

"From where?" I want to know, turning my attention to Luna, who's been sticking close to Blackfoot. I'm not sure if to gather information, or to offer silent support, but it is interesting to note that now she's talking to me, his eyes keep drifting this way.

"Off the West Hall parking lot at the college. The one right by the lookout."

I know the one she means. The road we're on runs up the side of the mountain to the college, which overlooks Durango. The lookout she's talking about is off Rim Drive, which curves around the outside of the college grounds.

"Isn't there a hiking trail you can access from there?"

Luna nods. "Yup, there is. Runs all the way down to 6th Street. I've taken it a few times."

"The only way up or down the mountain is this road, right?" I'm thinking out loud, not really needing an answer. "And with a general call going out, I would assume he'd avoid going in the direction where more emergency vehicles were likely to come from. He'd avoid the road all together."

"He's on foot," Luna fills in, nodding in agreement.

"Yup, and my guess is, he'll want to get as far away from the scene, as fast as possible. How far from here to the trail?" I ask her.

"Maybe a mile, a mile and a half? That is if he followed the road. Only half the distance, if that, cutting through the trees. He could have theoretically made it to the head of the trail and down the other side to 6th Street, before we even got to the scene," Luna suggests.

"It'd be a decent climb, he'd have to be in shape. We should run this by Keith."

"Run what by me?" Blackfoot walks up behind Luna.

Luna does the honors and gives him the gist of it, and he's on the radio before she's even finished talking. He directs units to cover both ends of the trail, blocking access.

"Be difficult to find anything in the dark. We'll secure the exits and send guys out at first light," he explains to us. "Doubt many of my guys will get any sleep anyway."

Two white vans pull up to the side of the road. One with the La Plata County Medical Examiner's logo on the side, and the other holds the CBI forensics team, who immediately start unloading large floodlights to illuminate the scene below.

"Sorry it took me a bit," Doc Franco, a portly man, apologizes before getting down to business. "What do we have?"

From the corner of my eye, I see Bella climb out of the rig and walk over to her, leaving Blackfoot to sort out how to get the aging coroner down the damn slope.

"How's it going?" I ask when I reach her.

"Hanging in."

I'm surprised at her honesty, I'd expected her to brush me off again. "That's all you can do, honey. Do your thing with the coroner and then I'm taking you home."

Her head whips around.

"Don't boss me around," she snaps. "Ryan already called the supervisor, who is getting an additional unit rolling to cover us, but I'll be driving back to Mercy with him. We go on calls as a team, and we return as a team." She leans in close and hisses, "This is my job."

I grab her by the shoulders and drop my forehead to hers, ignoring the fire she's shooting in my direction.

"Compromise. You go with Ryan to take the rig back to Mercy, but I'll be following behind, and you let me drive you home from there."

Her eyes slowly close, as she leans her weight into me.

"But my car…"

"We deal with your car tomorrow."

It takes a moment, but I finally feel her small nod before she pulls away, and walks over to Doc Franco.

"Are you hungry? I could do with something."

I glance over at Bella, who's been quiet since she got into the truck at the hospital.

"Nothing's open," she says in a flat voice, staring straight ahead.

"True. Not for another hour at least, but I could make us something."

"If you want."

"Okay, we'll see what you have in your fridge. It's gotta be better than what's in mine." She says nothing to that, and I give up trying to engage her. For now, anyway.

I'm starting to worry about her lack of emotion, though. It's like she's completely shut down. Granted, she seems to have had a particularly tough week, but I still wonder if there's not something to Damian's concern for her. It looks and sounds like an overprotective big brother worrying about his younger sister, but perhaps it's for good reason.

I know a bit of the history behind Bella moving to Durango. I know she was involved with a guy from work, a doctor, who apparently was the subject of an investigation into several complaints of sexual misconduct at the hospital where they both worked. I also know the fucker took off, leaving her to face the fallout by herself. Things were bad enough, she ended up leaving her job. The douchebag had the balls to resurface last year, only to beg her to provide him with a fake alibi. If I didn't know, for a fact, Damian made sure he would never bother his sister again, I might've done those honors myself.

What I don't know is: what happened in the months after she quit and before she came to Durango.

"Give me your keys, Squirt." I hold out my hand when we pull up in front of her house.

This time she doesn't even argue when I ask her, she just hands over the bag she's been clutching in her lap. I dig out the keys, mildly surprised at what all she carries around in that plus-sized tote of hers. When I notice she's not moving, I unclip her seat belt, and get out, rounding the truck to help her down from the cab.

She doesn't even object when I sling her bag over my shoulder and grab her hand as we walk up her steps.

The instant I unlock the door, she slips past me and immediately turns right toward her bedroom. I rush after her to make sure it's secure and walk in on her starting to undress by the side of the bed.

"Give me a second to check," I suggest, walking to the window to make sure it's locked and closing the blinds.

Clearly she doesn't listen, because when I turn back, she's stripped down to just her panties as she climbs onto the mattress. *Fuck*, I'm trying not to notice her heavy breasts with large dark aureoles, swaying with each movement as she gets settled in bed, but we can strike that as a fail. My eyes noticed, blood pressure noticed, and my fucking dick sure as shit noticed.

Bella, on the other hand, doesn't seem to notice a thing. She pulls the sheet over her ear as she curls on her side. I round the bed to her and press a kiss to the side of her head, my knuckles white with restraint. No matter how tempting it is to strip down myself and climb in with her, I'm not about to take advantage of a woman who currently is more like a zombie than a living, breathing human being.

No matter how fucking breathtakingly gorgeous she is.

Resigned, I snatch a throw from the bottom of the bed, and flick off the lights as I walk out, pulling the door shut. I check my phone for updates, before I pull off my boots and jeans, and finally get settled in for a couple of hours of sleep on her couch.

BELLA

I'm numb.

Frozen.

I remember this feeling of desperately keeping the lid on the swirling emotions that lie just below the surface. The times when there is no longer anything there to distract me from the fact I'm sliding down a hole where darkness is waiting for me. Afraid if I let only a single emotion slip at this point, the chasm will rip open and swallow me whole.

I wish for sleep to take me but am scared to let myself drift off. So I lie in bed—all concept of time forgotten—my eyes burning as I keep them open until the soft light of dawn filters in through the blinds.

I don't even move when I hear the sound of my bedroom door opening. I know it's Jasper and steel myself not to let him see this side of me. The side that has branded me as the emotionally fragile one with my family. The side that feels too deep, and makes me wonder if I'm cut out to look after other people, when I can't seem to look after myself. I fight every day to keep that side hidden, by working hard to prove I can handle the stress of my job, by battling insecurity with defiance and attitude. I try so hard not to live up to what I know the expectations are: an emotionally weak failure.

"Have you slept at all?"

Jasper's blurry face appears in my line of vision, and I blink a few times to clear the grit. I don't say anything, just look into the warm blue depths of his eyes and wish I could float away.

"*Jesus*," I hear him mutter.

The mattress shifts as he climbs in beside me, and panic sets in when his arms come around me, cradling me to his warm chest. I remind myself that the feeling of safety in his embrace is not real. That the moment I let go, and he discovers the real me, he won't see me the same way again either.

"Let it go, beautiful," he coos softly, his cheek firm against the top of my head. "Just let it go."

That's all it takes; a few gentle words, a kind embrace, and my desperate hold on impassion rips away with the first strangled sob from my throat.

The wave of churning shadows crashes over me.

JASPER

I fucking curse myself for leaving her alone in the first place.

The moment I see her face with those sunken, red-rimmed eyes, I know she has not closed them yet. I fucked up.

Her body is cold and stiff when I gather her against me, desperate to will some warmth into her soul.

I thought she'd hold strong in her almost catatonic state, but when I encourage her to let go, the first sob breaks free. And another. And another. Each one deeper and more gut-wrenching than the last. Some so violent, her entire body convulses as they rip from her chest.

I keep waiting for them to subside, but it's endless and agonizing. The sun shines full into her window now, and when I check her alarm clock on the nightstand, I see over an hour has expired. This can't be healthy.

My phone is on the coffee table in the living room, where Bella's purse is too.

"Sweetheart." I try to slip out from under her. "I'll be right back, I promise." The moment the warmth of my body leaves her, she curls back up in a ball, but the sobbing doesn't wane.

My first stop is the bathroom, to check if there are any meds she's supposed to be taking, but other than ibuprofen and something for menstrual cramps, there's nothing in her medicine cabinet. Next up is the kitchen, but that doesn't hold much either.

I need help.

Any other person; I'd load them up and take them to the hospital, but if one thing hammered home last night, her job is everything to her. If I take her into Mercy when she's in the middle of...I'm not even sure what to call this, but if I show up with Bella in this state, the entire hospital will know eventually. Even if it doesn't put her at risk of losing her job, it will certainly impact her working relationships. I can't do that to her.

I dig through her purse to find her phone. Only one person, who might be able to help, and I don't have his number.

Locating the phone, I open her contacts and find Ryan's name right below Damian's.

"How are you doing?"

It's clear from the sound of his voice, he was still sleeping, and he obviously thinks I'm Bella.

"It's Jasper Greene, I took Bella home this morning, and she's not doing well. I'm gonna need your help."

"What do you mean, not doing well?" he asks, suddenly sharp.

"She was out of it earlier, not sleeping but cold and unresponsive. But now…here, listen." Rather than trying to explain, I hold up the phone and he should be able to hear for himself.

"How long has she been like this?" he asks when I put the phone back to my ear. I can hear rustling in the background, like he's getting dressed.

"Well over an hour. I'd take her into the hospital, but—"

"Don't," he interrupts me sharply. "Let me see if I can help before you do that. Can you hold out for twenty minutes?"

"I can. I'll leave the door unlocked."

Hanging up, I take the phone with me into the bedroom, where Bella lies much the same as I left her, still making the same god-awful noises. Like a tortured animal. I crawl back in bed with her, and like before, have to physically move her onto my chest.

Almost thirty minutes later, when I hear the front door open, I'm about ready to fucking cry myself. I can't remember ever feeling as fucking useless as I've felt in the past couple of hours.

Or maybe I just never cared enough.

"Sorry," Ryan says walking in, and I belatedly realize Bella is virtually naked in my arms. Quickly I pull the sheet up to cover her as best I can. I'm not sure what the man thinks as he's taking in the situation, and frankly I don't give a flying fuck, as long as he can do something for her. "I had to swing by the hospital to get something from the rig."

I flinch when he comes over to the side of the bed and leans over me to brush the hair plastered to Bella's face. If not for my concern for her, this might've been awkward.

"Hey, gorgeous," he tries to get through to her. "Shit just hit the fan, huh? Gonna give you some good stuff to help you sleep. You need to get you some rest." There is no distinct reaction noticeable from Bella, but Ryan doesn't seem to expect it. He opens the small bag he carried in on the nightstand, and pulls out a prefilled syringe while keeping up his continuous chatter. "You'll probably have my balls later for sticking a needle in you, but it can't be helped. And at the risk of completely alienating you, I will notify our supervisor that you seem to have come down with a nasty case of strep throat, and will be off for at least a week." He wipes an area of Bella's upper arm with a disinfectant, and slides the needle easily into her skin.

"What are you giving her?"

"Midazolam. It's fast-acting. Don't worry, I'm only giving her half a dose, hopefully just enough to help her sleep."

In minutes, she settles down a little, her eyes closed and the sobbing down to an occasional involuntary hiccup.

"Now is probably a good time to grab a shower, I'm going to stick around for another forty-five minutes or so, to make sure she has no adverse effects, but she can't be left alone today, someone will have to check in on her regularly."

"How long do you figure she'll be out?" I ask, when I feel her body go heavy with sleep and gently slide her head off my chest and onto her pillow.

"Hard to tell. The drug alone, not necessarily that long, but given that she was already exhausted, I wouldn't be surprised if she slept the day away."

"I can work from here," I say, more to myself than anyone else, as I make a mental list of what I will need either Dylan or Luna to drop off.

As suggested, I grab a quick shower, after supplying Ryan with a well-deserved cup of coffee I manage to wrangle from Bella's Keurig machine.

"She seems to be comfortable, but call me if anything changes," he offers, when he's ready to go a little later. "My shift doesn't start until three, but I'll call in to check how things are before that."

I shake the man's hand and clap a hand on his shoulder.

"Appreciate it. I hope this won't get you into hot

water."

"Nah," he answers with a grin, brushing it off. "Not unless you or Bella decide to spill the beans."

"No chance of that happening."

"Figured as much." I expect him to leave but he hesitates in the doorway. "Look, you realize she may need help that extends beyond this, right? She's never come right out and admitted to it, but I've suspected there are emotional issues she struggles with. She's a damn good partner, and I'd hate to lose her because she is not taking care of them. I don't know who you are to her, but from what I can see, you care. I suggest you get her to talk to someone this week. She may need medication to help her cope."

"I'll see to it," I promise. "I care more than I probably should."

CHAPTER 9

BELLA

I wake up with a pounding headache, eyes caked shut, a dry throat, and a bladder that is about to burst. This time without the pleasure of a bottle of wine and pint or so of ice cream.

Bits and pieces are coming back to me, most of them ones I'd rather have forgotten. Yet somewhere in between those was the memory of a pair of strong arms and soft words, which somehow kept me from getting sucked under completely.

Swinging my legs over the side, I sit up, holding onto my head for fear it'll explode. A glance at my nightstand shows it's close to four. *Shit*, I slept the day away.

I reach for my old ratty robe and make my way to the bathroom on wobbly legs. While relieving my bladder, I rummage through the drawers of the vanity looking for relief of another kind. I'm positive I had some ibuprofen left somewhere. I find it in the medicine cabinet and palm four. I'm not even sure that'll make a dent in this doozy of a headache.

With drugs on board, my mouth no longer tasting like the bottom of a trashcan, and a splash of cold water on my face, I feel somewhat human. I need coffee.

"Hey, sweetheart."

Startled, my head swivels around a little too fast at the rumble of Jasper's voice when I walk into the kitchen. It was so quiet in the house, I thought he might have left.

"Hey," I manage just seconds before I'm enveloped in those arms I remember. My arms slips around his waist where my fingers curl in the back of his shirt.

One of his big hands slowly rubs up and down my spine, making me want to purr like a cat. Despite the danger signs popping up, I nuzzle deeper in his shirt.

"Coffee?"

Dammit. He even knows the magic word.

Reluctantly, I let go as he walks over to my Keurig and hits the button. Clearly he'd been prepared, a mug already slowly filling.

"Sit," he orders, noticing me swaying on my feet.

I perch my ass on a stool and lean over, dropping my head on my arms on the counter. It's tempting to close my eyes and let myself drift off again, but I know sleep is just a way for me to hide.

The tender brush of fingers through my hair has my eyes well up. I can't believe he stayed. After my meltdown, I thought for sure he'd be running for the hills, but as he's done more than once recently, Jasper is proving to be nothing like the man I believed him to be, and everything like the man tentative dreams are made of.

His fingertips gently trace the scab left by my encounter with the underside of my car last week, reminding me of yet another instance where he looked after me. Of course, just minutes later he kissed me, only to walk out the door and drop off the face of the earth until yesterday. I'm not sure who he was running from; me or himself.

Afraid to fall under his spell again, I raise my head and his hand falls away.

"How are you feeling?" He scans my face with concern.

"Like I was run over by a freight train."

"I bet." He grins and again he reaches out, brushing a stray strand from my forehead. I'm mesmerized, getting lost in his eyes, until the welcome gurgle of my Keurig announces my much-needed coffee is ready.

"Black. Right?" I nod at his question, a little surprised. I guess being an FBI agent you're required to have above normal powers of observation.

He hands me my cup and I wrap my hands around it, taking a grateful sip.

"What do you remember?" he asks, as he drops

another dark roast cup in the machine and sets his mug under the drip.

The question may have come out casually, but that doesn't hide the weight behind it. It's a clear invitation to talk, to share…to explain. I'm not sure I want to, in fact, I'm pretty sure I don't, but I also don't want him to go to Damian to get answers, and he deserves at least some.

"Well, it's clear I had a little meltdown," I start, not just a little defensively, and working to put the usual snap in my tone. "I'm sure my low resistance after that bout of stomach flu, didn't help."

"I didn't know you were sick," he comments, almost accusatory as he turns to face me.

"Flu. Just went back to work on Tuesday."

"And you didn't call me?" I'm surprised he looks as irritated as he does.

"For what?" I feel a good head of steam build. "You're the one who ran out of here like you were being chased the night before I got sick, and yet you expect a call? Why? So you can be a knight in shining armor? You like swooping in and playing the hero. I'm sure it does wonders for the ego. Except apparently your armor disappears at the stroke of midnight."

I know I'm using attack to deflect from the conversation he was aiming for, it's an ingrained response for me; an automatic defense mechanism that seems to kick in when I feel cornered.

"At midnight, huh?" he says, dripping with sarcasm as he sharply sets his cup down on the counter and checks his watch. "Then I guess my ego overstayed its welcome."

In three large strides, he's across the living room and out the front door, leaving me to gape after him with my mouth hanging open. The sharp sound of the door slamming shut has me jump in my seat, and I immediately regret my words.

For crying out loud, the man had walked away from the job, just to see me home. Stayed with me to make sure I was okay, and called help when he discovered I wasn't, still not leaving my side.

I'm a bitch. A grade A, bona fide bitch. So afraid I'll get hurt, I lash out and make sure I do injury first. It's no wonder only my family tolerates me. No friendships I've ever had stood the test of time, I even fail at those.

My head drops back down on my arms, and this time I make no effort to stop the tears, as the destructive thoughts play on repeat in my mind.

A warm hand touches the middle of my back and slides up to settle on the back of my neck. Jasper's voice is firm but kind.

"That's enough of that."

JASPER

I had to get some air before I'd say something I might

regret later.

To say my day had not run smoothly would be an understatement. Luna had been at the office early and kindly dropped off my files and laptop, plus a change of clothes from my locker. All I told her in explanation was that Bella was feeling under the weather, but I don't think she quite believed it. Luna had been there last night; she would've noticed Bella's robot-like behavior and drawn her own conclusions. Nothing I could do about that. Typical Luna, she didn't ask any questions, just gave me a brief update on the status of the investigation and promised to call with anything new.

Still remembering the dress-down Damian gave me last week, I quickly called him before the grapevine could find its way to Europe. I gave him what details I had, as he fired off a barrage of questions. When I let slip that Bella had been the one to find Bert, he'd been ready to abort his vacation and hop on a plane home. I then compounded my mistake by mentioning I was at her house. I was hoping to put his mind at ease, but only succeeded in raising his suspicions when I told him she was sleeping. Not really my place to share Bella's breakdown with him, I went with the excuse Ryan came up with and just said she was sick and sleeping it off.

By the time I got off the phone, I could only hope I deterred him from cutting his honeymoon short.

There'd been occasional updates throughout the day, both the shell as well as the bullet were recovered from the scene this time, and looked to be consistent with a nine millimeter. Officers also found part of a bicycle pedal at the base of the trail. It was discovered wedged in the crack of a rock where some brush appeared trampled, and looked too clean to have been there for long. A bike might explain a few lingering questions around transportation. The shooter could easily get around, virtually undetected, on a bike.

Luna is the one who suggested if that were the case, we should probably be on the lookout for someone with a backpack, since it's highly unlikely the perp would ride around on a bike with a gun tucked in his pocket or waistband.

More leads to pursue, just as soon as the CBI forensics lab reports on their findings.

A day filled with waiting: for information to come through, for Bella to wake up. I'm not usually an impatient guy, but that is when I'm free to go run down any idea or lead that crosses my desk. I didn't have that luxury today. By the time I heard her in the bathroom, I'd been ready to wake her myself.

Too much time to think, consider, and second-guess, is rarely a good thing.

Perhaps that's why her words hit their mark. I'd been questioning my own motivations for sticking around earlier, so when she lashed out like that—and I'm well aware that's all it was—it was a little too close to the quick.

The moment I walk back in and see her slumped over the counter, I immediately regret walking out.

"That's enough of that," I order, worried I'll have to make another call to Ryan. I give her neck a squeeze before digging a clean kitchen towel from a drawer, wetting it under the cold tap and offering it to her. "Wipe your face, Squirt."

I use the pet name purposely, hoping for exactly the dirty look she throws me through her tears, before snatching the towel from my hands. The fire in her eyes is better than tears, or even worse, yesterday's blank pools.

"Figured you were gone," she says on a lingering sniffle, with a little bite. Not enough to hide the hurt underneath, though.

"Couldn't even if I tried," I establish, pointing in the direction of the coffee table holding my laptop and covered in paperwork. Her gaze follows mine and I see her shoulders slump.

"I'm sorry," she whispers with her back turned. "I didn't—"

"I know you didn't. I just needed to cool off." I round the counter and take a seat next to her, turning her to face me. "I'm not running," I assure her when her eyes finally come up. "I just didn't want to fire back and make you cry. And here I've made you cry anyway. Have I mentioned I'm not good with crying?"

She gives a little snort and tilts her head to the side. "You did fine this morning."

I grin; I recognize an opening when I see one. "So you remember this morning?"

"Mostly," she admits.

"Can I be honest?" I ask, but don't really wait for an answer. "That scared the hell out of me. Has that happened before?" She tries to look away, but I take her chin and force her to keep her eyes on me. "Isabella?"

"My dad calls me that." She smiles a little as she says it, but I'm not about to be distracted.

"Has it?"

She shrugs. "A few times when I was younger, but only once like that."

"And what causes it?"

"Mostly it's just stress building up. Feelings I don't know what to do with or get rid of. Then at some point the bucket is full—spills over—and I can't control it."

"Like it did last night."

"Yeah, like that."

I think for a minute, wondering how to phrase the next question without throwing her on the defensive.

"Do you have someone you can talk about these things with? A sister or a friend?" I know I've hit on something when she starts tearing up again and shakes her head.

"No one I'd trust," she confesses, before getting up and walking to the couch where she sits down in a corner. I don't like the way she pulls up her legs and wraps her arms around them defensively. As if she's in need of protection from me. But at her next words, I have a better understanding why she needed the distance. "My family probably would just have me committed again."

"When was that?" I ask, getting up and following her to the living room, purposely taking a seat right next to her, but looking straight ahead.

"When I ended up a mess at my parents' house a year and a half ago," she admits in a soft voice. "Mom called my sister, Chrissy, for help and between them they had me admitted for a seventy-two hour stay in the psychiatric ward. The same damn hospital where I just walked out on my job—where Philip worked," she huffs. "First thing the psychiatrist asked was whether I felt guilty for what my ex had done. After my seventy-two hours were up, he sent me off with a prescription and a diagnosis of clinical depression. I stopped talking after that."

My hands are fisted in my lap, and my jaw is clenched so tight, I wouldn't be surprised if I cracked a molar. The best I can do without losing my shit is make what I hope is a sympathetic sound, and I feel rather than see her shift in her seat to look at me.

"I'm sorry. I don't know how much Damian—"

"I know enough that if I ever bumped into your douchebag ex on the street, I'd castrate him," I grind out between my teeth, interrupting her. "Clearly I'd need a magnifying glass and a pair of tweezers to find his puny pecker, but I'd make sure he could never use it again."

Her soft giggle surprises me and I turn to face her.

"Puny pecker? Not saying it's not true, but how would you know?" she asks, and I'm more than happy to enlighten her.

"It's a known fact, only a guy with a tiny dick thinks he needs to prove his manhood by either sticking it in as many women as he can, or by driving a bigger truck than he can handle."

She's quiet for a moment, staring off in the distance when suddenly her mouth drops open, and she turns to me, mischief dancing in her eyes.

"You drive a big truck."

I grin right along with her, before I lean close, wiggle my eyebrows and share, "Difference is, I know how to handle a big stick."

After this morning's episode, I never thought I'd have Bella laughing so hard, this time the tears rolling down her face are those of hilarity.

Job done.

CHAPTER 10

BELLA

"So did it work?"

I look up at Jasper's question.

Laughing apparently makes you hungry, since my stomach hasn't stopped rumbling since. I'm frying up tortillas in my cast iron pan, while Jasper is doing something with the leftover roasted chicken and veggies that were in my fridge. Luckily, I always have tortillas and enough cheese in the house—my snack of preference—so putting a quick meal together is not a problem.

"Did what work?"

"You mentioned that doctor in the hospital gave you prescription; did the medication work?"

"I guess, but it also made me feel even more like a zombie. I didn't have any more emotional meltdowns, but then, I wasn't feeling much of anything at all. I hated it. I quit as soon as I moved out from under my mother's watchful eye."

"Did you ever try finding a decent doctor here in Durango? Maybe there's something you could take only as needed?"

It's strange, from anyone else I would find this line of questioning invasive—even judgmental—but I'm not getting that from Jasper. I find myself talking freely about things I've kept close to the chest.

"Other than the odd family physician, most doctors in Durango are affiliated one way or another with Mercy. I really don't want to mix work and private lives ever again. Besides, I don't know how this might impact my job. It's the one thing I'm good at."

I hear the clatter of the knife on the cutting board, but don't have a chance to look before I find myself pinned to the counter, Jasper's much larger body pressed against my back, his chin on my shoulder.

"I still have a lot to learn about you, but I'm willing to swear that your job, by far, isn't the only thing you're good at." His warm breath brushes my cheek, as my body instinctively presses deeper into his.

It feels good, both the words and the solid presence of his body behind me. I drop my head back, giving myself over to the moment, and he responds by opening his mouth on the exposed column of my neck, where I know he can feel the pounding of my heart against his tongue. He slides a hand from my hip, around to my stomach, and up between my breasts. When his fingers find their way under the edge of my robe, their soft stroke on my skin sends a shiver through me.

I'm floating on sensation, head back and eyes closed, afraid if I move I'll lose the feel of his breath brushing my skin, the heat of his palm curving around my breast. My knees feel weak and I lift my arm to hook behind his neck, anchoring myself.

He groans deeply—a delicious rumble I can feel to my toes—his free hand spreading on my lower stomach, holding me firm as he rubs his very noticeable erection against my ass.

"*Jas...*"

No sooner has his name left my lips, when the shrill peal of the smoke alarm goes off. Instantly the heat of his body is gone as he grabs a towel, wraps it around the handle of my smoking cast iron pan, and lifts it off the stove.

"Get the door, babe," he instructs, moving fast through the house to the front.

My brain and my legs, both still wobbly, don't respond immediately.

"Bella—door," he barks over the din of the alarm.

This time the message filters through and I mumble, "I'm not a dog," under my breath, as I rush to do as he asks.

He slips past me, down the porch steps and sets the pan in the dirt of my driveway, as I rush back, grab a towel, and start waving it in front of the offensive alarm mounted high on the wall.

I turn my head when I hear him come walk in, a shit-eating grin on his face.

"What?" I snap, firmly tugging the sides of my robe closed, but he ignores my bite, puts a hand in my waist and drops a hard kiss on my lips.

"We almost set the place on fire."

Still looking smug, he pushes me aside, reaches up and with annoying ease, dismantles my alarm and pulls the battery loose.

Luckily, it's only my last tortilla charred in the cooling pan outside, there are plenty left for dinner, which we eat in complete silence.

With the endorphin rush from our earlier encounter—and the flood of adrenaline at the near fire—fading, the heavy blanket of depression settles back on my shoulders. So when my phone rings while we're clearing dishes, my voice is tired when I answer it.

"What's wrong, *mi hija*?"

Ma doesn't bother saying hello, but goes straight into mother mode.

"Nothing, Ma. Just a bit under the weather."

"You're not looking after yourself. I was just saying to your *papa*, I worry about you with Damian away. And now with this awful business of someone shooting at policemen. I think you should come home."

I roll my eyes to the ceiling as I walk into the living room, slumping down on the couch. This is typical of my conversations with my mother, or anyone in my family for that matter. They ask how I am, only to dismiss whatever answer I give, and proceed to tell me what my problem really is.

"I *am* home, Ma. This is my home," I assert myself, but as usual it falls to deaf ears.

"Nonsense. You're renting someone else's home. I still don't get why you insist on living out there. No stores nearby, no neighbors—you scream—and no one would hear you. What if something happened?"

"Nothing is going to happen to me, and I like it here, Ma."

Jasper quietly sits down beside me, and I'm grateful for the hand he puts on my knee in silent support as my mother rants on.

"How can you say that? You think you're safe when police officers get killed in the streets? I can't sleep at night, worrying about you out on those same streets. That's not a job for someone like you."

I'm familiar with the jab of disappointment her words cause. Not like I haven't heard them before.

"Same job I did in Farmington for many years, Ma." I'm so tired of this same discussion, time and time again. Yet here I am, voluntarily banging my head into the same wall.

"And look how that turned out," she fires off, also not unexpected, but no less damaging. "At least your family was here to pick up the pieces."

As if my job had anything to do with my breakdown, but apparently that's more palatable than the hell Philip put me through, or the fact I may have suffered from depression most of my life. Those are shameful things one does not talk about in my family.

"Why did you call?" I ask, exasperated.

"To check up on my baby, of course. Someone has to." The kicker is, she sounds genuinely surprised I should ask.

"I'm fine, Ma. Just fine," I lie, suddenly bone-tired. "It's just a little cold."

"You sure? I could be there in a couple of hours if you need me."

"Positive. Give my love to Papa."

The moment I end the call, Jasper's arms circle me and pull me to his side. I close my eyes and lay my head on his shoulder.

"That sounded painful," he shares, pressing a kiss in my hair and I almost laugh out loud.

"You have no fucking idea."

J ASPER

No, I don't, but after listening to her side of the conversation and picking up at parts of what her mother was saying, I'm starting to get a clearer picture of Bella. A keener understanding of her.

I realize while I'm getting to know her better, because she's trusting me with parts of her she clearly holds close to her chest, I haven't been quite as forthcoming.

"You're right," I find myself saying. "I don't know much, if anything, about family dynamics. I grew up in foster care. I know little about where I come from, other than apparently I was found curled up, sleeping in a church pew in Hannover, Pennsylvania." I hear a small gasp coming from her, and immediately following, feel her body snuggle in closer, her arm crossing over my stomach.

"How old were you?"

"Three. There was a piece of paper pinned to the blanket I was covered with. It had my age and my name; Jasper."

"So were you adopted?"

I bark out a laugh. In hindsight it is a little funny. "No, but not for lack of trying. You could say I was bounced around by the system, mostly because people were fooled by my angelic looks, when I was really a holy terror."

This time it's Bella's turn to chuckle. "Doesn't surprise me." Her teasing words are immediately followed by a deep yawn.

"So yeah, the concept of family has always been rather alien to me. I'd look at yours, the way you care for each other, look out for each other, and I have to admit it never occurred to me that kind of closeness could be confining. I'm starting to see how it might."

"Do you miss it?" she asks, stifling yet another yawn.

"Can't miss what you never had." I shrug, before

untangling myself from her hold and getting to my feet. "Besides, my team is my family," I share, pulling her up from the couch.

"Where are we going?"

"I'm putting you to bed before you fall asleep on my lap."

"I wouldn't be averse to that." She smiles coyly, and I stop to capture her face in my hands and kiss those pouty lips.

"Maybe, but it would put serious strain on my control," I admit, and the moment she opens her mouth for a smart retort, I press a forefinger to her lips. "Don't tease me more, you'll make me forget I'm trying hard to be a gentleman."

She purses her lips against my finger, but follows me into the bedroom without another word and sits on the edge of the bed, about to untie her robe.

"Don't you have something to sleep in?"

"Top drawer," she says, pointing at her dresser.

Jesus fucking Christ. That's all I need, a drawer full of lacy confections. I'd hoped for more of the decent cotton panties I saw her wear in the hospital a few weeks back, but I guess I caught her on laundry day.

The only thing of any substance I can find is what looks like a flowy tank top with thin straps and a matching pair of panties. A fucking baby doll nightie—at least the cotton isn't see-through.

I hand it to her just as my phone buzzes in my pocket, and I use the excuse to hurry out of the room.

"Greene."

"Jas, it's Luna. I just got a call from Blackfoot, he's expecting us at his office in half an hour for a briefing on the shootings. Wants us to bring whatever we have."

Shit. That means Bella will be alone.

"I'm in a fucking tough spot here."

"I know. I tried, but he was adamant everyone be there."

"Fine, I'll figure something out," I concede, looking at my watch. I thought it was later than eight. "I'll be there."

I slide the phone in my pocket and head back to the bedroom, where I find Bella just coming out of the bathroom.

I was wrong.

The cotton does nothing to make the scant bits of clothing any less sinful. Bella's shapely curves are on full display, and they fucking make my mouth water.

I've never limited myself to any one particular body type when it comes to women. I've probably sampled all there was on offer at some point during my twenty-five years of sexual activity, but it all pales in comparison to the picture Bella makes in that less than innocent fucking nightie.

"Get in bed," I tell her, my voice hoarse as I hang on the doorknob like a life vest.

Thank God she does, but not without flashing me her juicy backside as she climbs in. I have to close my eyes and take a deep breath before I approach the bed.

"I have to go out for a bit."

"I know," she says, batting her long lashes against the fatigue straining her face. "I heard you on the phone. I'll be fine," she adds.

"I don't want to." I sit down on the edge beside her.

"I know that too," she says, smiling as she reaches out and lays her hand against my cheek. "But I really will be fine. I feel like I could sleep for a century."

I turn my head and kiss the inside of her palm.

"I'll get your phone, put it on your nightstand, in case you need me before I get back, and I'll lock the house up tight before I go."

"You're coming back?" The genuine surprise is evident on her face, and I lean down, plant my elbows on either side of her head, and rub her nose with mine.

"That shouldn't even be a question," I assure her, taking a quick taste of her sleepy lips. "I should be back by ten, but if I run late for whatever reason, I'll send you a message. Just turn off the ringer so it doesn't wake you up. Need me to bring back anything?"

Her eyes already closing, she hums as she shakes her head. I drop another kiss on her forehead and make my way out of the room to fetch her phone. By the time I return and drop her phone on the nightstand, she looks to be already asleep.

"Fries," she mumbles, as I'm about to shut her bedroom door.

"What?"

"Bring me back McDonald's fries."

"Sure thing," I promise, before pulling the door shut behind me, a smile on my face.

Fries it is.

I make sure the stove and oven are off, gather up my files and laptop, grab her house key, and do one last check of windows before I lock her safely inside.

I don't care what it takes, but come hell or high water, I'll be back here with her fries before McDonald's closes.

My hopes this meeting will be a fast one are dashed when I walk into the Durango PD boardroom, fifteen minutes later.

The room is packed with anyone remotely involved in the investigation: CBI, Colorado State Patrol, La Plata County Sheriff's Office, and half the Durango PD, along with their chief of police, Tom McMahan. Everybody is fucking present, up to and including the blasted mayor of Durango.

This may take a while.

CHAPTER 11

JASPER

"Hey, Luna, hold up!"

The damn briefing had taken much longer than I'd hoped, but at least we came away with a few more questions answered, and a few more leads added.

The CBI forensics lab had made quick work processing the shell and bullet from the second scene, confirming the same weapon was used as in the first shooting. They also reported, based on some rubber residue found on the slugs, the use of a suppressor was likely. The one bit of real news was the partial thumb print they found on the shell. All good information, but only if we have a gun and a suspect to match it to.

Nonetheless, there are still too many questions around the suspect; motivation being one. Why would someone start picking off police officers one by one? The only concrete pieces of evidence, which might be helpful identifying him, are that fingerprint and the partial bike pedal recovered from the trail.

No one questioned the conclusion that the police department is the target, or that the perp is likely local, since we were unable to find any incidents with a similar MO in neighboring areas.

The last hour and a half was spent setting a tighter protocol in place for all law enforcement, to ensure safety. Not an easy task, since the department budget doesn't stretch far enough to double up officers in every cruiser.

I anxiously watched the clock during that part of the discussion, and ended up shooting Bella a message around eleven thirty to let her know things were running late. I figure she's sleeping since I never heard back.

It's a little after midnight when I walk to my truck, a thicker file tucked under my arm, and see Luna in the parking lot up ahead.

"What's up?" she asks, turning around at the sound of my voice.

"I want you to grab a few hours of sleep, and tomorrow hit up gun shops and shooting ranges."

"I thought Blackfoot had someone look—"

"I know, but it can't hurt to do it again. You have a way of getting answers. Go shoot a few rounds, look around, and talk to other patrons, not just staff."

"Gotcha."

"Ask Dylan to follow up on that pedal. There's a bike out there with half of one missing."

"I'm going to focus on motive, check arrest records, police involved incidents, anything that may have put a target on their back."

"Will you be in the office tomorrow?" She tilts her head slightly and raises an eyebrow.

"At some point I plan to be."

"How *is* Bella?"

"She's…" I want to say she's okay, but Luna already knows that's a lie, so I try for the truth instead. "Struggling, and it's not just because she knew Bert."

"I figured." Luna taps her forefinger against her chin. "The eyes tell a lot about a person. Bella seems so well-adjusted, appears so upbeat and generally happy, but the eyes give it away. There's a detachment from the person she puts out there for the world to see."

I nod my agreement. "Apparently it's not new."

"Depression rarely is. I'm actually surprised she's talking to you."

"So am I," I admit. "But I'm out of my depth with this."

She pulls a pen from her pocket, rips a corner of her file folder, and jots down something on it, then hands it to me.

"What's this?"

"Gary Patterson, that's his number. He's a psychologist in Aztec, in private practice and certified in psychopharmacology."

"What does that mean?"

"He can prescribe certain medications. Only

a few states allow psychologists to prescribe with appropriate certification, and New Mexico happens to be one. He's good."

This time it's my turn to tilt my head and raise my eyebrow. "You seem well-informed?"

She's quiet for a moment, staring at the ground, and I wonder if she'll answer or blow me off.

"If you breathe a word, I will shoot your dick off. You know I will," she suddenly says, throwing me a heated look. I don't argue—I believe every word she says. She pauses to make sure I understand before she clarifies. "He's my therapist."

"Appreciate it," is all I say in return, and I mean it. Luna is extremely private, and it's pretty fucking big she's willing to share as much as that with me.

I tuck the number in my pocket without breaking eye contact, and put two fingers to my forehead in mock salute, before turning toward my truck.

Making a quick stop at my apartment, I grab a few clean clothes, my shaving kit with a few necessities, and put it all into an overnight bag. In the kitchen, I do a fruitless scan of my virtually empty fridge. I'm starving, it's been hours since we had the chicken fajitas we threw together, and my fuel gauge is on empty. As an afterthought, I unplug my scanner and stuff that in my bag as well. At this point, I'm not sure what the day will bring, but at least I'll be prepared.

When I drive up to the window at McDonald's my dashboard clock reads quarter to one. Fifteen minutes to spare.

"I just turned off the fryer," the kid in the window says when I place my order.

"Dude, it's not even one yet. You can't claim to be open until one if you stop serving fifteen minutes before."

Ten minutes later, and forty dollars poorer, I drive off with my order of fries for Bella and a Quarter Pounder with Cheese for me. The house is as I left it, with just the kitchen light on and not a peep coming from the bedroom. When I stick my head around the door, I find Bella still sleeping, her breathing deep and even. I don't really want to wake her up, so I close the door again and take the food to the kitchen.

Halfway through my burger, I hear the bedroom door open and the soft pad of bare feet on the floor.

"I smell fries," Bella says, as she walks into the kitchen, rubbing her eyes with her knuckles.

I try not to stare at her top, barely clinging to her tits, as one strap dangles uselessly from her shoulder.

"Good nose," I say, shoving the bag in her direction as she sits down on the stool beside me.

Much like last time I saw her chow down on these, she eats the fries with gusto, stuffing a few at a time in her mouth, barely aware of her surroundings or me. I try to eat the rest of my burger, but the little moans she elicits with every bite are starting to have an effect on me.

I never considered eating sexy, but fuck…

The loud crumple of paper disrupts thoughts I should probably not be having.

"Are you done with that?" Bella points at the empty McDonald's wrapper in front of me.

"I'll take care of it. Go back to bed," I grumble, probably a bit more brusquely than I need to be.

Bella doesn't seem to notice, though. She slides off her stool right beside me, hooks a hand behind my neck and pulls me down for a sweet, almost innocent kiss, before she pads back toward her bedroom, lush ass jiggling with every step.

I work for another hour, scouring through the Durango PD's online records, until my eyes cross. I shut my laptop, turn off lights, strip off my shirt, and shuck my jeans before trying to get comfortable on the couch.

I last maybe five minutes.

Bella is once again deep asleep, curled on her side. I slide under the covers, plump up the pillow, and tuck a hand under my head, trying to pretend I'm back in college, sharing a bed with a buddy too drunk to make it home.

There is no mistaking the little whimper, or the round butt scooting back to press against my hip. Can't say I don't appreciate the fact—even in sleep— she's looking for me, but she's making it awful hard to keep a lid on my libido.

Yielding to her draw, I roll on my side, hook an arm around her waist and tuck her close. I groan when her ass nestles against a rather hopeful boner, but I still manage to drift off just minutes later, the scent of her filling my senses.

I look at the clock on my kitchen wall again. I've done little else since I got up at a little after four this morning, Jasper's large body pressed against my back. My inner clock is completely fucked.

I slipped out of bed to use the washroom, ended up having a shower, which I realized I failed to do yesterday, and then tried to distract myself with some mindless TV.

It is now almost eight and there's still no sound from the bedroom.

I felt him slide into bed last night. I purposely rubbed up against him when he didn't look for contact himself. I was desperate for a continuation of what started in the kitchen yesterday and left me aching for some kind of release.

When he left the house after kissing me goodnight, I'd slipped my hand between my legs, trying to give myself some relief, but my own fingers rolling my clit didn't even come close to having the effect the chastest of his kisses has.

Eight o'clock.

I tiptoe to the bedroom, peeking around the door I left on a crack, to find him still sleeping, lying half on his stomach, one knee pulled up. His back is broad, muscles defined and tapering to his firm ass. His strong legs are covered in light down, just a shade darker than his hair.

I watch him for a while, indecisive whether to go back to watching TV, or be bold and climb back in bed. Jasper inadvertently makes that choice easy for me when he flips on his back and then over on his other side. I don't miss the substantial tent in his boxers before he rolls though.

Tiptoeing over to the bed, I climb in behind him, molding myself against his back as I slip a hand around him and under his waistband, feeling the heat of his cock against my palm. Carefully folding my fingers around his girth, I slowly stroke as I rock my hips into his.

I'm not sure at what point he becomes aware, but when one of his hands reaches behind and grabs onto my ass, I know he's well awake. His own hips take up fucking my fist.

It's the sexiest thing I've ever felt, the ripple of muscle in his back, the dig of his fingers into my flesh, and the heat of his rock-hard cock in my hand. I almost come from that alone.

"Bella, sweetheart..." his raspy voice groans my name, before suddenly I find myself on my back, his large body leaning over mine, his breath choppy. "Are you sure this is what you want? Because, baby, waking up with your hand on me—I'm already about past the point of no return."

Instead of answering, I grab the hem of my top and whip it over my head.

"Fuck yeah," I hear him mumble, just before his hot mouth sucks my nipple so deep, my back arches off the bed. While he moves his mouth to the other breast, giving it the same treatment, he one-handedly yanks down my panties. Firmly stroking two fingers along my wet crease, he finds my opening and plunges them deep.

There is nothing gentle about this. Nothing held back. Pure unbridled lust after a long leisurely buildup. Not even the wild scramble for a condom— which luckily he stocked his shaving kit with—abates the clawing need.

He holds himself over me, but when I open my legs wide in invitation, he instead curves an arm around my waist and hoists me further up the bed. I know why, seconds later, when he scoots down and his head disappears between my legs.

Bliss at the first stroke of his tongue. Apparently he works out all over; the hard flicks and deep probes have me teetering on the brink in no time.

"Not yet," he mumbles against my soft inner thigh, before climbing back up my body, letting his body rub along the length of mine.

He braces, an elbow on either side of my head, as he effortlessly lines up his cock at my entrance. I've already stopped breathing in anticipation when his mouth covers mine. In contrast to the wild, passionate ride so far, his kiss is soft, tentative almost, as his eyes remain open and alert on mine. He's giving me a last out.

All it takes is the tight clutch of my hands on his ass to answer his unspoken question, and with one firm drive, he buries himself to the root.

***

"What are you doing?" Jasper asks as he walks into the kitchen. He just came out of the shower, dressed in only a pair of jeans and rubbing a towel through his wet hair.

"Calling into work."

Jasper ditches the towel on my counter and stalks over, fishing the phone from my hand and tossing it on the couch as he wraps me in his arms.

"Why?"

"Why?" I repeat, confused why he'd ask.

"Yeah, why? Don't you remember Ryan coming here? Saying he'd make sure you'd be covered for a week. You have strep throat, remember?"

I remember Ryan being here, but I clearly don't remember everything that was discussed, which is irritating to say the least.

"I don't, actually. I remember a lot but not all, given that I spent most of the time he was here sedated." There may have been a hint of sarcasm in my delivery, but Jasper is not fazed.

"That's my bad. I could've reminded you," he says calmly.

I hate to admit, but I now vaguely recall Ryan saying something about alienating me and calling the supervisor, right before he stuck a needle in my arm.

"I need to work, though. I like staying busy."

Meaning I'm afraid I'll lose my shit once Jasper goes into work, and I'm left with nothing but my thoughts—but I don't say that.

"I have a better idea," he says, digging through his pocket and coming up with a piece of paper with a name and number on it. "Why don't you see if you can talk to this guy instead? He's a therapist, I have it from a reliable source he is good, he has a practice in Aztec and is not affiliated with any hospitals. Also, he can prescribe."

Panic claws at me at the thought of baring my soul to another stranger.

"I'd much rather just work, I'm feeling a lot better—clearly."

His hands come up to cup my face. "I'm sure you do—for now—but we both know you can't bury this with work and attitude, Squirt. Gotta treat it from the root, or it'll keep growing through the cracks."

I want to throw sass, but I can't for the life of me come up with anything scathing or particularly smart to say. Instead I voice what I feel.

"I hate that you're right."

He grins, dropping his forehead to mine.

"I know you do, sweetheart."

CHAPTER 12

JASPER

"You're cooking again?"

As she has been for most of yesterday afternoon and evening, Bella is in the kitchen, pulling shit out of the cupboards and the fridge.

"Breakfast," she throws over her shoulder when I walk in.

"We could've eaten some of those enchiladas you made yesterday," I suggest, leaning my ass against the counter, which earns me an eye roll.

"Those are for Bert's family. Besides, I already stuck them in the freezer."

"And the muffins?"

"Those too," she snaps.

One thing I'm learning about Bella, she cannot sit still. In part I'm sure it's a way to cope for her, but I'm guessing being industrious in one way or another is part of her upbringing as well. I've seen her family in action at Damian's house. They swarm in en masse and get shit done.

Her phone rings on the counter and she leaves the eggs on the stove to check the caller, immediately placing the phone facedown on the counter again.

"Are you ever gonna answer her calls?"

Bella has been avoiding her mother, who's tried calling a multitude of times.

Stubborn. Something else I figure as a family trait.

"When I'm ready."

I grab her hand, which is wielding a spatula, and pull her away from the stove and into my arms. My mouth cuts her off mid-protest as it covers hers. She goes rigid in my arms, but when I rub a hand along her spine—something I've discovered she responds to—she relaxes, kissing me back.

"Morning," I mumble against her lips.

"Let me go. You're making me burn my food again." Her words are testy, but when I do as she asks and she turns back to the stove, she does so with soft lips and a pretty blush on her cheeks.

There's been a lot of that since she surprised the fuck out of me in bed yesterday morning. Me touching or kissing her, and Bella blushing as she tries hard to hold onto the prickly persona she likes to display.

I get it. There are moments I feel exposed, and my instinct tells me to hide in my digital world, so I imagine it's no different for her. Habits are hard to break, especially when they've become a shield you protect yourself with from the world.

She did end up calling the number Luna gave me, and I was surprised at how forthcoming she was with this Dr. Patterson over the phone. It had been enough for him to make room in his weekend to see her right away on an emergency basis. She'd balked at first, but conceded eventually.

By ten, we were on our way to Aztec. I dropped her off at the therapist, before heading to Safeway with a grocery list she'd prepared on the drive down. I do my own shopping 'off the cuff,' basically throwing in my basket what looks good at that time, so shopping with a very specific list was a bit of a challenge. By the time I got back she was already waiting outside, face a little blotchy and clutching a prescription in her hand.

I didn't ask, but she shared a little on the way back to Durango, said he seemed nice and had persuaded her to try a new low-dose medication, with a minimum of side effects, to help stabilize her.

Leaving her to her cooking, I open my laptop on the coffee table to check emails. I'd sent one off last night to Keith, with a list of police arrests and incidents for the past twelve months I had flagged for him to look into. There's an email back from him, saying he's on it and to call him when I have a minute.

"You're up," he says when he answers my call.

"And you sound like you haven't been to bed in a while," I fire back.

These past few weeks have worn on the man.

Everyone wants answers: the chief, the mayor, the victims' families, and since the shooting last Wednesday there's the added pressure of the press hounding him.

"Not really," he admits, sounding exhausted. "Let me find a quiet spot. Hang on."

I wait until I hear the background noise fade, and the sound of a door closing.

"You asked me to call?" I prompt.

"Yeah. Sorry, I need some privacy for this. I'm in my office now." His words pique my interest. "I have my guys working on the list you sent me, and I'd like you to go further back, maybe do one with anything you can find two to five years back."

"Okay." I'm not quite sure why he had to lock himself in his office to ask me that.

"You'll find an incident that probably will raise all your flags, but I want you to leave it off the list. A traffic stop that went wrong in the spring of 2013."

"Have any more for me to go on?" I ask, when no further information appears forthcoming.

"I'm putting my job on the line telling you this much."

"Why do you want me to leave it off the list?" I ask, suddenly uneasy with the request.

"Because I want you to look into that one quietly. Not sure if it has anything to do with this, but I can't have it shoved under the rug again when I've already lost two guys."

"All right, what if it does turn out relevant? I

won't keep anything quiet then, you know I won't."

"I know, which is why I'm asking you. Look, I've gotta go. No emails on this, and to answer your question, if the incident turns out to be relevant, it's about fucking time the lid came off. If not, then it's up to your office what to do with what you find." He ends the call before I can respond.

A little pissed, but mostly intrigued, I immediately sign into the police department's reports and start looking through 2013. It doesn't take long for me to find it.

I'm just about to start reading when Bella calls me for breakfast.

"This stuff has some serious bite," I comment, my mouth full of *huevos rancheros*.

"Too hot for you?" Bella tosses me a teasing grin.

"I can take any heat you dish out, Squirt," I shoot back with a wink, which has her return a dramatic roll of her eyes.

Breakfast is interrupted by the ringing of my phone. Ryan's name pops up on the screen. Bella sees it too and raises an eyebrow in question.

"Morning."

"Ditto. How is she?"

I look at Bella, who has a storm brewing on her face. "Sitting right beside me with a face like thunder," I tell him bluntly.

Ryan chuckles. "Better then," he deduces.

"Getting there, but why don't I hand you over to her, you can ask her yourself?"

Bella almost snatches the phone from my hand, and proceeds to tear a strip off her partner, while I turn my attention back to my plate.

BELLA

"I'm not a child, you know. I'm more than capable of speaking for myself, so if you want to know how I am, fucking ask *me*."

From the corner of my eye, I see Jasper grin around his fork. I'll get to him later.

"I don't need to ask now," Ryan answers, an annoying smile in his voice. "I can tell just by listening to you."

"Quit being a smartass, Ryan. I'm not in the mood."

"Aunt Flo coming for a visit?"

I grind my teeth, my partner has a finely honed sixth sense for PMS, which he claims is imperative for survival in his family. He has a sister, a wife, and two teenage daughters. I think it was the second month I was riding with him that he asked me if I was on my period. I almost slugged him, but he explained, being a man, he couldn't be held accountable for pissing me off, if he didn't have fair warning. He actually keeps a calendar on his phone. Weird for sure, however, as I've found out since, he's one of the few people who actually doesn't piss me off. Guess it's working for him.

"You know damn well she is," I bite off.

"Good, then by the time you're scheduled to come back to work, she'll be good and gone."

"What do you mean by the time I'm scheduled to come back? I'm good to go now."

"Bella," Jasper growls beside me, but I wave him off and take my call to the living room.

"You're bored. That doesn't mean you're ready to come back. You should know the difference. Have you seen someone yet?"

I throw an accusing glare at Jasper, who just shrugs and shoves another forkful in his mouth. "I see you two have been talking behind my back." I don't bother softening my scathing tone. I'm allergic to being managed.

"If you mean, have your boyfriend and I stayed in touch after sitting by your bedside, watching you withdraw from life before our eyes? Then yes, we've been fucking talking behind your back. Not because we don't trust you, but because we care and are affected by what is happening to you."

"He's not my boyfriend," I return, trying to deflect. It sounds petty—even to my own ears. I know Ryan doesn't patronize, nor would he say anything derogatory about me, and neither would Jasper. I don't know a whole lot, but I know that. I'm not being fair to either of them.

"Coulda fooled me," Ryan says casually. "Has he been there every night since Wednesday? Sleeping in your bed?"

"I don't see how that is—"

"Has he, Gomez?"

"I guess," I give in meekly, having been put in my place.

"Then he's your boyfriend. Get over it, he seems like a stand-up guy."

"He found me a therapist in Aztec. Took me to see him yesterday."

"See?" Ryan comes right back, hammering his point home. "A good guy. Not a douchewipe like Scott with the limp dick, or that other creep back in Farmington. Good things can happen to you, Gomez. You just have to believe it."

I've got nothing to say to that, so I don't. Jasper looks at me curiously and I give him an embarrassed little smile.

"I should get going. The girls are waiting for me in the car. Going to see the in-laws; pray for my soul, theirs are beyond saving."

When Ryan ends the call and I drop my phone on the table, I look up to find Jasper crooking a finger at me.

"Come here, Bella," he prompts when I don't move right away.

"What?" The attitude is moot, since my feet are already heading in his direction. I walk straight up between his knees and into his arms, pressing my nose in the hollow of his neck. He smells good.

"Want to go on a date with me?"

"A what?" I tip my head back to look at him.

"A date," he grins. "We kind of jumped over that part, and I wouldn't be much of a boyfriend if I didn't take you out at least once. Tell me something you've always wanted to do but never got around to?"

"Vegas?" It flies out without much thought. It's true, I've always wanted to experience Vegas, but it's not something you do on your own.

"That's a vacation, I'm talking something around town. Something we could do on the spur of the moment. We'll save Vegas for after this case is resolved. Why don't you think about it? *Fuck.*" His eyes are focused somewhere behind me when he curses. "We've got company."

I hear the sound of a key turning the lock and swing around to see the front door open.

Fuck indeed.

A goddamn invasion, that's what this is.

I should never have given my mother the spare key she insisted on. I could've prevented myself a scene just like this.

"Isabella, maybe you should put some clothes on?" is the first thing out of my mother's mouth, as her critical eyes scan first me—and then the rigid form of Jasper behind me—including his arm which is anchored around my waist. I'm still prancing around in my nightie, and he never bothered putting on a shirt.

Papa steps inside behind her, toting a suitcase, the sight of which has my stomach ball up in a sudden cramp. His eyebrows shoot up when he sees us. I can only imagine the picture we make, half-naked.

"Be right back," I mumble, wiggling my way out of Jasper's hold, I grab his hand, pulling him behind me into the bedroom.

"This is a nightmare," I hiss, closing the door behind us.

"I'm guessing you should've answered her calls," Jasper comments dryly, yanking a shirt from his overnight bag and pulling it over his head.

I freeze with only one leg in my yoga pants.

"You think that would've made a difference? You don't know my mother, she's relentless. Where are you going?" I ask in a panic when he reaches for the door.

"Get dressed, Squirt. I'm going to say hello to your parents."

Before I have a chance to warn him about the viper pit he's about to step into, he closes the door firmly behind him. I struggle into my pants, grab the first shirt I find, and yank a brush through my tangled hair. No more than two minutes, and already I can hear raised voices.

When I rush into the kitchen, I find Jasper calmly making coffee. My parents, however, are nose to nose in my living room.

"She's my baby, a mother can sense when there's

trouble," Ma hisses at my father, who does his own version of the eye roll.

"She's clearly not a baby. I told you to knock first when we saw the truck parked out there, but you just couldn't help yourself. Isabella is a grown woman."

"She needs me," Ma insists.

"She looks like she's doing just fine without you, Carmella."

I feel Jasper step up behind me, his hand comes to rest on my hip and his warm breath brushes my cheek.

"Want me to grab the hose? Just say the word." I bite down on a chuckle at his whispered words, as my parents battle it out in my living room—at my expense.

"Coffee?"

Jasper's offer draws their attention, and in the next moment, I find myself folded in Mama's arms, pressed against her chest. She's is tall, much taller than my five two, even taller than Papa. Texas-born, and yet more Mexican than most Mexican mothers I know. It's all about the food and the nurturing—those two go hand in hand—but it's also about attempting to control the whole family. That's something Papa usually lets her get away with, but clearly not today. He may look like a pushover, but he may well be the only match for my mother.

"Ma," I plead, trying to untangle myself. "I can't breathe."

She lets me go, but then sets her sights on Jasper.

"Does Damian know you play with his baby sister?"

"Ma!"

"Carmella!" Papa and I exclaim at the same time.

"It's okay," Jasper says calmly, throwing a wink in my direction before turning to Ma. "He will, although, I have a feeling it may not come as a complete surprise. Bella and I together may be a new development, but we weren't exactly strangers before. I'm pretty sure this was bound to happen at some point, circumstances just sped up the timeline."

"Circumstances?"

"Ma!" I try again, and this time she turns to me.

"What circumstances, Bella? I call, you sound horrible. You say you're under the weather, but I hear these things about shootings, and all I can think is my baby is out there. You won't talk to me. What are you not telling me?"

My eyes shoot over to Jasper for rescue, but all he does is walk over, tuck me to his side, and give my shoulder an encouraging squeeze. I have a choice, I can play it off as work-related stress—but that will only enforce her position that I should find something more suitable to do—or I admit to my problem."

"I'm on medication for depression, Ma."

Her response is almost funny, it's so predictable. Her eyes shoot immediately over my shoulder to Jasper, and I know she's worried what he might think.

"Everyone feels a little blue now and then. Nothing a good meal and a mother's love can't fix," she comments with a fake little smile, more to him than to me.

"This isn't something you can fix with your chili rellenos or a hug, Mama. I struggle every day, and what makes it worse is not being able to talk about it because it shames the family."

Her eyes shoot to me and I'm surprised to see both shock and fear, when I was expecting anger and disappointment. "Isabella, you can always talk to me."

"Really? Because I've tried and you end up brushing it off; telling me I have to get thicker skin, make better choices. You say I should trust you to know what's best for me—but, Mama—you've never once trusted me. None of you have."

JASPER

"Greene."

Of course my phone has to buzz, right in the middle of a showdown between Bella and her mother. I try to surreptitiously fish it from my pocket to check the caller, but Mr. Gomez catches me.

"Take it. I've got these two," he mumbles from the side of his mouth.

"Be right back," I whisper in Bella's ear, as I release my hold on her, but I doubt she even hears me. Her dad takes a step closer, and his calm nod assures me she'll be fine, as I step outside on the front porch to take Luna's call.

"I may have a lead," she gets right to the point. "A small shooting range up in the mountains, just north of town. Off Junction Creek Road. It's on the property of the Arrow's Edge MC."

From what I understand, the motorcycle club has been around for a few decades, and mostly keeps a low profile. I know Damian looked in on them when he took over the La Plata County office, but the last run-in those guys had with the law predates the legalization of pot in 2012. You see the guys sometimes, they own a few businesses in town they check in on, all legal as far as I know. From what I gather, most of them are veterans who had trouble adjusting to civilian life.

"Take Dylan?" I suggest.

"Max has soccer practice."

"Shit."

Normally Luna doesn't need anyone holding her hand, and I know she resents having to call in for back up, but MCs are a brotherhood. A men's club. They can be testy when law enforcement comes knocking, let alone in the form of a woman no bigger than a sprite.

"Sorry, Jas."

"No, you made the right call. You at the office?"

"I am."

"Give me twenty minutes and I'll swing by to pick you up."

"Sure thing."

Inside, the mood has shifted some. I find Bella and her mother on the couch, deep in conversation, while her dad keeps a close eye from the kitchen, where he's doing the dishes. I walk over to him.

"I've gotta run out. We've got this case—"

"I know, the cop shootings. Go. Carmella came prepared to stay a while if she was needed. No holding that woman back when she has her mind set on something. We'll stick around. You go get that *pendejo* off the streets."

"About Damian—" Again, the older man stops me, raising his hand as he shakes his head.

"You sort whatever needs sorting with my son when he gets home from his honeymoon. It's not our business."

"Much appreciated."

I offer my hand, which he clasps tightly, pulling me toward him.

"Told you my youngest is a handful. Glad to see you're made of stern stuff."

CHAPTER 13

"It'll be the first left."

I follow Luna's directions and drive through thick trees, up a winding dirt road that's got to be hell in winter. When we round the last bend, the trees open up to a large clearing with several buildings. The eight foot high, chain-link fence surrounding it looks out of place in the natural setting.

I drive up to the gate, which is opened by a rough-looking kid, with a red bandana tied around long greasy hair and a huge gun hanging off his skinny hips in an open holster. Some modern-day Billy the Kid wannabe.

"What do you want?" he asks me when I roll down my window, but I let Luna answer.

"Special Agent Luna Roosberg," she says, flashing her badge. "I spoke to someone at the shooting range earlier, who said I should talk to Ouray."

"Chief don't talk to Feds. 'Specially skinny bitch Feds. We ain't got nothin' to say to you."

I'm this close to reaching out the window and grabbing his scrawny little neck, but I manage keep a lid on it.

"We're investigating the recent murder of two police officers, we'd like to ask him some questions."

"Only good cop is a dead cop," the punk says, with a grin I want to permanently engrave on his face with my fist.

"Enough." The deep baritone comes from behind the kid, where a man who looks like he's a couple of years older than me walks up. Gray threads his beard and the short buzz on his head, and his face looks weathered by the road. The guy is solid, built like a bull, with a set of shoulders that strain the seams of his shirt.

"But, Chief—"

"Momma needs help with the propane, Rowtag. Now."

The man never raises his voice but his words clearly command respect. The kid skulks off to the larger of the buildings.

"Ouray." I shake the hand he sticks through the window. He merely nods at Luna, with a mumbled, "Ma'am," and I have to bite down a grin when I hear her growl beside me.

I introduce us both and he shows us where to park. He leads us inside the main building and through what looks a bit like an American Legion hall: a cavernous space with a large American flag on the wall behind the bar, mismatched tables and chairs, and a couple of old couches. The handful of people inside watch with open curiosity as we pass.

"Sit." He waves at a couple of chairs in front of the desk in, what I assume is, his office at the end of a hallway.

I glance over at Luna, who is sending off agitated vibes. Her eyes are slits as she watches Ouray move behind the desk and sit down in the old leather office chair. He pays her no mind whatsoever and keeps his focus on me.

"You've got questions for me."

"Actually, *I* do," Luna speaks up, and the man ever so slowly turns his head to her, one eyebrow raised. I just sit back and cross my arms. This should be interesting.

"That so?" There is no mistaking the mocking tone, and for a moment, it looks like I'll have to stop Luna from flying across the desk, but she reels it in, taking a deep breath.

"We're investigating the shooting—"

"Of two cops—I know."

"We understand you operate a shooting range?"

Ouray leans forward, planting his elbows on his desk. "Is that a fuckin' question? 'Cause we'll be here for hours if you don't get on with why you're here."

I'm tempted to jump in before this goes off the rails, but Luna is able to shake it off.

"The shooter is a good shot. Accurate. Every nine millimeter strikes target. It's possible he practiced with a suppressor at some point."

"Nine millimeter? Fuck. Hang on." He gets up, walks to the door, and sticks his head in the hallway. "*Momma!* Nosh here yet?" Something is yelled back, but I can't quite make it out.

He sits back down when an old man—at least seventy—walks in, barely glances our way, and leans against the wall, his eyes on Ouray, who surprises me when he starts signing with lightning speed. The two engage in a silent conversation that's starting to wear on my nerves.

"Care to share?" Ouray's eyes flash my way, before burning on Luna when she starts to talk.

"The old man manages the shooting range. One of his regulars, a guy who showed up—maybe a year ago—with a Glock he said he inherited from his dad and wanted to learn how to shoot, brought in a silencer the last few times he was here," she answers, surprising everyone in the room. Even more so when she turns to the old guy and shows off her American Sign Language skills, by taking over the conversation. This time it's Ouray's turn to cross his arms and sit back in his chair. Amusement clear on his face.

By the time we walk out, Luna is apparently enlightened but I'm still in the fucking dark.

"I'd like to think I didn't just come as a doorstop," I bitch, as I drive the truck off the property. Something Luna apparently finds amusing.

"Guy's name is Connor. Nosh says he checked his license first time he showed up, maybe a year ago. Can't remember the last name, though. Says he would help out from time to time in return for gun storage and use of the shooting range. Last time he saw him was three weeks, maybe a month ago, when he spent a day shooting rounds with a new suppressor he'd brought. Says the guy's a crack shot. When he left, he must have taken his gun, because his safe is empty. He hasn't been seen since."

"So no last name. Description?"

"Dark hair, tall, and lanky."

"No distinguishing marks? Tats?"

"Not that he could see. He drives a navy Ford F-150. The guess is early nineties."

"Plates?"

"No number, but he remembers they were New Mexico plates."

"Good start. Let's head back to the office and see what we can do with that."

It's close to nine o'clock by the time I pull up to Bella's place. Her parents' car is still parked in the drive.

I sent her a text when I got back to the office to see how things were.

Bella: Ma is out shopping. She insists on making

tamales. Emergency food for a Gomez. I'm fine, do your thing.

Me: Save me some.

Bella: There'll be enough for a battalion. They reheat well.

Me: xox

I chuckled when I realized what I just sent. Pretty sure it's the first time I resorted to sending hugs and kisses in code. Or any other way for that matter.

"Ma wants to stay the night."

It's the first thing out of Bella's mouth when I walk in. If not for the look of sheer panic on her face, I might have thought she was sending me packing.

"Where's she going to sleep?" I tease, loud enough for everyone in the house to hear, as I fold Bella in my arms. Her father chuckles from the couch, she hides her face in my shirt, and her mother is shooting daggers from the kitchen. Clearly, I'm not gaining points with Mom.

"See, Carmella?" Mr. Gomez, who is evidently more sympatico. "The man wants to look after his girl. You just come back to the hotel with me."

"But we don't even know him!" Exasperated, the woman throws up her hands. "He's almost a stranger."

"To us, maybe, but I think it's pretty obvious not to Bella." The older man shoots me a wink over his daughter's head, before he heads into the kitchen to fetch his wife, who seems determined to stay, and another argument ensues.

"Do you want your mom to stay?" I ask Bella softly. She lifts her face and gives me her signature eye roll.

"Cuddling with you is a lot nicer," she says with a cheeky smile, before turning serious. "But we had some good talks, and I know she worries. Maybe?"

Good enough for me. I drop a peck on her lips before I let her go and walk into the kitchen. Time to make nice with Mom.

"Mrs. Gomez, it's actually a peace of mind if you could stay," I say, clearly surprising her. "Truth is, we've made some good strides in the investigation today and there's always a possibility I'll get called away. I don't want to run the risk having to leave your daughter alone in the middle of the night."

I pretend I don't see the triumphant look she throws her husband before she turns to me. "Of course. Sit down, you must be starving. Have some tamales," she offers. Not waiting for my answer, she grabs a plate from the cupboard and loads on three tamales from the pan on the stove. She misses her husband clapping me on the shoulder as he passes by me, a grin on his face.

"Well played, son. Well played."

BELLA

"You sure you'll be okay?"

I smile up at Jasper.

We're standing out on my porch, saying goodbye, while Papa is doing the same with my mom inside. Although, I hope they limit it to the saying of goodbye, and not the butt-clutching, heat-fueled kiss goodbye we just shared out here.

"I'll be fine. You should be focusing on finding this guy, and not be stuck here holding my hand."

"Hasn't exactly been a hardship, sweetheart." He grins and tucks a strand of hair behind my ear.

"Might've been now, though. Damn Ryan was right," I confess. "Apparently, it's my time of the month." For a moment, it looks like I might have to elaborate, but luckily realization dawns on his handsome face.

"I see."

"Yeah," I sigh, stroking a hand up his chest, feeling the solid muscle underneath.

"Although you should know, I'm not exactly a one-trick pony," he adds, but before I can question what exactly he means by that, my father steps out on the porch.

"Heading out, *mi hija*," Papa says, and I swing around to give him a peck on the cheek.

"I still don't get why you don't save yourself the money and crash at Damian's place."

"Your mother didn't want to be too far from you. She wanted the hotel—I got her the hotel."

"But since she's staying here, you can always—"

"Isabella," my father says, tapping the tip of my nose like he did when I was twelve, "I'll feel better being close too. Your mama, she may not always say the right things, but I promise you she always means the right things."

"I know," I mumble into his neck, when he gives me one of his teddy bear hugs.

Jasper's hand rubs along my spine as we watch my father's taillights disappear down the road. He doesn't have far to go, just down to the Best Western along the 160 into town.

"You should head back inside," he says, stepping past me off the porch. Standing two steps down from me, he's still almost eye to eye. "Call me tomorrow morning?"

"I will." I lean in for one more kiss, and then watch until his lights disappear down the mountain as well.

"Can I get you anything?" my mother asks when I walk inside. She's in the kitchen, packing up the leftovers and tucking them in my freezer.

"I'm fine, Ma."

As long as I can remember, my mother could always be found in the kitchen. It's her domain. Maybe even her safe zone. It's also the way she cares, with cooking. Whatever she can't express with words, she does with food.

Papa would come home from work and sit in his lazy chair, watch the news on TV, or sometimes toss a ball with Damian. I would usually climb on his lap and put my ear to his chest, because I loved to hear the deep thud of his heartbeat and rumble of his voice. Papa has always been safe, less critical, and definitely the easier parent to talk to.

That's what I did this afternoon while Ma was at the store, I sat beside him on the couch, put my ear to his chest and talked. After that I listened. He gave me some insight into my mother, told me how she was raised without any physical affection. How she would call her parents 'Sir' and 'Ma'am.' He explained how he saw her; trying to compensate for what she never had herself growing up, but in doing so had no sense of boundaries. She'd simply never learned. He said she was tough on us girls, not because she preferred Damian, but because life had taught her girls had to be tougher to survive.

He also pointed out that me being the youngest, always last in line, I might have become conditioned to assume everything was criticism, when sometimes it was simply concern. That he and Ma both have long known that I struggled, and avoided talking about it much, not because they were ashamed, but because I would become defensive.

Not the easiest thing, when someone holds up a mirror, but certainly eye-opening.

When Ma came home, she saw my blotchy face, raised her eyebrows at my dad, and then ordered me into the kitchen to help her put the groceries away. We spent the rest of the afternoon making tamales. For the first time, I was able to hear my mother's truth behind her sometimes brusque words, instead of my interpretation of them. It was a revelation.

"Wanna watch a movie?" I flop down on the couch and grab the remote.

"What kind of movie?" Mom says, wiping down

the counter.

"I'm not sure, I'll see what's on."

"Should I make popcorn?" she asks, and I hide a grin behind my hand. Always with the food.

"Sure. There's some in the—"

"Cupboard above the fridge, I know," Mom finishes for me, as she dries her hands on a towel. She probably took stock before she went shopping. It means she saw what else I stock up there as well.

"Grab the wine while you're at it."

Ten minutes later, she walks in with a tray holding the wine, two glasses, a bowl of popcorn, one with nachos, a small bowl of salsa, and another with the fresh guacamole she just whipped up on the spot.

I'm ready with a box of tissues and *Steel Magnolias* lined up on Netflix.

Two hours later I roll into bed, stomach full, completely cried out, and oddly satisfied as I listen to Ma's soft snores on the other side of the mattress.

I grab my phone and shoot off a quick message.

Me: Goodnight xox

Jasper: Night, Squirt. I'd much rather cuddle you than my pillow.

I chuckle softly as I put my phone on the nightstand and tuck the covers over my ear.

From behind me I hear my mother's sleepy voice.

"He seems like a nice boy."

CHAPTER 14

We've been digging for days with little to show for it.

Between the demands of the investigation and Bella's parents in town, I've kept a low profile, limited to a few calls and nightly texts since the weekend.

Luna is putting together a suspect analysis, based on what we know so far. Dylan has been looking at every navy Ford F-150 in a fifty-mile radius, and ever since I discovered the police report Blackfoot hinted at over the weekend, I've had my nose to the grindstone trying to make sense of the multiple red flags that went up when I read it.

The report describes a simple traffic stop on a white pickup with a taillight out, which resulted in the death of one Franklin Davis, a forty-three-year-old general laborer, on his way home from a job site up near Hermosa. According to the report, the man had reached under his seat, despite repeated requests by the officer to stop moving. The moment the officer spotted a weapon in the man's hand, he fired a shot, instantly killing the single occupant of the vehicle.

The first red flag went up when I saw the officer's name: Tom McMahan, the current chief of police. The second was the time lapse between when the initial notification of a traffic stop went out to dispatch, and when the second call reporting the shooting came in. Twenty minutes separated the two, which did not exactly line up with details in the report. The third red flag was the notation at the bottom of the file that certain items in evidence had gone missing, most notably the reported weapon.

A sick feeling has been eating at my gut, and for once, since Damian went on his honeymoon, I am tempted to call and tell him to get his ass home. Blackfoot may have asked me to look into this on my own, but after trying to sort through bits and pieces of it, I'd feel a fuck of a lot better if I had Damian at my back. I'm not going to keep my boss out of the loop on this. I'm increasingly uneasy carrying this on my own, given the potential scale of what should be a full-fledged investigation.

"Did you hear?" Dylan asks, as he walks into the office. "The funeral for Cummings is this coming Friday."

There had been no funeral for Belker, whose family had the body shipped home to Nebraska for a quiet cremation. Law enforcement was bound to come out strong for this one, with full pomp and circumstance.

"Where'd you find that out?"

"I bumped into one of the dispatchers when I was grabbing lunch at Applebee's, she mentioned it."

"I didn't know you had a contact in dispatch." This from Luna, who's been quiet most of the afternoon, but likes to try and get a rise out of Dylan on occasion. Her tone is teasing.

"Wouldn't call her a contact, exactly," he admits a tad sheepish. "She's a girl I dated a few times, who happens to be a dispatcher."

"She been there long?"

"Trish? I think about six or seven years. Why?"

Both sets of eyes are focused on me and I only hesitate a moment. "Because I need someone to talk to in dispatch, who's been there for a while, and can keep their mouth shut."

"Have you called the boss?" is Dylan's first question, when I finish filling them in on what I've been doing.

"Been tempted, but—"

"Guys, quiet!" Luna suddenly barks, diving for the scanner on her desk and cranking up the volume.

"...*Suspect Caucasian, in his late teens, early twenties, black shirt, pants, and ballcap, camo backpack, riding a small silver-colored bicycle. Was last seen heading into the residential area between Columbine and Delwood...*"

"Attempted car theft behind the Frontier Baptist

Church on Forest," Luna clarifies when I look at her questioningly. "Could be our suspect."

"I'm heading out there," Dylan announces, already on the move.

I'm left looking over at Luna. "It's Wednesday."

"I know," she says with a grin. "It's a pattern." She gets up and walks over to the large whiteboard on the wall, adding the suspect description, and Wednesday in large red letters.

"Looks like, but what the fuck does it mean?"

"Not a clue," she admits. "But I'm positive it's important."

"You look tired," Bella says when I show up on her doorstep unannounced.

I was on my way home, frustrated with another day of running down leads and forming theories, when I found myself turning right instead of left coming down from Rock Point Drive.

Luna kicked me out, after helping me to dig into Franklin Davis' family and discovered that not quite six months after Davis was shot, his wife committed suicide, leaving their almost fourteen-year-old son, James, an orphan. He'd been placed with his maternal grandfather in Shiprock, the fall of 2013, but the grandfather since had moved into a seniors' facility in Farmington. No record of where James ended up. His name is now at the top of our whiteboard.

"I am," I freely admit, coaxing her out on the porch and pulling the front door closed behind her. "How are you?" I ask, wrapping my arms around her tightly and looking down in her large brown eyes. Without waiting for an answer, I kiss her like I've been starved to do since Sunday.

"Better now," she says, when I finally let her up for air. "Although my mother is trying hard to eradicate what little sanity I have left. I get she means well, but God I'd shoot myself if I had to live with her. I've been trying to convince her to go back to the hotel the last two nights, so I can breathe a little, but I can't get her to go." Suddenly her eyes light up, and I know she's up to something when she drags me inside, straight through to the kitchen. "Ma, look; Jasper is here. Why don't you go with Papa? Have a nice meal at the Strater, you guys love that Diamond Belle Saloon. Jasper will keep me company, won't you, Jas?" I bite back a grin. Conniving little thing, but I'm not about to complain.

"*Majaderías,* I have dinner cooked already. Why would we go spend money when we can eat right here?"

"Carmella," her father's voice is firm. "We're leaving."

"I made pollo mole poblano, your favorite," she tries, but he won't have any of it.

"I feel like roast beef."

"*Pero...*"

"Ma, really. Go."

It takes ten more minutes for her to grab her stuff after her husband informs her, in no uncertain terms, she is sleeping in *his* bed tonight, but we're finally on our own.

"Are you ready to go back to work Friday?" I ask, stuffing the last bite in my mouth. If I ate like this every day, I'd be sporting a pot belly in no time.

"Tomorrow, actually. Ryan called this afternoon. The flu has been doing the rounds apparently. On nights for another two weeks, and then off for a long weekend before we go back on days."

"Sounds like our date will have to wait a bit longer."

"I do get a day or two off, you know," she says, sliding off her stool and inserting herself between my knees, draping her arms around my neck. "And in the meantime, we have tonight."

I slip my hands around her waist and down to her ass.

"Mmmm. Have all your visitors left?" Her face shows confusion, before she clues in and her bottom lip juts out.

"Not quite," she admits grudgingly, but I kiss the pout from her lips.

"Then I guess we'll have to get inventive."

BELLA

The house has been quiet since my parents left after lunch.

They'd shown up this morning, just minutes after giving Jasper a lazy kiss goodbye on my porch. The man had made true to his promise. He got very inventive last night and discovered erogenous zones I wasn't even aware I had. Which reminds me, I have to wash my sheets, before my mother's spicy chocolate sauce won't come out anymore. I will have very sweet memories to go with my mother's pollo mole poblano from here on in. I hope to God she never finds out.

My parents dragged me out of the house for breakfast at CJ's Diner, which was nice. We chitchatted about my sisters, their kids—well at least Chrissy and Gaby's, since Fran, like me, is still childless to my mother's great disappointment—and their plans for the summer. The previous days have been so focused on me and my issues, it was almost a relief to have someone else as the subject of conversation for a change.

Ma made sure there was plenty of food in the house before they left—seriously, I could be stranded in my house for a month, and I'd still be laughing— and Papa took my little red Fiat to the gas station to make sure all the fluids were topped up and there was enough air in my tires. It's actually been nice, letting myself be looked after for a while. For me, but I think also for them. I don't often let them.

Still, I'm glad to have my house back to myself.

I'm stuffing my sheets into the washer when my

phone rings. I don't recognize the number.

"Hey, Bella? It's Joanne. I hope you don't mind, I finagled your number from Ryan."

"Hi—no, not at all."

"I hear you're feeling better and coming in for your shift tonight?"

"Much better, thanks." I feel a little awkward and a lot awful for lying. "And yes, I start at seven."

"Ryan told me. I'm on at seven as well and was wondering if you wanted to grab a bite before?"

The question throws me a little and the silence on my part becomes uncomfortable. That's how socially inept I've become. Poor Joanne starts scrambling.

"You probably have stuff to do. I shouldn't have dropped this last minute, but it's just that my mom is keeping the baby until tomorrow so I can sleep a little when I get home. Except the house is so quiet now, and—"

"I'd love to," I interrupt her ramble, coming to a firm decision. I could do with a few friends.

"You sure?"

"Absolutely. Where do you want to go?"

We end up agreeing on Digs, near the hospital. A casual place, with decent food, and they have a flourless chocolate torte that is to die for, which was the clincher for me.

By the time it's ready for me to head out, I have the washed sheets in the dryer and clean sheets on the bed, and all the food Ma left me packed away and stored. The ping of a message stops me on the way out the door, and I quickly check, chuckling as I read.

Jasper: FYI, I just sent an email to Hershey with some new marketing ideas.
Me: And I'm going out with a friend for another chocolate induced orgasm.

I grab my keys, stuff my flip-flops in my bag with comfy clothes for after my shift, and lock the door behind me. The smell of new car hits me when I climb behind the wheel for the first time in over a week. I have to smile when I spot the new air freshener clipped to the vent—typical Papa. One last check of my messages shows two consecutive ones.

Jasper: What???
Jasper: Bella????
Me: LOL. Dinner (mostly chocolate torte) with friend Joanne at Digs. Gotta run.

Immediately a message pings back. He must've been waiting.

Jasper: Cruel. Someone needs a spanking.
Me: Promises. Promises.

I don't see his final message until I park the car at the restaurant.

Jasper: Pure evil.

I'm still chuckling when I walk into Digs and see Joanne waving me over to a table by the far wall.

"What's funny?" Joanne asks, when I slide into the seat across from her.

"This guy I'm seeing."

"Tell me more," she prompts, signaling the waitress. "I've been married for eight years, and with Mark for six more than that. I've forgotten about the excitement of dating. I'll have to live vicariously through you." When the girl comes up to the table, Joanne orders for both of us. "Two coffees and two large servings of your chocolate torte."

A girl after my own heart.

That's how within seconds of sitting down, I'm spilling as if we've been friends our whole lives. The things chocolate can make me do.

-

"You didn't have to get dressed up for me."

We've barely cleared the hospital lobby when I hear the voice behind us, and a shiver runs down my spine.

"If it isn't Dr. Lipczyk," Joanne sneers beside me as she swings around. "Still stalking the hallways I see? Not much has changed since high school."

"Ah, look, it's the lovely Joanne, I've caught a twofer tonight. Like old times."

I'm stunned this man has the gall to even talk to us, although I'm sure he thinks he's untouchable. I'd never taken the time to check the board of directors, as he'd suggested the last time I saw him in the parking lot, but it doesn't take a genius to figure out he probably has a family member in one of those chairs. I wouldn't doubt it.

Truth is, I haven't given him much thought at all. I never even mentioned the incident in the parking lot to Jasper. Maybe that was a mistake.

I grab Joanne by the arm and start walking toward the locker room, but she pulls back and turns to poke a finger in the smirking man's chest. "You were a bully then and you're a bully now, Scott. I may have been too timid at sixteen to stand up to you, but I'll be damned if I let you harass me or my friends now, and I don't care who your daddy is."

Whoa.

From the reference to high school earlier, I figured she knew him. This outburst suggests it might have been a little less innocent than I thought.

Joanne's blowup is drawing a bit of an audience in the lobby, when I see Ryan come stalking through the small crowd gathered right inside the front doors. He walks up, just in time to hear the good doctor's softly spoken response to Joanne's outrage.

"Say bye to your job, little girl."

"Try," Joanne taunts, getting ready to poke him again, but this time Ryan pulls her back.

"Hold up, Tiger," he mumbles when she struggles against his hold. "There are better ways."

By the time Ryan herds us down the hallway to the locker rooms, Joanne is shaking and looks near tears. I'm not sure what to expect when I lead her over to the sink so she can splash some cold water on her face.

"Why do I let him do this to me? He gets me spitting mad and then uses it to threaten me. Same damn game, just with bigger stakes."

"What do you mean?"

"Ugh. I hate to even admit it," she says, plopping down on a bench. "I may have had a few run-ins with him over the years, starting in high school. He was interested, I was not, but to this day Scott does not take rejection well and is used to getting what he wants. Let's just say he found ways to make my life miserable after that. It didn't help my dad worked for his father, at the time, something he would lord over me to keep me quiet. Nothing's changed; the man is still a bully."

There's a knock on the door and then Ryan's voice calling out, "We've gotta roll, Gomez.

I rush to strip out of my summer dress and get into my uniform.

"Will you be okay?" I ask Joanne, who is getting changed as well.

"I'll be fine. I generally avoid being around him, and he should know by now I can't be pushed around anymore. He's a coward, who still hides behind his daddy at his age. He doesn't scare me."

I hope she's right.

Ryan is waiting in the hallway, impatiently jiggling the keys.

"We have a pick up from the seniors' home.

Advanced heart failure. Let's go."

It's a steady night. In addition to that first call, we bring another three patients into Mercy during the course of our shift.

The last one is a young woman in labor, who ends up having her baby in the back of the rig. In all my years as EMT, this is my first birth, and I carry that baby into the hospital as proudly as if I'd given birth to it myself. I'm still on a high when I walk out of the hospital at the end of our shift.

"Wait up!" I swing around to see Ryan jogging to catch up with me. "I wish you'd fucking wait for me so I can walk you to your car," he grumbles, looking at me sideways. "Head still in the clouds I see?"

I grin widely. "That was the *best*. Wasn't that the best?"

"Good you think so, because after being verbally and very publicly eviscerated by my normally sweet wife in the throes of labor—not once, but twice—I think I'll take a pass."

"Come on," I nudge him as we get to my car. "It's a beautiful thing, new life."

"I'm sure it is, but I'd still rather have a vasectomy with a spoon than go through one more childbirth with Beth." He opens my door, waits until I'm behind the wheel, and then leans down. "But you did well out there tonight, Gomez. Glad your first shift back ended on a high note."

CHAPTER 15

JASPER

"Thanks."

I take the tray with coffee and the brown bag with food, and pass them through to Luna. We're on our way to Farmington at the butt crack of dawn, having breakfast on the fly. We're hoping to catch one Hiram Miller, before he goes down for his morning nap.

The last few days have been spent fruitlessly looking for James Davis, other than forensic evidence, the only real lead we have. We found three by that exact name in Durango, but only one of them was the right age, and that James Davis spends his days in a wheelchair and lives with his mother.

Looking up his grandfather is the only avenue left open. We chased down the nursing home in Farmington and I called yesterday afternoon, hoping to speak to him. I didn't get much further than the nurse assigned to his care, and was told Hiram sleeps most of the time, and is rarely lucid anymore. She was able to inform us that he doesn't really get visitors, only the occasional church volunteer who'll come and sit with him for a while. She indicated the best time to come would be during or right after breakfast, it's apparently his clearest time of day.

Luna had offered to go, but I figured two were better. One of us could see what information to get from the old man, and the other could talk to some of the other residents and staff. Hiram had been in the nursing home a little over two years, surely he'd mentioned his grandson at some point in time.

"What time is the funeral?" Luna asks, her mouth full of hash brown.

"Service at one, interment immediately following. I'm guessing around two, two-thirty?"

Bert Cummings will be buried with full honors, which means there will be officers from all over flocking to Durango to see him off. For someone with a hard-on for cops, it makes for a tempting scenario. It would be like shooting fish in a barrel.

While everyone is focused on the funeral, we'll be focused on the crowd.

Bella will be there too. She's planning to go with Ryan, which I was happy to hear, since I won't be able to sit with her.

I saw her briefly yesterday, and again this morning, when she came home from work around three thirty. She doesn't think it's necessary that I come check her house every day, but I need to make sure she's safe. I don't mind, I just start my day a little earlier. Getting in my Bella fix to start the day doesn't hurt either.

"Wow, nice place," Luna comments when we pull into the parking lot of the nursing home. It looks more like a luxury hotel, a newer structure with beautiful landscaping—which costs a sweet penny in the New Mexico drought—and a driveway that curves under a large portico over the front doors.

I park the car and lean over the steering wheel, staring at the building.

"Tell, me. How does a retired welder, living off a senior's pension, end up in a place like this?"

"That's a very good question," Luna agrees, pushing open her door.

She ends up seeking out Hiram, who is still eating his breakfast when we get there, while I chase down the administrator.

"How can I help you?" the man asks, when introductions are exchanged and we sit down in his office.

"I'm hoping to get a few questions answered that might help our investigation. Am I correct in assuming this is a private facility?"

"You are."

He goes into a sales pitch about the luxury accommodations and the high quality care provided to the residents. It takes a while for me to get to the answers I'm looking for.

"So it would be safe to say, your average resident

is at the very least well-to-do, to afford living here."

"I guess that would be fair to say," he says with a shrug.

"Then how is it possible that a retired welder—who draws Social Security—and whose last residence was a trailer park in Shiprock, can afford this place?"

It takes a little arm wrestling, but I finally walk out of there with the name of the obscure trust fund financing Hiram Miller's monthly bill. I have a lot of digging to do, but this is the kind of stuff I'm really good at.

"I need you to drive back," I announce to Luna when I meet her in the lobby. "I have to look into something." She takes the keys from my hand without question. "How did you make out with the old man?"

"I got most from his neighbor, who was here when Hiram moved in. He's clear of mind and remembers Hiram talking about his grandson, he was worried about him. Apparently the kid never came to visit, not even once. When he'd asked Hiram about it, he mentioned he hoped his grandson was living it up in Mexico by now."

"What about the old man himself?" I ask when we get to the car. "He just seemed confused when I asked about James Davis. Swore he knew no one by that name. When I said *grandson*, he mentioned the name Connor."

"Why does that name sound familiar?"

"Because it's the kid's middle name; James Connor Davis."

We've been looking for the wrong name.

By the time we get back to Durango, I've made some headway on unraveling the mystery trust fund benefiting Hiram Miller. I was able to lead it back to a consortium of pharmaceutical and other medical supply companies.

One partner name stands out; Eugene Lipczyk, owner of ELS—a company manufacturing surgical supplies. I'm not sure why the name is familiar, but when I look closer at the man's resume, Mercy Regional Medical Center catches my eye immediately.

Eugene Lipczyk is on the board of directors, and the circle gets smaller. A quick scan through the hospital website, and suddenly I realize where I've seen that name before. On the name tag of the asshole who was bothering Bella in the ER back in May. Doctor Scott Lipczyk.

Father and son.

Small world.

BELLA

I'm glad Ryan is meeting me at the church. To be honest, I'm not sure how well my emotions will hold up at this funeral.

These past few days, I've done mostly okay on my own, although I have to admit, it's been nice to have Jasper pop over in the middle of the night. It's usually during those hours of darkness that the weight of everything seems to grow. Having him show up, to get me inside my dark lonely house, has helped me get to sleep, but I feel guilty about the disruption to his schedule. The only time I am truly alone are the hours before I go back in for my next shift, which is when I struggle most with the thoughts threatening to pull me down.

This morning I set my alarm for ten thirty. Jas left here at about four thirty, so I've had six hours at best. I'm still a little groggy as I dig through my closet trying to find something appropriate to wear. All those little slinky dresses I usually wear are inappropriate. Besides, they're part of the role I've played to the outside world, and hiding behind them seems to have become a moot point. It's only a matter of time before everyone knows I'm not as okay as I pretend to be.

I'm actually surprised my sisters haven't showed up at my door by now. Tomorrow Damian and Kerry get back, and I have no doubt before the day is out, my mother will be on the phone with him, if she hasn't interrupted their vacation already.

This reminds me, I should get up to Hermosa this afternoon to air their place out and turn on the AC, it's bound to be stuffy.

Sick of my indecision, I snatch a pair of black crop pants off a hanger and pair it with a floral tank and my little three-quarter sleeve bolero jacket. I almost don't recognize myself: my hair back in a low ponytail, a minimum of makeup, and dressed in the modest outfit.

Yet, oddly, I feel more exposed wearing it.

—

"Sorry I'm late," Ryan huffs when he makes his way to the steps outside the church. "I had to park way the hell over at the high school. This place is gonna be packed."

"It is already. I doubt we can find a spot in the pews. Looks like all of Durango has turned out for this one. It'll be standing room only."

I take the arm he offers and walk inside the blessedly cool church. It's already getting pretty hot out there and we're not even into summer yet.

As suspected, even half an hour before the service is scheduled to start, the pews are packed, but Ryan spots a couple of seats on the far aisle in the back.

I scan the church, to see if I can spot Jasper, who is supposed to be here in an official capacity, but don't see him. I do see a host of other familiar faces, and I'm struck by how many people I've come to know in the year I've been in Durango. I may not get out much, but my work certainly connects me with people.

Almost all first responders, but there are a few faces I recognize from the hospital as well. Bert clearly was well-loved.

"You okay?" Ryan asks beside me, when I dab at a leaking eye with my tissue.

"I'm fine."

I send him a reassuring smile when two rows

down a head turns, eyes zooming right in on me.

"Are you shitting me?" Ryan hisses beside me when he spots Scott Lipczyk throwing me a wink.

"Tell me if he needs another attitude adjustment, Squirt," I hear behind me, just as Jasper leans in between Ryan and me.

"Hey, I didn't see you when I came in."

"That's 'cause we're paid to look, not to be seen."

"Whatever." I roll my eyes, but the effect is nonexistent because I'm doing it with a smile on my face.

Jasper drops a quick kiss to my lips, which I suspect is more for Scott's benefit, since he straightens up, staring down Scott, who quickly swings back to face the front. At least the man seems to have a healthy respect for law enforcement.

"I have to go, look after her?" Jasper claps Ryan on the shoulder.

"On it," he answers.

"I'll see if I can swing by before you go off to work, otherwise I'll see you after."

I don't get a chance to answer because he's already walking away with long strides. Instead of irritated, which would be my usual response when I'm being managed, his concern settles around me like a soft blanket.

"After?" Ryan whispers beside me, and I elbow him in the side.

"He just checks my house when I get home."

"No shit?"

I open my mouth for a retort, when organ music starts and a long line of first responders—in full uniform—files into the church. They fill the outside aisles and line the center aisle as an honor guard for their fallen comrade. The casket is slowly rolled in, Bert's mourning family follows close behind. Already I've lost the battle with my tears.

All I can say is the man was clearly loved by both his community and his peers. The service is solemn and moving, and when Bert's oldest son delivers a eulogy that sheds a heartfelt personal light on the man, there isn't a dry eye in the house.

Ryan convinces me to ride with him to the cemetery, promising to drop me back at my car after.

The procession from Sacred Heart to Greenmount Cemetery is led by police vehicles, and snakes through the town and up the mountain. The whole town comes to a halt as Bert is escorted to his resting place.

"Sure you don't want to come have dinner with us? Beth would love to see you." Ryan is leaning against his open car door as I unlock mine.

"Thanks for the invite, but maybe some other time? I have some stuff to do and will grab a bite to eat at home. I'll see you at seven."

I lucked out when I was paired up with Ryan. It's like having another brother. Don't get me wrong, I love Damian to distraction, but he can be overbearing.

Ryan shows his care for me too, but does it in a way that doesn't make me feel inadequate. He sees and values me as an equal, and that means a lot.

The town is back to its usual bustle when I make my way through, heading to Damian and Kerry's place. No sign of the earlier solemn goodbye to one of its finest.

Life goes on.

Other than a message wishing me a good shift, I haven't seen Jasper since the funeral, and I'm looking forward to getting home.

As I was going through Damian's place earlier—putting the groceries I picked up away and letting some air in, while I put fresh sheets on the bed—I realized that although I look forward to having both him and Kerry home again, it may also cause some tension. They've only been gone three weeks and yet so much has happened in the interim.

Undoubtedly, Damian will get swept up in the hunt for the killer who is still out there somewhere. But what has me a bit nervous with trepidation is how he'll respond when he finds out Jasper and I are a thing. It's likely not what he meant when he asked Jas to keep an eye out for me while he was gone.

Knowing my brother, he will not only give me a hard time, but he'll surely rake Jasper over the coals. Last he knew was we barely tolerated each other.

It's hard to put a label on what we have, given the circumstances, but I'm starting to believe there is something there. Even though these past few days we've done little more than say hi and bye in the middle of the night, there's not a doubt in my mind he'll be waiting for me when I get home. Even if only to do his walk-through of my house, kiss the stress from my body, and tuck me into bed.

I never got around to eating a proper dinner before my shift. All I've had are some crackers with fake cheese from the vending machine at the hospital, and my stomach is growling. I wish I could swing by McDonald's for a snack, but they close at midnight or one. It's three-thirty now.

I head north toward town and spot the lights of the Walmart store up ahead. I blame my loudly complaining stomach for pulling into the parking lot. Second only to McDonald's fries is Ben & Jerry's and my supply at home is long depleted.

JASPER

Jesus what a day.

Part of me expected something to happen at the funeral. I mean, someone who is shooting cops would have had a heyday there. It was uneventful. We tried scanning the crowds, in hopes he'd show up to gloat at his handiwork, but without any idea who to look for, that got us nowhere.

The pressure to come up with some answers, especially with the boss coming back tomorrow, had the three of us at the office until well after midnight. Going over Hiram Miller's financials, Luna found an interesting trail of payments coming into his bank account—starting about six months after Franklin Davis was killed—from the same trust fund financing the man's current living expenses. Most of it was transferred by Hiram himself into a savings account, which, coincidentally, was cleared out after the man moved into the seniors' facility, two weeks' worth of daily maximum withdrawals of $1000. A grand total of $14,000 gone.

My money is on the grandson: James Connor Davis.

No record of the kid though, not even a driver's license through DMV.

Luna offered to scour high school websites in and around Shiprock to see if his name would pop up, but I called it a night. We all needed some sleep.

Not that I had a lot of it, driving up to Bella's house at three-thirty in the morning, but maybe I'll catch a few more hours in her bed.

I let myself in with the spare key she gave me a couple of days ago and flick on the coffee machine before doing a quick check. It's become habit.

I flip through emails on my phone while I wait for my coffee to brew, answering some of them. When it's done, I take it outside on her small porch and sit down in the Adirondack chair.

She's a little late. Other nights she'd be home by now, but they may have caught a call at the end of their shift. I shoot off a quick text:

Me: Busy night?

Leaning back I briefly close my eyes, waiting for her response.

The sound of birds wakes me up and I blink against the early morning light. My watch shows it's after five, I must've dozed off, and I quickly realize Bella never came home. My phone shows no return message either, and I'm suddenly wide awake. What the fuck?

"I fucking just hit the sack. This better be good," Ryan answers on the second ring, and the bottom drops out of my stomach at his words.

"Where's Bella?"

"What do you mean? She left same time I did, three thirty or so."

"She's not home, Ryan. She never fucking got home."

CHAPTER 16

JASPER

It's been three hours since I called Ryan, who was the first to show up at Bella's place. Luna had not been far behind. She'd already spoken to Dylan, who would hit the streets as soon as he dropped his son off at his mom's.

Luna and Ryan both understood my growing panic, given Bella's recent state of mind. Ryan started calling around, starting with the Mercy Emergency Room, and I'd already checked with Durango PD, to see if any accidents had been reported since three thirty this morning. I was tempted to file a missing persons report, but Luna suggested we look for her ourselves first, before making the fact she suffers from depression public knowledge.

I looked at some places in town, Dylan was checking hospital grounds and the route she would've taken home, while Luna drove all the way up to Hermosa to see if perhaps Bella had gone to Damian's place. She just came back empty-handed as well. Dylan hasn't shown yet, so I give him a call.

"Where are you?"

"Just pulling into the parking lot at Walmart. I just spotted emergency vehicles pulling around the back. Do you have your scanner on?"

"No, it's at home. Go see what's going on."

"*Shit*," I hear Dylan hiss.

"Fucking talk to me, what's going on?"

"Hang on, let me talk to…" I listen to a muffled conversation, picking up an odd word or two that has my blood run cold.

"What?" Luna prompts beside me. I have the phone on speaker and drop it on the counter, hauling my fist out and slamming it into the stainless steel fridge door.

"Jesus, man." I turn, ignoring Ryan who starts fussing with my hand, and instead looks at Luna, whose face is draining of all color as she's taking in what I just heard.

When Dylan comes back on the phone, we are both braced for the worst.

"Walmart staff found a car parked at an odd angle, not far from the dumpster this morning. It's Bella's Fiat. Her purse and keys are still inside. There was a body hidden from view between the back door and the dumpster that looks to be of a male, gunshot wound to the chest."

The breath I've been holding whooshes from my lungs, and I have to hold on to the counter to stay upright.

"Male victim?" Luna sharply asks for confirmation.

"Male, mid-to-late-forties, and a lot of fucking blood everywhere. That's all I know for now."

"On our way. Hang tight there," she says before hanging up the phone. To me she says sharply, "Wrap some fucking shit around that hand and let's go. Pull yourself together."

—

There are maybe six cars parked in the employee parking lot behind Walmart, not counting the numerous emergency vehicles and Bella's red Fiat, the trunk open. The sight of her car makes everything all too real.

"What happened to you?" Blackfoot asks, as we walk up to the group that includes the coroner. He points at my hand, which Ryan had quickly wrapped.

"He had a disagreement with a fridge. Now what do we have?" Luna swiftly directs the conversation away from my hand and to more important matters.

"Single shot to the chest. There's a great amount of blood here, and more over there." Keith points to a spot about ten feet away from Bella's haphazardly parked car, where an officer is marking the parking lot with yellow tags. "But no trail connecting the two. The victim is an employee. According to the cashier who found him, that was where the man usually parked his truck."

"We've got a gun!" Everyone turns to the investigator taking pictures of the victim. "Looks like he fell on it."

"Two shooters," Luna concludes. "One dead, one alive?"

Hard to believe no one would've heard a shootout. Even at three or four in the morning.

"Dylan," I finally speak up. "Find out who of the employees were here between three and four."

"There's three of them. I have them in the lunchroom with one of my guys," Keith contributes. "I didn't want them going home before we have a chance to talk to them."

"Good. You got a problem if Dylan starts questioning them?" I ask, aware I may be treading on toes here. Blackfoot gestures for him to go ahead. "Find out what you can," I instruct him. "See if anyone saw Bella, either driving up, or inside."

Dylan jogs off, and Luna walks closer to the victim, leaving Blackfoot and me alone.

"What is Bella's car doing here, Jasper? And where the fuck is Bella?"

Goddammit, I wish I had answers. "She never showed up at home. She must've pulled in here, coming from work."

"Why park in the back though?"

"Maybe she saw something?" I turn around to look at the entrance to the main parking lot, which is directly in line with where the Fiat is parked next to the second pool of blood. "What if she saw someone in trouble—hurt—as she was pulling in? Her training would've kicked in."

"She probably wouldn't have seen the body if she was focused on the second shooter," Keith muses. "So Bella stops to help, walks over, and then what?"

That's the million dollar question, and I don't have a fucking clue where to start. "Given that she is gone, along with the victim's truck, we have to assume she was forced."

"How is this for a theory?" he proposes, looking over his shoulder at the victim and the back door before turning around to the secondary scene. "Our victim finishes his shift, walks outside and spots someone trying to get into his truck, maybe he calls out a warning first. It's not the first time a car was stolen from this lot, if you recall."

"Our cop shooter?" I have to admit, the thought had crossed my mind. It's not like there are that many trigger-happy folks walking the streets of Durango.

"We have to keep an open mind, but yeah, I think it's possible our guy was back here stealing another car—maybe he was planning another murder—when he got shot. Either way, the guy clearly was bleeding profusely, he would need medical attention."

"Unless a paramedic happened to drive up to help."

"How about Damian? Have you called him yet?"

The sudden topic change threw me for a second.

I had thought about contacting him, but he was likely already on his way home as we speak.

"He's actually arriving home from his honeymoon, early this afternoon. I should probably call her parents though."

I have no idea how they will react. They left her in my care just days ago. Damian's reaction is not even in question, I know he'll hold me personally responsible. I deserve it; I totally fucked up.

BELLA

I think I'm still in shock.

Concentrating on driving, I try not to think about the bleeding young man in the passenger seat—or the large gun and silencer he has aimed at my head.

When I saw a person slumped beside a truck—I didn't even think—I just drove right up, pulled my kit from the trunk and turned to him, noticing the blood pooling under him for the first time. It was coming from an injury to his left leg. I'm not sure what I assumed, maybe a heart attack or something, but the blood suggested something more nefarious than that. It wasn't until I knelt by his side, opening the paramedic kit I keep in my car, when I was first introduced to that same gun. Everything was pretty much a blur after that. He refused calling for help and threatened to shoot me if I tried.

I know I helped him up into the cab. I also

remember having the presence of mind to slip my hand in my pocket and find the small button on the side of my iPhone to turn off the ringer, as he was trying to scoot to the passenger side. Then I climbed behind the wheel as ordered. Bits and pieces were hanging down from the steering column, and I received an on the spot tutorial in hot-wiring.

"Left up there."

I do as he says, turning on a road that seems to lead us up the mountain. I can't say I've ever been this way, although it's hard to tell in the dark. Leaving behind the city lights peels away the last bit of security I held onto. It feels like diving off a cliff, and I wonder if I'll come out of this alive.

I throw a careful sideways glance at my captor, who is slumped against the passenger side door. A black baseball cap is pulled low over his face. There's something familiar about him I can't quite place.

"You really need medical attention," I try again. "You're losing a lot of blood."

"That's what I have you for," he bites off. "Keep driving."

I briefly consider running the truck off the road, even if I could incapacitate him for a moment, I might be able to get away. I lift a hand off the wheel and covertly test my seat belt. I know he's not wearing one.

"Don't even think about it." I startle at his voice, as he is clearly able to read my mind. Not quite as covert as I thought.

The road makes a sharp left, and then comes up to an intersection, I automatically slow down.

"Stick to this road. In about half a mile you'll see a sign to your left. There's a dirt road going into the woods right past it. Take that."

I have to stop at the stop sign. Two motorcycles approach from the right, and I'm about to throw myself at their mercy, when I feel the gun poke between my ribs.

"I *will* shoot you."

Tears spring to my eyes as I watch the two turn, pass my window, and drive completely oblivious the way we just came. Someone with bigger balls would've given it a shot.

"Let's go," he prompts when I'm not moving.

I'm actually contemplating the irony of it all. You see, I'm pretty sure the man sitting beside me is the same one whose actions triggered last week's breakdown when he shot Bert with the same gun and silencer. Which brought me to a point where I was voluntarily withdrawing from life, and might have welcomed the promise of an easy exit. Yet here I am, a week later, desperate to stay alive.

Obediently I continue up the mountain until I spot the sign—Ridgeview Rentals, 1 mile—and turn left onto the dirt road just beyond. What little illumination the night provides is almost completely obliterated by the canopy of trees covering us, and I'm completely dependent on the truck's headlights to guide me through.

The dirt road is quickly reduced to a narrow trail, until it ends suddenly.

"Pull in between those boulders," he orders, indicating a couple of large rocks to my left. "We'll have to walk the rest of the way."

"How are you going to walk?" I look pointedly at his incapacitated left leg.

"You're gonna help me. It's not far."

He has me get out the driver's side before scooting over on the seat and exiting the same door, never taking the gun off me.

He's right, it isn't far; maybe fifty yards from where we parked the truck. He has his left arm hooked around my neck, I have mine around his waist, supporting him as we make our way through the brush. Just in case I might get any ideas, his other hand is pressing the barrel of the gun in my side.

The small log cabin is mostly obscured from view by trees. At least on the back side, where we approach. All I see are two small windows, but not much else; it's pitch dark out. Around the front there is a bit of a clearing and a gravel pathway leads into the woods to the left. The cabin sports two steps up to a small covered porch.

"Key is in my right pocket," he says a little out of breath when we come up to the door.

He leans against the doorpost, while I have to use both hands to get the lock to turn. I note the large oblong tag on the key ring, like an old-fashioned hotel key. The number matches the one on the door: 12.

It's not until I flick on the light switch on the right side of the door that I get my first good look at the punk who has me at gunpoint, and I'm stunned.

"You?

CHAPTER 17
BELLA

"So now you recognize me. I knew who you were right off the bat."

The young man, who always seemed so shy with his sweet smiles, looks menacing now, with a painful grimace exposing his teeth and hatred in his dark eyes. What gives him away are the acne scars that mar his face.

"What's your name?" I ask, hoping to find some way to connect with the nice kid I remember from the McDonald's window.

"Does it matter?" he snaps, as he drops a small backpack I never noticed on the couch, the sound of metal hitting metal implying it's much heavier than it looks. Then he makes is way over to a Formica kitchen table and sits down heavily in one of the chairs.

"Maybe not, but it makes communication a little

easier," I suggest, and he seems to think about that. "I'm Bella," I add, to prompt him.

"Connor," he finally mumbles. "Now can you fix me up?"

I look at his wound and notice fresh blood dripping down his pant leg onto the vinyl kitchen floor.

"I can try."

I walk over and drop the medical kit, I had slung over my shoulder, on the kitchen table, zipping it open. The first thing I grab is a pair of bandage scissors, which seems to make him nervous.

"Watch what you do with those."

"They're blunt, see?" I show him the flat, rounded ends, designed especially to avoid injuring. "I need to cut away your jeans, unless you want to try and take them off?" Judging by the sweat starting to drip from his forehead, he's in no shape for any gymnastics. He waves his free hand, urging me to go ahead.

I methodically cut up both legs, along the zipper and through the waistband, so all he has to do is lift his butt and I can discard the jeans. When I see the skinny white legs sticking out of a pair of well-worn Power Rangers boxers, I almost forget the kid is aiming a gun at me. A gun he's used to kill trained police officers. I have no doubt he'll use it on me if I give him reason. My immediate objective is not to give him one.

"I'm just going to grab some water," I say, moving cautiously to the sink. "Is this clean to drink?"

"Spring fed."

Scouring the cabinets, I find a metal bowl and fill it up at the tap before returning to the table. I carefully wash around the bullet hole and check the back of his leg for an exit wound. There is none. He has a nice sized hole in his upper thigh.

"You'll need to have that bullet removed," I point out, kneeling on the floor by his feet. "I don't know if it's hit bone, or what kind of damage it's done on the inside, but you're still bleeding. Unless we can at least pack—if not close this hole,—you might be in bigger trouble than you already are."

"Then you take it out."

"I can't do that. I'm a paramedic, not a surgeon."

The hand with the gun slowly lifts from the table and drops down, pressing the barrel against my forehead.

"If you can't do it, then what good are you to me?"

The malice is dripping from his voice, and there are no more words necessary to drive home his threat. I get it.

"I'll try," I concede. It's all I can promise.

"Grab my pack." I do as asked and note that indeed, the pack is heavy. "You'll find a bicycle lock in there; a long chain with a coded padlock. Get those out."

He has me chain myself by an ankle to the old refrigerator door. "In case I pass out," he says by way of explanation. "Don't want you running off."

The chain is long enough that I can reach the table and the sink, but not much else. I'd hoped to leave the lock shut only partway, so if he does pass out, I could get away, but apparently he's anticipated that.

"Lift your foot on the table."

With one hand, he makes sure the lock is closed properly before scrambling the numbered wheels with his thumb. So much for that plan.

"Do you have any alcohol?" I ask and he looks at me surprised.

"I'm not twenty-one yet."

I think my mouth may have dropped open at the ridiculousness of that statement. Here he is, toting around a man-sized gun, shooting and killing people, but he's worried about drinking before he's legal?

Whether the absurdity of his words, or the slow buildup of hysteria, I sink to the ground on my ass, laughing until the tears are running down my face. My mind can't quite wrap around my situation, and it feels like sanity is slipping.

A firm kick to my leg, snaps me back to reality.

"Get on with it," he grinds out between clenched teeth.

I use the hem of my shirt to wipe my wet cheeks and get to my feet.

Five minutes later, I have all I think I need lined up on the kitchen table and peel the paper backing off the sterile scalpel. I look up into Connor's eyes; instead of the dark hate I saw there before, there is only pain and fear left.

He looks innocent and scared, even though I know better.

JASPER

I watch through the window of the terminal as first Kerry, and then Damian, come down the stairs rolled up against the plane on the tarmac.

Luna had offered to pick them up, but I wouldn't let her. It's my responsibility. Just as it was my job to contact her parents. That was a painful phone call. Her mother had answered and immediately, when I told her Bella was missing, she became irate—throwing blame squarely at my feet—and there wasn't a thing I could say. She was absolutely right in her anger. Mr. Gomez took the phone at some point and asked some pointed questions I was able to answer. They should be on their way by now.

I imagine this encounter won't go much better.

I know the exact moment Damian spots me. The smile he just gave his new wife, vanishes from his face, and his back goes ramrod straight as he stalks to the terminal doors, his eyes never leaving mine.

"Where is my sister?" he asks in a low, threatening voice when he walks up, Kerry half running to keep up. I expected him to figure out something was up as soon as he noticed Bella wasn't here to pick them up.

"She never made it home from work." All I hear is the sharp intake of breath from Kerry, who grabs onto Damian's arm, as I decide to rip off the Band-Aid. "Her car was found behind the Walmart store, just south of town. Her purse inside."

"And where were you?" Kerry hangs onto his arm when he growls his words, leaning in close enough our noses almost touch.

I don't move, whatever he wants to dole out—I have coming. "Waiting for her at her house, clearing the place like I've been doing every night."

Kerry finally manages to pull him back a little and automatically his arm curves around her, pulling her tight to his body.

"My parents…"

"On their way. Let's get your bags."

I don't wait for his answer, but turn and head for the luggage belt.

It's not until we're in the Bureau's Explorer, I opted to take instead of my truck, that Damian speaks again.

"What have you got?"

I try to be careful in my description, for Kerry's benefit, but there's no way to sugarcoat a dead body and blood at the scene. By the time we pull up to Bella's house—which is where Kerry insisted we go—the rest of the Gomez family has already arrived.

Chaos ensues the moment Damian gets out of the car. He's instantly surrounded by his mother and sisters, while I help Kerry from the back seat. Mr. Gomez comes around our side and kisses Kerry on the cheek before turning to me. He looks like he's aged twenty years in one week.

"Sir, I'm so—" I start, but he stops me with a sharp shake of his head.

"No, son. No blame. Not from me. The girls, they are…upset. Scared. It's easier they have someone to point at. It will pass. I will handle them. You go find my Isabella."

I can do little more than nod, tied up with a host of unfamiliar emotions.

"Greene," Damian calls from the other side of the vehicle. "Let's go, I want to touch base with Blackfoot."

Ignoring the glares from the womenfolk, with the exception of Kerry, who gives me a sad little smile; I get behind the wheel and head back out to the road.

-

Luna is by the whiteboard in the Durango PD operations room, adding in information we compiled resulting from our trip to Farmington, only yesterday, about our suspected shooter. As agreed, she's keeping some details off the board. It sure as fuck feels like weeks ago.

I'm living on maybe two and a half hours of sleep, a cocktail of adrenaline and fear, and as much coffee as I can get my hands on. I've had nothing to eat since the pizza we shared back at the office last night after the funeral. Something apparently Dylan is intent on rectifying, as he walks in with a Subway bag and makes his way over to where I'm sitting.

"Eat," he orders. "You'll give yourself a doozy of an ulcer if you don't get something in your stomach to absorb that toxic waste they call coffee here."

"Thanks," I mumble, unwrapping the sandwich,

even though I am not in the least hungry.

"Don't thank me, thank the boss," he says, stepping aside to reveal Damian right behind him.

"Thanks," I repeat, this time to Damian, who nods and takes a chair on the other side of the table.

"You look like shit and you're no good to me incapacitated. Now, fucking eat."

Small groups of people start filling the room for the briefing. I keep my eye on the door and nudge Damian when Tom McMahan walks in. I'd filled Damian in on everything on our way here. Including the possible motive Keith pointed me to. The man works the room like a true politician, smiling and shaking hands like it's some kind of goddamn social gathering, not an operations briefing for a missing woman who may be held by a cop killer.

The moment he spots the large whiteboard Luna has been updating, he freezes on the spot, and I know he's seen her note behind 'motive.'

"Can I have your attention please?" Blackfoot is at the front, getting everyone's attention. "I have requested the FBI to lead a task force on this investigation."

Immediately sounds of objection go up, and I notice the chief still standing, staring down Keith, who continues undeterred.

"Quiet! Ballistics came back on bullets recovered from this morning's shooting victim. They match the ones recovered from Officers Belker and Cummings. We are dealing with a serial killer, who apparently is adding abduction to his litany of offenses. SAC Gomez? Please?"

Damian gets up and moves to the front, taking a moment to look around the room.

"Approximately twelve hours ago, my youngest sister, Isabella Maria Gomez, was taken from the employee parking lot behind the Walmart at 1115 South Camina Del Rio, presumably at gunpoint."

"Excuse me," McMahan suddenly interrupts, focusing on Blackfoot. "I don't recall approving such a request."

"Oh, but you did," Keith answers, producing a piece of paper. "You signed it this morning."

"Yes, for a task force to be formed, but you never mentioned requesting the FBI take the lead on this."

"It's right here in black and white."

The paper is snatched from Blackfoot's hands and scrutinized.

"I assume that is cleared up?" Damian doesn't expect an answer and forges on. "As you can see, some new information has come to light on a potential motive and suspect. We've put together the details in the package that's being handed out now."

Luna goes around with the updated files, handing everyone a copy, including the chief of police, who tosses it on a table and stalks out of the meeting room.

Keith looks over at me, and I raise my eyebrows. This is not unexpected. Chief McMahan may be of questionable ethics, but no one said he wasn't quick on the uptake. This move was carefully planned, just forty-five minutes ago, behind the closed doors of Blackfoot's office. We needed to make sure that once the death of Franklin Davis was introduced as possible motive, there was no possibility for undue influence on the resulting investigation. This goes to possible police corruption, and McMahan knows it, even if it simply looks like a task force formation to everybody else. And that was exactly the idea.

We cannot afford to lose any time or focus. Not with Bella out there at the mercy of a killer.

I know all too well the depravity of mankind, I've seen enough evidence over the years. The thought of Bella subjected to that kind of evil has my stomach revolt, and I have to fight to keep my sandwich down.

It's not until we are on our way back to the office on Rock Point, after a clear direction and the division of tasks was accomplished at the briefing, that I share the details of Bella's recent emotional struggle with her brother.

I don't want to betray her trust, but under these circumstances, I feel I don't have a choice. He needs to know.

Suffice it to say he doesn't take it well.

BELLA

I lean my head back against the kitchen cupboard and look into Connor's dark eyes. His face has an unhealthy grayish tinge. I'm concerned.

After making the initial cut to widen the wound in his leg, he stopped me to toss the gun behind him on the couch. Within reach for him but out of reach for me. I didn't mind; his hand had been shaking so badly, I was afraid he'd shoot me by accident.

I rolled up a kitchen towel and gave it to him to bite on, since I had nothing around to sedate him with. Those types of medications are kept in the ambulance, not in my kit.

It was hard, trying to ignore his muffled screams as I used a straight hemostat to attempt dislodging the bullet I could feel with my pinkie finger. I finally managed, though, but as I explained to him, I can't guarantee there aren't fragments of the bullet or bone splinters floating around, potentially wreaking havoc. After I rinsed out and packed the wound, wrapping a tight compression bandage around his leg to stop the bleeding, I slid back along the floor until I hit the cupboard behind me.

It probably was a combination of stress, adrenaline let down, and sheer exhaustion, but at some point I must've fallen asleep. When I open my eyes, the light inside the cottage is on, but it's dark outside. I'm a bit disoriented, is it still Saturday?

I take stock of my surroundings and it's everywhere—blood.

I've seen lots of blood in my day, but I've never been covered in it. The linoleum looks like the floor of a slaughterhouse and the front of my shirt is stiff with it. I strip off the gloves I'm still wearing, and

I see that it's even seeped underneath, staining the skin of my hands. Scrambling to my feet, I hold them under the tap, using dish soap to try and scrub the stain from my fingers. With my luck, he'll end up being HIV positive or something, but there's nothing I can do about that now.

I feel strange, detached, as I turn around, almost hoping he's dead. Connor's eyes are closed, but he's breathing, albeit shallowly. I feel both disappointment and relief. I've been waiting for an opportunity to use my phone and this may be it. I slowly slip my hand under my oversized shirt, keeping my eyes on him, and sneak my fingers into my pocket.

"What are you doing?"

It takes everything out of me not to jump at the sound of his voice. His eyes slowly open and I scramble, pretending to wipe my hands on my shirt.

"Washing my hands, why? You don't expect me to wipe them on that towel you had in your mouth do you?" It's not hard to fall back on attitude as a cover-up. It's worked for me for years and seems to do the trick now.

"Do you have any painkillers in that bag?" His face is drawn with pain.

"I may have a few ibuprofen." I dig though my bag and find a container that seems to have a few remaining. I fill a glass with water, shake a few tablets in his hand, and watch him swallow it down. "Any chance you can take off the chain? I need to use the bathroom and the floor could use a wash."

He stares at me for the longest time, before reaching over and grabbing his gun from the couch. I freeze, afraid he's realized he doesn't really have further use for me, but he motions me over. I lift my foot and he quickly opens the padlock. I try to catch a glimpse of the numbers, but he's too fast, and I'm at the wrong angle.

Unchained, I start walking toward the small hallway in the back, where I assume I can find the bathroom.

"You get two minutes, and keep the door open," Connor says behind me and I turn around. "Don't bother trying the window, I haven't been able to open it since I moved in here."

I nod my understanding, and continue moving through the main room, making note of as much as I can take in. A PlayStation is set up beside a small flat-screen TV, a pile of dirty clothes is tossed in the corner of the couch, and the coffee table is littered with dirty dishes. Looks like Connor has been here a while.

There is a door on either side of the doorway, and I start pushing open the one on the right when he calls out. "Stay out of there!"

A quick glance, before pulling it shut again, shows a cache of weapons and ammunition on the unmade bed. I quickly scoot into the bathroom and close the door not quite all the way.

The bathroom is disgusting, but I actually do have to pee, so I quickly pull my phone from my pocket before pushing down my pants and hovering over the seat. A glance at my screen shows eleven voice messages and even more texts. I don't want to waste time reading them so I tap the last one, which is from Jasper. Just as I'm about to type in a message, I hear shuffling on the other side of the door. I one-handedly type in the first thing that comes to mind, as I pull up my pants with the other. I quickly hit send, and am about to flush when the door slams open.

"Drop it," he barks, spotting the phone in my hand. "Fucking drop it in the toilet. NOW!"

The sharply barked order startles me and I open my hand, letting my connection to the outside world drop in the bowl.

"Now flush," he instructs.

CHAPTER 18

JASPER

Twenty-four hours.

She's been gone for twenty-four hours and we are no closer to finding her.

I drop my head onto my arms on the desk. Sunday morning and I've had maybe three hours of sleep total since the butt crack of dawn Friday. The urgency to find Bella is all that's kept me on my feet. That and copious amounts of coffee, and the occasional food that is forced on me.

Damian has barely spoken to me since finding out his sister has been struggling with depression for years. He'd been under the impression that the episode after her troubles with her ex had been an isolated incident. He's been close to her this past year, and to find out she opened up to me about something he knew nothing about, clearly stung.

It may all be moot, since we both know the more time passes, the less likely it becomes we'll find her alive. Especially since the guy holding her has nothing to lose.

I've gone over the surveillance footage from the single camera behind the Walmart for hours. Hoping to pick up some little detail I may have missed on an earlier pass. In the footage, we just see part of the parked truck, but you can make out the suspect riding up on a bike, looking around, and then lifting the bike into the back of the parked truck, before using a Slim Jim to open the door. The next few moments, his body disappears from view behind the open door. A flash of light at the bottom of the screen shows the exact moment the owner steps out the back door, and even though he's off screen, it's clear he yells something when the suspect's head pops up.

The scenario plays out much as we'd assumed, but the last part—the reason I keep watching it over and over again—shows Bella arriving on the scene. I must've played back those last moments, before you see her get behind the wheel and drive off, a hundred times by now.

"We need fresh blood," Damian says. I lift my head as he sits down across my desk from me. "We're spinning our wheels, you and me. Too tired to come up with any fresh ideas."

Like me, Damian has not had any sleep since getting back from Europe. He's dealing with jet lag to boot.

"We may get some feedback from the picture of a truck similar to the missing burgundy Dodge belonging to our victim. There can't be that many around of the 1993 models, and the silver hood is pretty distinctive."

The image is set to go out on mainstream media first thing this morning. It's been blasted around social media since the briefing yesterday afternoon.

"You care for her," he suddenly says, taking me by surprise, and I'm not quite sure how to respond to that.

Fuck yeah, I care about her, but I'm not sure where Damian is going with this, so I just shrug.

"Clearly you do, or you wouldn't have spent so much time at her place," he prompts.

"Hey, just doing what you asked—looking out for her while you were away." The words even taste like a lie, and Damian doesn't seem too impressed either, but at least he seems to drop the subject.

He slaps his hand on my desk. "All right, call Luna and Dylan in. We're gonna go over everything from the top with their fresh eyes."

He had sent them home around midnight last night, so at best they've had some four hours of sleep, but it's better than nothing.

I fish my phone from my pocket, only to discover it's run out of juice. Not surprising, since the last time I charged it was Thursday night. Pulling a spare cord from my drawer, I plug it into a USB port, and walk over to Dylan's desk, which holds the only landline.

Luna answers the phone right away, apparently already on her way out the door. She promises to pick up some food and fresh coffees on the way in.

Dylan is not so fast, but when I finally get him on the phone, he indicates he'll be here in twenty.

By the time they get here, the sun is coming up. Fresh eyes, coffee, sandwiches, and daylight infuse me with new hope.

"Anything from Blackfoot's crew this morning?" Dylan asks, his mouth full of egg sandwich.

Damian grabs for his phone and I look around for mine, when I remember it's charging. I walk over to my desk, pick it up and almost drop it.

Bella: Cabin 12

"Fuck!"

All heads at the conference table turn in my direction.

"It's Bella." I look at the time signature. "Eleven forty-five she sent a message."

Damian is out of his chair like a shot and snatches the phone from my hand.

"Cabin 12?"

"Call her back," Dylan suggests.

"No. She's clearly had her phone hidden on her, I'm not going to risk alerting the suspect by drawing attention to it," I point out.

"How did we miss that?" Damian asks, stalking over to his desk where he's been going over the details of the case all night. He shuffles through the paperwork and comes up with a report. "Here—it says her phone was found inside the car, in her purse."

"Must be her work phone," Luna points out. "Do you have a tracker installed on her phone?" she asks Damian, but since I know the man, I already know the answer and immediately slide behind my computer.

With Luna leaning over my shoulder, I type Bella's number into my tracking software, and we watch the little color wheel turn as the system is scanning for a signal.

"Anything?" Damian asks, getting impatient.

"Nothing."

"Did you plug in the right number?"

I try again, punching each one in carefully.

"No signal."

"Could her battery have run out?" Damian wants to know.

"The tracker requires a bare minimum of power. Even if there's not enough power to run the operating system on the phone and it shuts itself down, there's usually enough residue left for the tracker to work."

I see realization dawn on his face, and I'm sure mine shows the defeat I feel.

"So what does that mean?" Dylan asks, and while Damian and I stare at each other with painfully clear understanding, Luna is first to answer.

"It means sometime between eleven forty-five last night and this morning, the battery on Bella's phone was destroyed."

My face hurts.

I try to move and discover it's not the only thing hurting, my whole body seems to throb.

For a lanky kid, Connor packs quite a punch.

I almost cried when he made me flush. I didn't even know if my message had sent before the surge of water surely killed my phone. I should've waited for a better moment instead of panicking and trying to get a message out. If I'd slipped the phone back in my pocket as soon as I heard him moving around, I still would have a chance. A better one than now, because even if Jasper received my message, what could he do with it?

Hindsight being twenty-twenty, I would've done better giving him the name, Ridgeview Rentals. At least he'd have a location. Now all he possibly has is a fucking number.

Connor had backhanded me so hard, I stumbled and fell into the bathtub, which I am feeling this morning.

It does not make for a comfortable sleep, lying on a dirty kitchen floor, chained up to the refrigerator. Especially when your body is bruised.

I peek at the couch from under my eyelids, not that I can see much from my vantage point. That's where he collapsed last night, after chaining me back up. I guess I should count myself lucky I'm still alive.

He could just as easily have shot me, but for some reason didn't. I somehow have to make sure to keep it that way.

There's no movement from the couch at all, but then I hear the toilet flush. I close my eyes the moment I hear his unsteady steps walk into the room.

"Bella?"

I'm surprised to hear him use my name and inadvertently my eyes pop open, as I try to sit up, wincing against my stiff limbs.

He looks almost contrite standing over me. "I'm sorry I hurt you." If not for the gun in his hand, I could almost believe it.

Still, I wouldn't be surprised if a part of him did regret hitting me. I'm not a psychiatrist, but from what I've observed of him, I'd bet that he suffers from some kind of mental disorder. Schizophrenia or perhaps multiple personality disorder, I don't know, but there are definitely two sides to him.

My job is to keep the shy and contrite side engaged, and make myself as indispensable as I can.

"I should probably clean those dressings," I suggest, completely ignoring his apology. "We don't have any antibiotics, so I have to make sure the wound doesn't get infected."

He appears to consider it for a moment before finally sitting down at the kitchen table, still in his boxer shorts. A rank odor hits my nose, but I can't be sure if it's him, me, or the floor that is still disgusting.

"Are there any cleaning solutions around?"

He squints his eyes looking at me. "I'm not letting you out of my sight."

"No, I didn't mean that. I just want to clean a little before I take off the bandages. I don't want to expose you to more possible bacteria. I'll just check under the sink."

I find a small bucket and a rag, and in the back there's an almost empty bottle of Mr. Clean. It's enough to fill the bucket with warm soapy water and I turn to tackle the table first. After that I concentrate on the floor, getting as much caked-on blood off as I can. I have to change the water twice, and each time I get close to Connor, he lifts his feet off the floor without the need for prompting.

During the time it takes me to get the worst of the crud removed, his gaze has not left me.

"It won't be nearly as bad as yesterday, but it'll still be uncomfortable when I take the packing out."

"Okay."

I carefully unwrap the bandage from his leg, and pull the stack of gauze from the wound. It sticks a little, and I hear him hiss.

"Sorry. I'll be more careful." With a little bit of isopropyl alcohol, I soften the spots that adhere, and gently peel it back.

I'm actually surprised the wound doesn't look more inflamed than it does. I use the alcohol to clean the hemostat and use it to remove the packing.

"So how long have you worked at McDonald's?" I purposely don't look at him but stay focused on his injury. It takes him a moment to answer.

"Almost a year," he finally shares.

"Oh, yeah? I remember my first job was at McDonald's, but I was still in high school in Farmington."

"You lived in Farmington?" I look up at his surprised question.

"Yeah, was born and raised there. I only moved to Durango last year."

"My grandfather lives in Farmington. Well, he does now. When I lived with him, he was in Shiprock. He's in a seniors' home."

"I see. So you moved here when he went to Farmington? What about your parents?"

I knew it was a risky question the moment it left my mouth, and the sudden tension in the muscle under my hands confirms it.

"They're dead."

"I'm so sorry." I quickly try to desensitize the situation when I hear the change in his voice, but I'm afraid the damage is done.

"They killed my dad, killed my mom too, when she started asking too many questions. They claim the first was self-defense and the second suicide, but none of that is true. None of it!"

His voice had been steadily rising until he actually shouts the last few words, making me flinch.

I stay quiet for a few minutes, waiting for his breathing to return to normal while I carefully put clean dressings on the wound.

"Who did that?" I finally ask, curiosity getting the better of me.

"Fucking cops, that's who. Swept it under the rug, and when Mom asked around, they hung her from the rafters in the attic. She never would've left me alone."

"I'm so sorry that happened to you."

He suddenly grins in my face. "Don't be. I'm making them pay. Kept my grandpa quiet for years, by paying him off, but money don't work on me."

He's getting agitated and the leg I'm trying to work on starts bouncing.

"Connor, you have to keep still so I don't hurt you," I try, putting a restrictive hand on his knee.

Suddenly he latches on to my wrist, squeezing so hard I'm sure my bones will snap. "Let's see how he likes me killing his cops. I'm saving him for last."

Attempting to stay calm, I plead with him, "Please let me go, that hurts." But it's as if he doesn't hear me.

"How is that for justice? He deserves all the pain I can give him."

"I don't know who you're talking about, but you're hurting me, Connor."

"Officer McMahan. Or maybe I should call him Chief now. Dad never had a gun. Didn't believe in violence. Your chief of police shot an innocent man, and then tried to bury it, paid off my grandpa, but I'm not gonna let him."

"Okay, Connor. Okay, I believe you."

Finally he releases his tight grip on my wrist, and I rub to get the blood flowing again.

"Did you know my dad was killed on a Wednesday night?" he asks.

"No, I didn't." I carefully start wrapping his leg, hoping I can keep him calm.

"Yeah. I don't work on Wednesdays."

"Is that in memory of your dad?" I want to know.

"No. It's because I planned to be busy handing out payback on Wednesdays; the same day he died."

JASPER

"Fucking Sunday morning," Luna grumbles. "Everyone's either at church or still in bed. Can't get an answer anywhere."

Without a phone to trace, all we have is Bella's cryptic message. It was her idea to look for lodges, ranches, and resorts that advertise cabin rentals.

Damian's been on the phone with Keith already, filling him in and getting his input, since he was born and raised in Durango. He provided us with a list of possibles, and Dylan had found a few online, but we couldn't afford to eliminate any other lodgings or even rental condos either. Anywhere they might have a room twelve, unit twelve, or cabin twelve.

So far though, our calls have netted zero. Either because they didn't have a number twelve of anything, the rooms weren't occupied, or because the renters didn't match the description of the suspect by a mile. Anything close we would check out.

"Found another one east of town, up in the mountains. About forty minutes out," Dylan pipes up. "Owner says the cabin is rented for the month. Small one bedroom, secluded from the others. Renter is a single guy by the name of Robert Patton."

"Could be using a fake name and ID," Luna points out.

"I'd expect him to be closer to town, but fuck, it's better than nothing. Dylan, let's go." Damian stands up and pockets his phone, but when I make a move to get up as well, he stops me. "Need you and Luna to keep digging. We can't afford to all go on what might be a wild goose chase. You two are more familiar with the facts of the case than either Dylan or me."

Even though I'm itching for fucking something to do, I can't argue his point, and watch as they walk out the door.

"We'll find her," Luna says, when I turn back to my screen. "She's a tough cookie. We'll find her."

"Not so tough," I point out, but Luna shakes her head.

"You're wrong. Just because someone is depressed doesn't mean they're not resilient. I'd actually like to wager most people suffering from depression are stronger, because they often have fight to get up and keep going every single day. And the majority face that battle alone. Don't count Bella out."

It's about half an hour later that my phone rings and I snatch it up, hoping for some news.

"Greene."

"I may have seen that truck." I don't immediately recognize the voice until he introduces himself. "It's Ouray, you came sniffin' around the compound last week, left me your card."

Right, the Arrow's Edge MC.

"I remember."

"Been out of town since early yesterday mornin', just got back, readin' the newspaper, see a picture of this fuckin' truck."

I shoot up straight in my chair and put the call on speaker right away, so Luna can listen in. "Where'd you see it, and what time was that?"

"Rode out at four, woulda been shortly after, since I saw it right at the intersection at Junction Creek Road, where it turns into County 204, headin' north."

I'm already pulling up the map on my screen.

"Which direction was it going?" Luna asks from behind me.

"Well, hello, darlin'. North. Fuckin' saw the woman behind the wheel and it nagged at me at the time. Shoulda stopped. No reason a woman'd be drivin' up the mountain at that hour. No reason that can stand the light'a day, anyways. There ain't nothin' up there. Paper says she's missin'?"

"Taken at gunpoint," I specify. "Look, do you know of any places up that way where he might've taken her? Anywhere they rent cabins?"

"Not anymore. Used to be. Riverview or Ridgeview—somethin' like that. Most of them got leveled, but they sold a few to some hunters, I believe.

Can't be sure."

"Would you happen to know the last owners? A name at least?"

"That won't be hard, it's the old man's brother, he still owns most'a that land."

CHAPTER 19

JASPER

"Fucking wait for me, Greene," Damian barks.

I called him the minute I hung up with Ouray. He's about half an hour out, and I'm not about to sit on my ass and wait around for him to get here.

"You can meet us up at the Arrow's Edge compound. I'm not going in half-assed, Boss, but I won't sit here and twiddle my fucking thumbs until you get back."

"Tell him I'll load up their gear, save them a stop at the office first," Luna says, heading over to the large locker in the hallway that stores a variety of weapons, ammo, and tactical gear. She pulls out two large duffels and starts stuffing them.

I relay the message to Damian when he asks, "Call Blackfoot yet?"

"Premature," I point out. "First, I doubt a full

show of force at the MC compound will help with information gathering, and second, I don't want to have law enforcement crawling all over that mountain without a strategic plan."

According to Ouray, the former chief's brother's name is Jimmy Wells, who apparently is traveling somewhere up the West Coast with his wife in an RV. It may be tough to get hold of him, but Luna can talk to Nosh, see what he can tell us. There are probably others who could provide helpful information, but not when we get their hackles up with a show of force.

"Agreed," Damian grumbles. "In the meantime, give me fucking updates."

"Will do."

I grab my laptop and the files off my desk and stuff them in a backpack, looking over where Luna is zipping up the duffels.

"Radios?"

"All in here," she confirms, patting the bag.

"Let's go. We're taking my truck."

"Why?"

"Because it doesn't scream law enforcement."

The same kid is at the gate when we drive up. No lip this time, he simply steps aside when we drive through.

Ouray is waiting in front of the main building, smoking a cigarette.

"Greene. Darlin'." I can feel Luna bristle beside me at his greeting. "You can find Nosh in the kitchen," he directs at her. "Momma's cooking breakfast, you may wanna grab some while you're there. You could use some meat on those bones."

I manage to grab Luna's arm and pull her back when she makes a move toward him. Having her wipe the ground with his ass wouldn't be a good idea. And I have no doubt she would.

"Shelve it," I grind out under my breath. "You'll get your chance."

With a scathing glare at a grinning Ouray, she brushes past into the building.

"She's a fiery one." The man is still grinning, watching her disappear inside.

"Word of caution; there is a whole lot of power packed in that little package. Don't be fooled."

He turns to me with a wink. "Never could say no to a challenge."

Ten minutes later, I find myself sitting at a table in the clubhouse, satellite images of the area open on my laptop, and a plate of bacon, eggs, biscuits and gravy in front of me. Apparently you don't refuse Momma's breakfast.

Luna's hands are signing at a furious pace as she tries to get details out of a slightly reluctant Nosh.

"He says the original entrance to the place is about two miles north of the intersection on the left."

I locate the entrance on the satellite image and try to pinpoint any structures. I count three.

"Ask him if he recalls which one is number twelve."

More signing back and forth before the old man leans over the table, and taps his finger against the screen on a more densely treed section.

"He says he can't remember numbers, but there may be one or two cabins in the woods."

I try to zoom in as close as I can on the image, but I can't pinpoint any buildings.

"Ask Rowtag," Ouray suggests, leaning over my shoulder. "Boy spends enough time up there. Takes his dirt bike up on the Colorado Trail all the time, which cuts right alongside those trees." He points out a faint line running almost parallel to the road. "Anything up there, he'd know. Honon," he calls out to a massive guy, who comes lumbering in from the back. "Go relieve Rowtag at the gate. Tell him to get his ass in here."

The man utters some colorful expletives in response, but heads out the door nonetheless. They may not stand on protocol here, and clearly aren't afraid to throw attitude, but there's no doubt who's in charge.

A couple of minutes later, the scrawny kid comes sauntering in, same greasy looking red bandanna tied around his hair, same cocky attitude.

"Dagnabbit, Rowtag," Momma calls out when she sees him come in. "How many times I told ya to get rid o' that dang lice-infested do-rag. Don't be bringin' that back in here. Burn it."

Beside me Ouray chuckles and I bite off a grin. The swagger is gone from his step as he rushes outside and comes back in a second later, bareheaded and with considerably less attitude.

"Boy's as wayward as they come, but he sure listens to Momma."

"Helps when you hold the keys to the kitchen," Luna points out, earning an appreciative grin from the chief.

I leave it to him to ask the kid for information, figuring that would get answers faster than if I were to try.

It does, five minutes later we head outside, Ouray and Rowtag getting on their bikes to show us a back way the boy knows onto the Ridgeview property.

The big man is just opening the gate for us when a familiar Explorer drives up on the other side. I make quick introductions and tell Damian to follow us.

The Ridgeview Rentals sign is partially overgrown but still visible from the road, and up ahead the two motorcycles turn left onto a dirt road but stop about a hundred feet in. Ouray gets off his bike and comes jogging over as I roll down my window.

"Bikes are noisy," he explains. "Thinkin' you don't wanna announce your presence."

"Good point."

"Boy says the road narrows down to a trail that dead-ends shortly after, the cabin's another quarter mile from there. Thick brush, though. Best to walk in."

I agree, and pull the truck as far off the road as I can without hitting a tree. Damian follows suit behind me. Luna and I pull gear from the truck, as Damian and Ouray seem to be sizing each other up. The contrast is stark. Damian: ramrod straight, authoritarian, head to toe the agency man, but looks like he could've stepped off the cover of *Esquire*. Ouray, on the other hand, is casually leaning against his bike looking amused, his big tattooed arms crossed over his chest, in torn jeans and formerly white T-shirt; toothpick sticking out from his gray beard, looking like he owns the space he occupies, wherever that may be.

"Just you guys going in?"

"For now. We have backup on standby," Damian answers the burly biker, before turning to Luna. "You head in. Recon only, no engagement."

Luna nods and starts strapping on her gear and fitting the earpiece and microphone of the two-way radio headset, before throwing a salute and jogging into the woods.

"You're shittin' me," Ouray comments, turning to watch as Luna disappears from view. "Sending a woman in by herself?"

Damian visibly bristles and takes a step closer. "Sending an *agent* to do what she's trained for and damn good at. You'd do best not to underestimate any member of my team. Most especially Agent Roosberg; she's touchy about things like that."

I have to give it to the man, he takes the dressing-down with unexpected grace.

"So noted, Agent Gomez. So noted."

BELLA

One minute my bladder is about to explode, and the next I can't even squeeze a damn drop out. Then again, I don't usually have an audience when I pee.

I tried to hold it. Even managed until after I finished rewrapping Connor's wound, and made us some stale sandwiches on his instructions. But I lost the battle after that.

He wasn't gonna let me go without following close behind, and I didn't bother objecting when he leaned against the door, keeping it open. I figured I had that coming, after he caught me with the phone last time. So I grabbed a grungy towel from beside the sink, covered my front as with the limited material, and squatted down, leaving it draped over my lap. The best I could do under the circumstances.

Still, apparently my bladder is still desperately clinging on to what little dignity is left and won't cooperate.

"Could you at least turn your back?"

"Oh for fuck's sake," he mumbles, turning slightly so he is looking toward the living room, but still keeps half an eye on me in the bathroom mirror.

I close my eyes and try to pretend the door is closed. I wish it was as easy for me as it apparently is for him. Not that he even bothered using the bathroom, he's been peeing into an old milk carton, making me empty it in the sink.

Fucking disgusting, just like the smell in this place. I'm mortified to realize part of the rank odor is emanating from me. Fear and stress, a body that hasn't seen a shower in two days, and clothes that have dried blood all over them, make for a potent assault on the senses.

Finally, I manage to release enough to take the pressure off, but to add insult to injury, there's only a single sheet of paper stuck to the toilet roll. It will have to do. I'm not about to do something as intimate as ask him to pass me a full one. Fuck no.

I rinse my hands at the sink and forfeit wiping my hands, considering the state of the towel, and let them air-dry instead.

He swiftly chains me back to the fridge, and sits on the couch himself, putting the gun down beside him as he picks up the controller for his PlayStation. It concerns me. I noticed earlier he was moving around much easier than yesterday.

How long will it take for him to decide he doesn't need me anymore? And then what? Is he going to shoot me? Leave me here chained up? From what he told me earlier, I'm pretty sure he's not done yet. Should I try and fight him? Wait until he eventually leaves and somehow get myself free?

Christ, I don't know. I don't know what the wisest thing would be.

Instead of sitting on the floor, I pull out one of

the kitchen chairs I can reach, and sit down at the table. He's long discarded the scalpel I used on him yesterday. I try to glance into my kit, which is still sitting open on the table, without him seeing me. If the padlock bouncing against my ankle was a regular one, I might be able to find something to try and wiggle in the keyhole, but it's not. It's numeric.

Shy of trying to overpower him next time I'm allowed a bathroom break—which is not really an option to begin with, since he has that blasted gun pointed at me the whole time—the only other option seems to be to wait until he leaves, then somehow try to get myself unchained.

I take a look at the old fridge with the chain looped through the molded horizontal handlebar on the freezer drawer at the bottom. I'm sure if I exert enough power, I could eventually break that bar off, but it would not be a quick or quiet process.

Turning my head the other way, I can look out the window. I ignore the loud sounds of the evidently violent game he is playing, and lean my head on my arms on the table. The view is peaceful, even if the audio is not.

Trees at the front of the cabin are far less dense than at the back, and I can partially see down to the edge of the large ridge we're on, another mountain rising up on the other side. From the corner of my eye, I see slight movement outside, and my head snaps up.

"What are you looking at out there?"

"Elk," I blurt out the first thing that comes to

mind, trying to keep the adrenaline surge from my voice. "Just one, he's gone now." I turn my head to find Connor engrossed back in his game.

That was close.

No way I want him to know that I just saw a head pop up from behind a rock on the left of the window, a finger pressed to the lips.

I'm pretty sure it was Luna.

It feels like it's been hours.

Connor started complaining a while ago about being hungry, and I heated up a can of Campbell's tomato soup I found in one of the cupboards. My own growling stomach quieted quickly since anxiety took over, and the smell of the soup didn't do much for the overall bouquet.

No sooner had he slurped down the last bit straight from the pan, when the sounds of gunfire and explosions from the TV filled the cabin again, and I could resume my vigil at the kitchen table.

I'm not sure how they're going to come in, but I want to make sure I'm as far removed from Connor as I can get. I assume they won't be knocking on the door.

Almost at a point I wonder if I imagined seeing what I did, I close my eyes, giving them a rest.

Next thing I know all hell breaks loose.

CHAPTER 20

JASPER

"I have eyes on Bella. She's alive. I repeat; Bella is alive…No eyes on suspect, but someone is playing Call of Duty."

The sound of Luna's voice crackles in my earpiece, and my eyes find Damian, who has his fingers pressed against his. We both know alive does not mean unharmed.

I listen to her describe the setting and as much of the layout as she can see, before Damian cuts in. "Get back here on the double. I need a sketch with all entry and exit points. Let's plan this."

Ouray has been observing us from a distance as we gear up, but when he sees Luna come jogging down the path, he swings a leg over his bike and motions for the kid to do the same. Before she even reaches us, he's already pulling out on the county road.

"Best cover around the back, two small sliding windows with bracers. One is the bathroom and the other a bedroom. That's a room we don't want the suspect near; he has an arsenal spread out on the bed. Unfortunately the easiest access is the front. There's only one door and a single large window." Luna sketches a rough layout, and we're considering options when two cruisers and the SWAT unit turn onto the dirt road and park behind the Bureau's Explorer.

We're joined by Blackfoot, the SWAT commander, and for some reason Chief McMahan comes walking up in full gear.

"So what do we have?" he butts in, grabbing Luna's sketch pad off the hood of my truck.

"I don't think so," Damian says, snatching the pad back and blocking it with his body, crossing his arms over his chest. "Not sure what you think you're doing here, McMahan, but let me remind you; you don't run this show."

The man raises his hands defensively. "Force of habit, Agent. Don't bite my head off."

"Just stay out of the way and we're good."

Turning his back squarely on the chief of police, he goes over possible strategies with the rest of us. It's not until we have a plan in place and tasks divided that McMahan addresses Damian again.

"Where do you want me?"

Just then two ambulances pull in, followed by a KRQE News van. Damian raises an eyebrow and turns to face him. "All due respect, my sister is back there with some trigger-happy goon and an arsenal of guns. I don't have time or inclination to indulge your need for a sound bite."

"I had nothing to do with that." He plays dumb but everyone knows better. The man hasn't stopped campaigning since he first put his name in the hat.

"Let's quit fucking around," I bite off, my patience running thin. I don't have the stomach for politics.

"He's right," Damian agrees. "Stay well back." He pokes his finger at the chief. "You can come in when the suspect is apprehended."

It's clear the man is here to take credit for the arrest. It looks good on his resume.

Luna is told to take the lead, since she knows the landscape and we follow in an easy jog behind her.

The plan is for Dylan to boost Luna and me in through the bedroom window, so I can approach from behind, and Luna can secure the bedroom and the weapons stash. The SWAT team will take the front with Damian and Keith close behind. Timing will be everything.

"*...Everybody in position?*"

Damian's transmission is followed by several responses of '*Affirmative.*' I will be first through the window. I manage to slide it open partway without alerting anyone inside. As soon as I hear the countdown, I brace myself on the ledge.

"*...Three, two, one. Go-go-go!*"

The moment the large picture window shatters, I dive under the table.

There's chaos as officers push their way in through the window and front door, which hangs splintered from its hinges, everyone shouting orders. I see Connor leap up from the couch, gun in hand, and I cover my head with my arms. I don't want to see what happens next.

The shot is loud, and the immediate silence that follows is deafening.

I jump when I feel a hand on my back, curling up in an even tighter ball, my eyes tightly shut.

"Get her out of here!" I hear Damian yell.

Hands grab my hips and pull me out of my hiding place. That's when I hear his voice.

"You're okay, Squirt. You're gonna be okay," he mumbles behind me, before calling out, "Someone get that fucking chain off!"

I feel tugging on my ankle, hear a loud clank, and then I'm swept up in strong arms and carried out.

I focus on my heartbeat and shut the rest out.

JASPER

I don't want to let her go, afraid to hand her over to the EMTs. Afraid of what they'll find.

Her clothes and skin are caked with blood and

she's so still in my arms. I never got a good look at her, I just scooped her up and ran.

"Sir, you have to put her down so we can check her out," I'm urged again, and this time I comply, reluctantly laying her on the stretcher they had waiting. The loud clang startles me as the handle I ripped from the fridge still dangles from the chain around her ankle and hits the frame.

She seems to mutter a protest when they gently straighten her out and I see her face for the first time. One side of her face is bruised and swollen, but I can't see any other obvious injury.

One of the EMTs looks up and seems to stare at something over my shoulder. "Let's load her up in the rig."

I turn my head and look straight into the lens of a camera.

"Get the fuck out of here!" I bellow, just as Dylan comes jogging up.

"I've got it." He blocks my view of the camera, and gets in my face. "Jas, I'll take care of it. Go see after her."

With one last glare over his shoulder, I turn and climb up in the rig, making sure to block Bella from view as they cut her shirt down the middle.

"Hey, lady," the older of the two EMTs talks to Bella as he examines her. "Your vitals are fine. Heart rate a little elevated and you're breathing could be a little deeper, but no visible injuries other than that shiner. You're a mess, but it's not your mess, is it?

Let's get you cleaned up a little."

"Are you sure?" I want to know.

"I'm fine," Bella suddenly says, her eyes cracking open and for the first time in thirty-two hours, I can breathe.

"There you go." The guy smiles at her as he wets some gauze with distilled water. But when he goes to wipe it over her skin, I step in.

"I'll do that."

"It's okay, I—"

"I said I'll take care of it," I repeat, moving him out of the way and sitting down next to the stretcher. "Hey, Sweetheart." I pull the sheet out from underneath her and partially cover her up.

"Hey." Her smile is a little wobbly, but still the most beautiful thing I've ever seen.

I'm handed the bottle of distilled water and a stack of pads over my shoulder, and I gently start wiping the grime off her face. "What about Connor?" she asks suddenly.

I force my hand to keep moving as I weigh my answer, but the EMT behind me solves my dilemma when he says, "The other crew is looking after him."

Truth is, I'm pretty sure the kid is dead. I'll have to wait to find out what exactly happened, but I was coming up behind him when he suddenly dropped like a sack. The moment he hit the ground my entire focus became her.

"Bella!" I turn to see Damian running toward the ambulance.

"She's good," I assure him quickly, but I still move out of the way so he can see for himself.

"Fucking Christ, kid," he mutters, putting his hand on her ankle and dropping his head down. "Took twenty goddamn years off my life, I swear."

"I'm fine," she repeats. "How was your vacation?"

Damian snorts, shaking his head. "I think I need another one."

"Sir, we should take her into Mercy, get her checked out."

"Right," Damian acknowledges with a nod. "I've got shit I have to take care of here, but I'll call the family, tell them to meet you there."

"I'll go with her."

Damian's eyes snap to me, and he gives me a long hard look before nodding once. "Go on, get her out of here."

BELLA

By the time we pull up outside Mercy, I'm halfway presentable.

Jasper spent the entire half-hour trip painstakingly cleaning every trace of blood he could find off my skin. Gently folding back the sheet he covered me with, he would expose a little at a time, sweetly guarding my modesty.

"Thank you." I grab his hand when he's about to pull it away. "For finding me."

He closes his eyes and sighs deeply. "I shouldn't

have lost you to begin with."

Before I have a chance to set him straight, the doors open and the sounds of my family drown out everything else.

"*Mi preciosa!*"

My mother wrestles her way to the stretcher as they pull me out, and I swear would've thrown herself on top of me, if my father hadn't held her back.

Flashes of my sisters' worried faces fly by as I'm wheeled into the ER, repeating, "I'm fine."

I miss Jasper's touch already and try to look behind me to see if he's there, but my family crowding behind me blocks my view. I'm wheeled into a cubicle—my family held back at the door—and lifted onto a bed. I sigh in relief when it's not Dr. Lipczyk I see coming through the curtains, but one of the young female interns.

"I hear you've had quite an adventure," she says easily, palpating the swelling on my cheek and around my eye. I'm grateful for the lighter tone, it helps stave off the dark shadows lurking at the edge of my awareness. "Nothing looks broken," she concludes, peeling back the sheet they left me covered with. "Let's have a look at the rest of you."

"There's nothing, other than a couple of bruises," I inform her.

"Good. Lucky. Now, you know I have to ask this…" She lets her words trail off and looks at me with the question clear in her eyes.

"He never touched me," I assure her, and she

raises an eyebrow at the swelling on my face. "Not like that. He never touched me in any sexual way."

"All right. Well, then I think we'll get some X-rays done of your face and your ribs, since you've sustained quite a bit of bruising on your left side, but if nothing shows up on those, I think we'll be able to let you go home."

Two hours later, I'm wheeled out of the hospital to my father's waiting car, Ma and my sisters flanking me. There's been no sign of Jasper.

I'm installed in the front seat, while Ma and Chrissy get in the back. Gabby and Fran are in Gabby's car. When Papa gets behind the wheel I turn to him.

"Have you seen Jasper?"

Instead of looking at me, his eyes shoot up at the rearview mirror and he glares into the back seat.

"Papa?"

"Ask your Ma and your sister," he grinds out between clenched teeth, as he pulls away from the hospital.

I turn around in my seat and find those two looking at each other.

"Well?"

Chrissy is the first to look me in the eye. "I believe he mentioned something about needing to get back to his team."

My father snorts beside me.

"Was that before or after you guys jumped on him like a bunch of feral cats?" I guess, and judging from the guilty look on Chrissy's face, it's the latter.

"He was supposed to look after you," Ma says defensively. "This would never have happened if your family had been here."

"Bullshit," Papa and I say at the same time. I'm glad to know there's at least one person in my family with some sense.

"That man got up before dawn to make sure my house was safe to come home to at the end of my shift. Would any of you have? Do you think Damian would've gotten up at three o'clock and driven half an hour to do that?"

"He should never have let you go back to work." I can't quite believe what I'm hearing as my mother's mouth presses into a stubborn line. "I told you that job was too much and too dangerous for you."

"Ma," Chrissy cautions, putting a hand on her arm, but I'm already reeling with a retort.

"At least he respects and trusts me enough to let me decide for myself what I can and cannot do," I hiss before swinging back around in my seat, staring straight ahead, my eyes burning, knowing Ma won't let this go until she's had the last word. She doesn't keep me waiting long.

"And see where that got you?"

"Enough!" my father barks. "Carmella, no more. Stop before you do more damage."

The rest of the trip to my house is silent. Uncomfortably so. I dread seeing not only Gabby's car, but Damian's SUV as well, parked in front of my house.

Damian has the car door open and me wrapped in a bear hug in seconds.

"Love you, kid," he mumbles against my ear, and the tears I've been holding back suddenly tumble down my cheeks. He leans back and cups my face in his big hands, searching my eyes before looking over my shoulder. "Where is Greene?"

"Ma."

He doesn't need more explanation and shakes his head. "What do you need?" he whispers for my ears only.

"A shower and sleep," I tell him, the strain of the past two days making my legs weak.

"You've got it, honey. Kerry will give you a hand, she's inside waiting."

My big brother tucks me under his arm and walks me inside, ignoring my sisters and walking me straight to Kerry.

"I'm fine," I assure Gabby and Fran, who look a little bedraggled, although I'm not sure if I was successful, given the state of my face.

"She needs a shower and bed," Damian instructs his wife, and behind him Gabby pipes up.

"We'll take care of her."

"No," he says firmly, facing our family. "Kerry will, while we have a little chat."

-

"So," Kerry starts, while she's brushing through my wet hair. "Jasper Greene."

I look at our reflection in the mirror, her face

healthy and tanned, wearing a gentle smile, and mine red and blotchy from spilling my guts to her and having a good cry in the shower.

"I don't know," I confess. "I can't imagine he'll want much to do with me after what my family did to him."

"Pffft…I'm sure he's a bigger man than that. He'll understand your family's just been worried. They were scared, they'll turn around, and so will he."

"I'm not so sure."

"Why would you say that?"

"Because he told me he's never had a family. Let alone one like mine. Besides, I'm afraid what my mother and sisters said to him only enforced what he's beating himself up for."

I remember his last words in the back of the ambulance, "*I shouldn't have lost you to begin with.*"

Kerry has barely tucked me into bed when the bedroom door opens a crack and Damian cautiously peeks in.

"Ahh good, you're decent," he says, walking over to sit on the edge of the bed. "I've got to get back to work, but I'm sure Kerry won't mind staying with you."

"Where is everyone else gonna be?" his wife asks.

"I'm sending everyone over to our house, if that's okay with you?"

The two share a look in silent conversation, and Kerry nods. "Of course it is."

"Papa wants to have a word before he herds them

out of here, though."

"Sure."

"I'll send him in and, Isabella?" I look up in my brother's serious face. I can't remember the last time he used my full name. "I'm proud of you. I don't know many people, man or woman, who would've been able to keep a cool head under those kinds of circumstances. You did an amazing job holding it together. Keeping that kid calm. I found the slug on the kitchen floor. I know what you did and it's nothing shy of amazing."

My eyes instantly start welling up again, both at Damian's words and the fear that boy—barely an adult—didn't survive; despite my best efforts. I have to know for sure.

"Connor?"

"I'm sorry, honey. He didn't make it." I nod sharply, noting the sharp clench of my brother's jaw.

"I don't think he was always bad," I feel compelled to say. "Most of the time he was just a teenage kid, really. But life damaged him in a way I don't think he could ever have recovered from."

"I know."

"He told me some things you probably should know."

"Tomorrow, honey. We'll deal with that tomorrow. I'm sending Papa in and then you get some sleep."

He gets up, leans over, and kisses my forehead before leaving the room. My father walks in almost immediately.

"Your brother is right, *mi hija,* you were…are amazing. I want you to know he read us the riot act out there."

"But you—"

"Oh, me too. And I deserved it. Accused me of not speaking out when I know better. Keeping silent to keep the peace. He's right. I did that, and I'm sorry, Isabella."

"Papa, it's okay."

"*Bueno, nada mas.* I just needed to tell you that. *Te amo, querida.* Get some sleep."

"*Te amo, Papa.*"

CHAPTER 21

JASPER

"What the hell are you still doing here?"

I look up from my screen to see Damian walking in. I don't even know what time it is, but a quick glance at my watch shows nine thirty.

"I'm writing up my report. Almost done."

"Since when do you write up reports the same day?"

"Since I saw something you guys didn't because you had your back turned, and I want to make sure I remember every fucking detail, so there isn't a chance in fucking hell this kid's death will be brushed off like his father's was."

"Don't hold back on my account," Damian comments sardonically, taking a seat on the other side of my desk. "You're talking about McMahan? You know he didn't shoot the kid, right?"

"He might as well have."

"Okay, you're gonna have to explain, Jasper. As I recall, he didn't step foot into the cabin until after the shot was fired."

"But he was out on the porch, looking through the broken window. Fucking waving at the kid, Damian. There's no way that kid would've missed him."

"Are you saying McMahan manipulated the shooting?"

"That's exactly what I'm fucking saying. Think about it; he knows the kid, he knows we're looking into his connection to the kid, and he knows the kid is out for revenge. He knew the kid would go for his gun. He doesn't want to give us a chance to ask questions."

"And you saw him?"

"He was fucking waving, Boss. He doesn't know we're aware of the payoffs to the family. As far as he's concerned, his involvement dies with the kid."

Damian is quiet, tapping his fingers on my desk, processing the information. I leave him to it and finish writing my report.

"So show again me what you have on this payoff scheme so far," he finally says, when I print off a copy of what I wrote for my own records.

I lay it all out for him: Hiram Miller's bank statements showing all transactions after his daughter died, the trust fund, the connection to Eugene Lipczyk, and how he is affiliated with Mercy Hospital through his seat on the board. I even tell him about the run-in I had with his son in the ER the night Bella was cut.

"Do you have anything to show Lipczyk is connected to McMahan in any way?"

"Working on it. There's evidence the two know each other; they both grew up in Durango, were only a few years apart in high school, and they attend a lot of the same social events."

"That's not exactly much to go on," Damian points out. "That could apply to quite a few of the upper echelon in this town."

"You're right, it isn't, but it's interesting enough to keep digging."

"That, I agree with. Check college alma maters, find out any personal connections: golf, country club, wives. Dig through social media. Find me anything that shows a personal connection, anything more than what can be brushed off as coincidental."

"Working on it."

"As for what you saw today at the cabin, have you talked to any of the SWAT guys that were there? Blackfoot? Anyone who may have seen the same you did? I'm not doubting you, but two witnesses would be better than one."

"I was holding off. The moment I start asking questions, I'm sure word will get back to Chief McMahan, and I want to make sure I have full backing of the Bureau before I go ahead."

"You do, but tread carefully. The moment you can show me something concrete, we will launch a full investigation. Jesus, Jasper," he says, rubbing his hand over his face. "A cop shooter is bad enough, but police corruption in the highest possible ranks is a minefield. God only knows how far the tentacles reach.”

“I know, believe me. Blackfoot does too, which is why he slipped it to me.”

“Leave him out of it for now. I don’t want to put a target on his back.” Damian gets up and heads into his office, but I catch him just before he disappears.

“I meant to ask you, how is Bella doing?”

He turns and leans a shoulder against the doorpost, crossing his arms in front of him. “No injuries that won’t heal within a week or so. Emotionally? Only time will tell. Right now she’s sleeping. Kerry’s with her and I sent my family to my place. You’ve got something you want to tell me?” He squints his eyes, and I find myself wanting to squirm in my seat, but I resist, facing him head on.

“I like your sister,” I admit.

“Tell me something new, genius.”

That comment takes the wind out of my sails, and I need a moment to consider how to word things. I shouldn’t be surprised though, I was pretty adamant about going with her in the ambulance.

“I just think she’s better off with family. Safer. She’s going to need the support, and I…I should focus on the investigation.” I was going to say I’m not sure if I’m what she needs, but that would’ve given too much away.

“Good.” He pushes away from the doorpost and turns to into his office, but at the last minute he throws over his shoulder; "Go home, get some sleep. Tomorrow morning I want you to get a full statement from Bella. She mentioned something the kid told her, something important."

I'm not sure if he's being purposely obtuse or just an asshole, but the prospect of seeing Bella in the morning is already messing with my head. Still, I shut down my computer, pack up my laptop, and head out the door.

Last time I saw my bed was when I left it before dawn Saturday morning. When I rolled into it the moment I walk in the door, I didn't expect to fall asleep almost instantly.

Unfortunately, it's only three in the morning and I just shot straight up in bed. Bella is first on my mind, but then I remember she's already home, safely in bed—or so I hope. Nuts how quickly my body has settled into the routine of waking at this early hour. Too bad it'll be another five or six hours, at least, before I can decently show up on her doorstep to get her statement, and there's no way in hell I'll get back to sleep.

Work it is. I pad into the kitchen, get a pot of coffee going, and flick on the scanner before sitting down with my laptop. Work has always been my escape of choice, and fuck do I need an escape now. I don't do well with unpredictability.

I lead a simple life which consists mostly of work, sometimes the gym, and an occasional outdoor activity I enjoy. The only people I deal with are either part of an investigation I happen to be working on or my team. The last time I tried anything close to a relationship outside of those parameters was over twenty years ago. I was in college and really more invested in accomplishing the goals I'd set for myself than I was in her. I ended up hurting her, disappointing her family. I decided there and then I was probably better suited to a single life, and I've done fine by myself. Until Bella made me want something more.

I didn't disagree with Bella's mom and sister when they reminded me of my shortcomings in the relationship department. Her mother didn't mince words when she told me I was responsible for her daughter being taken, but it was the words of her sister that affected me most. She questioned whether I was the right person for her sister. Wondered what I thought I could offer her in terms of stability, given my chosen career, especially since Bella would always struggle with depression.

I had no answer for her. That in itself I found telling enough.

So instead of following my heart and sticking as close as I could to Bella's side, I walked out of the hospital, driven by my conscience.

BELLA

"Want me to make you some more?" Kerry points at my empty coffee cup.

I can't believe I slept straight through the night. I never noticed Kerry crawling into bed with me at some point, which she said she did. Almost eleven hours of solid sleep.

"I'll do it," I tell her. "You sit for a bit." She'd been up before me and had breakfast going when I padded into the kitchen earlier. "How long do you figure it'll take the family to show up?"

Kerry grins. "Damian's got it covered. At least for a while. I had him on the phone earlier, and he told me he begged Ma for tamales, threw in there he hadn't tasted a proper Mexican meal in three weeks, cranking up the guilt. Of course your mother had the whole house in overdrive, sent your dad out for groceries at the butt crack of dawn, and arm-wrestled your sisters into preparing a proper Mexican feast. I suggested he tell them I would bring you over there this afternoon, provided you feel up to it."

"I don't know if I can handle my mother right now."

"You won't have to. I'm pretty sure Damian will, and if he doesn't, you and I will get back in the car and beeline it out of there. If there was ever a time for you to assert yourself, it would be now. You have a choice as to how much you are willing to put up with, Bella."

"I know, but—"

"No buts. You've already proven you're no

wilting flower, for Pete's sake. Just because some in your family choose to treat you like one doesn't make it so. You should know better."

"God, I'm so happy you're home," I sniff, rounding the counter and grabbing my sister-in-law in a big hug.

"Me too. Although, I might tell you a different story tomorrow when I have to get up early for work."

A single knock sounds at the door and I snicker. "Apparently you're overestimating my brother's influence," I tease, looking back at the kitchen as I go to let in what I assume will be my family.

"Hey."

I whip around at the sound of Jasper's voice, who is leaning against one of the porch posts, looking at me from under his eyebrows.

"Oh. Hey," is all I manage, a bit tongue-tied, and more than a little embarrassed. I never even tried to contact him to thank him. Sure, I no longer have a phone, but I could easily have gotten the number off Damian.

"Damian asked me to come and take your statement."

The closed off look on his face, combined with those dispassionate words, send me straight from embarrassed to injured, and anger wraps around me like a protective cloak.

Really?

"Oh, he did, did he? Let me get this straight; you're telling me the reason you're here is because my brother asked you? That's priceless." I don't even bother holding back on the venom in my tone.

"Squirt…" he mumbles, but I'm already too far lost in my head of steam to let the nickname, which just days ago would make me feel safe and protected, sway me from my path.

"No. You don't get to call me that. Didn't take much to set you running did it? Did you suddenly decide I was too much of a challenge? Too damaged for ya? Too fragile?" Hot tears come spilling down my cheek as I rant, and I agitatedly brush at them.

"That's not—" he starts, but I stop him with a hand in his face.

I'm angry and so hurt. I trusted him, opened up for him in a way I never had for anyone. I feel exposed to the core, and found lacking. Again.

Suddenly deflated, I squeeze my eyes shut and drop my head. "Tell my brother he can come get his damn statement himself."

Without even looking at him, I turn back inside, swing the door shut behind me, and walk straight into Kerry, who closes me in her arms.

"Honey, maybe you should give him a chance to talk before—"

Behind me the door slams open and I'm suddenly pulled from Kerry's hold and swung around by an angry looking Jasper.

"Goddammit, Bella," he swears, cupping my face in his large hands and tilting it up. "Jesus, how can someone so smart get it so fucking backward?" He barely gets his words out before his lips take mine in a bruising kiss, laced with anger and regret. I find myself leaning in and almost whimper when he pulls back, leaving his forehead pressed against mine. "Don't you see?" he mumbles softly. "It's me who comes up short."

Next thing I know, he is stalking out the door.

"Oh my," Kerry whispers behind me.

"What just happened?" I ask no one in particular, trying to get my bearings after going through what feels like an emotional spin cycle. My eyes land on Kerry, who is inexplicably smiling. "What?"

"That boy's got it bad."

Not ten minutes later, there's another knock at the door and this time I let Kerry do the honors. She walks back in with Luna in tow.

"Let me guess; you're here to take my statement?"

Luna nods, the corners of her mouth quirking. "I am. Jasper needs some time to dislodge his head from his ass. I hear it can be a painful process."

Kerry bursts out laughing, and I can't hold back a snicker, even though I still feel like I'm standing on quicksand.

It takes well over two hours for Luna to take me through the details of the past few days, but the longest time is spent on the things Connor told me about his family. Luna wanted every detail, urged me to recall exact wording, tone, demeanor.

By the time she leaves, it's just after noon, and despite my eleven-hour night, I am wrung out and ready for a nap. I mention as much to Kerry.

"Then go lie down. I'll wake you up around three. That should give you enough time to get cleaned up before we head out for dinner."

Fuck. That's right, dinner with my family. I need all the rest I can get before wading into that.

JASPER

I couldn't let her think she was in any way the cause.

That's why I stalked in after her. Granted, kissing her may not have been the best idea, under the circumstances, mostly because it made my resolve waver, but at least I managed to get the beaten down look from her eyes.

The office is quiet. Dylan had to take Max in to the dentist, there's no sign yet of Damian, and Luna is taking her sweet time at Bella's. I just got off the phone with Jimmy Wells, the old man's brother and former owner of cabin twelve. He actually called me. Mentioned Momma left word for him yesterday, but he wasn't able to get to a phone until today. He was able to tell me he sold Connor the cabin the summer of last year. Said he'd been happy to take the ten thousand cash at the time. The kid didn't seem to feel the need for paperwork, and neither had Jimmy, who'd had to shut down operations when the IRS came after him for tax evasion. Apparently he'd been running his place off the books the whole time he had it, so he didn't look too closely when offered a plastic bag with five bundles of a hundred twenties each. He used the money to buy an old RV, packed up his wife, and has been on the road ever since. When I asked why he didn't seem too concerned telling me all this, he just laughed. Said he figured I had better things to do than chase him. He didn't sound even a bit worried. Quite the character.

Tying off the loose ends of an investigation is always a tedious job and can often take months to complete, but there's a sense of urgency in this case, since it's leading into a whole different investigation. Jimmy didn't have much to add, other than to confirm what we already know. I'm hoping my next call will be a little more productive.

"Trish? Hi, my name is Jasper Greene, FBI. I'm a colleague of Dylan's? He gave me your number, and I was wondering if this is a good time to talk."

"Talk? Is Dylan okay?"

"He's fine. I'm actually hoping you might be able to help with a rather sensitive investigation."

"I'm just on my way out the door. My shift starts at one."

"Understood. Perhaps I could meet you somewhere after?"

"Should I be worried?" she asks apprehensively.

"Not at all. In fact, I'll be happy to have Dylan come with me, if that makes it easier for you?"

"If you don't mind," she says, sounding relieved.

"Won't be a problem, just tell me when and where."

She tells me she should be done around nine, so to meet her at Durango Joe's, a coffee shop on the south side of town not far from her work, at nine twenty. I leave a message with Dylan to get him up to speed.

I return my focus on the outline I'm putting together to back up my case for an official investigation into the shooting death of Franklin Davis and the suspected police cover-up after. This cannot have been a one-man job. It's the reason I want to speak to Dylan's friend in dispatch. If she wasn't the one who took the call, she might know who did, or be able to help us find out. I'm on a fishing expedition, but I'll be damned if I let this go, especially after seeing what I saw yesterday.

I look up when Luna walks in.

"Took you long enough."

"Don't complain," she counters, flopping down in the chair at her desk. "I don't do things fast, I do them thoroughly, and if you weren't such an ass, you would've had the information already." I'm not sure how she concluded I am an ass, but I'm not really debating it. "And let me tell you, she was a treasure trove of information."

"How's that?" My interest is piqued.

"The mother's suicide? He swore to Bella his

mother was murdered. Hung from the rafters in the attic when she wouldn't stop asking questions about her husband's death, according to him. Said his grandfather was paid off to keep quiet."

"Holy shit. I didn't think this could get any more fucked up, but apparently it can."

"Yup. Once you set on a certain course, there's just no turning back," she says, with a meaningful look in my direction. I'm not sure she's referring to the case, to me, or to both, but she immediately follows it up, making her point clear. "You'd know."

CHAPTER 22

BELLA

"You must be exhausted."

Kerry clearly interpreted my pleading look correctly.

Dinner has been painfully awkward, starting with the bruising hug Ma gave me when we walked in the door. Not that anyone has said anything untoward, but more that nothing was said at all. Everyone seems to fall into their regular patterns—as if nothing has changed—when everything has. It shows in the way they leave me out of the banter. Like they're afraid to set off the crazy person in the family. I hate it.

Other than Kerry and my brother, the only person even close to normal is Papa. He's the one who asked if I was doing okay, something that earned him glares from Ma and the girls. I brushed it off with an easy, "I'm fine." Something that didn't please him but seemed to satisfy the rest.

No one mentioned Jasper.

After an hour, I was already fed up. I barely managed to eat anything, but even that went either unnoticed or ignored by most.

I love my mother, and my sisters, but I just can't be around them right now. I can't seem to settle in the place carved out for me in the family dynamic. It feels like taking off your shoe for a minute, after a day being on your feet, and finding you can't fit back into it.

That's when I caught Kerry's eye and sent her silent call for help.

"Actually, I am pretty tired," I play along, getting up from my seat.

"But we haven't had dessert yet," Ma points out.

"I'm not really that hungry."

"You need some decent food in you," she pushes on, and I know what's coming. "Things always look better on a full stomach. You need to eat better, that's your problem."

The line I grew up with whenever I was sad, disappointed, or upset. Food fixes everything, at least in my family. She doesn't even realize she trivializes the issue. My mother loves hard, but she loves tough too. She's one of those people you have to remind yourself 'means well.'

"I'm just gonna grab a few clean clothes for tomorrow," Kerry announces, I'm sure to break the tension.

"You should just stay home. I'll be fine," I tell her with a quick smile, to show her I didn't mean for that to sound quite as abrupt as it may have.

"I don't think it's a good idea for you to be alone," Chrissy contributes, only making me that more determined.

"Are you sure?" Kerry asks, efficiently dismissing my sister's opinion, while clearly valuing mine. It means everything.

"Positive. I could do with some solo time, and you should reacquaint yourself with your new husband."

"Good plan," Damian grumbles, getting up from the table, and I shoot him a grateful smile. Both for making this easy, even when I know he'd probably prefer to camp out on my doorstep himself, but also for making it clear my opinion is the only one that matters in this.

"Seriously, Damian?" Gabby pipes up, and my mother is not far behind.

"I still think—" she starts, but Papa's had enough

"*Basta.* I'm going to see Isabella out, and you girls start getting your things together—we'll be heading home to Farmington soon."

Not paying any mind to the collective protests following his declaration, he waits for me to say my goodbyes, takes my arm, and walks me outside.

"Are you going to call that young man?" he asks when we get to my car.

"I don't know, Papa. I think maybe I'm a bit too much for him to handle."

It wasn't meant to be funny, but apparently he thinks otherwise, laughing at me.

"*Mi hija*, you are no more too much for him than he is not enough for you, which is what your sister told him."

"Still," I dismiss him. "Maybe a little space is not so bad. You know what they say about relationships forged under extreme circumstances. They never last." That makes him laugh even harder.

"*Eres tonta*. If you learn anything from me, learn this: relationships are about the people in them, not the circumstances surrounding them."

—

I have to admit, there have been times this past week when I was tempted to call him. Especially that first night alone.

I came home after my father saw me off, and I was almost too scared to go inside by myself, but I did. Just like Jasper had done for me before, I checked every space in my house; under beds, behind curtains, and in closets—and made sure the windows were all properly locked—before I could even begin to relax.

Waking up alone in the middle of the night drenched in sweat, and with my heart racing a mile a minute because of a nightmare, had not been fun either, but I survived that too.

I spent some time at Kerry's store, helping her do inventory and picking up a few books for myself. I went to the hairdresser one day, and the next I had a pedicure. It's been a long time since I've allowed time to slow down to a pace where I was able to read or be pampered.

I even went out for dinner alone one night. Truth be told, I did try to call Joanne to go with me, but couldn't get hold of her.

On top of that, I drove to Aztec twice to see Dr. Patterson.

Ryan popped in this past weekend to see for himself I'm indeed good enough to be added onto the new schedule, starting today. No more night shifts. The bruising on my ribs is already fading, and other than a dark spot on the outside of my left eye, and some faint yellow at my hairline, my face is once again presentable.

I don't doubt he also wanted to get a bead on my emotional state.

Papa checked in with me a few times and put Ma on the phone last time he called. She couldn't help herself and asked if I was eating okay, but after that tentatively asked when I thought I might go back to work. Probably the first time she talked about my job without immediately feeling judgment.

It's with a piece of advice Dr. Patterson handed me—I can't control or change life around me or the people in it, but I can change my own response to it—that I'm able to start looking at things in a different light. Everything is not criticism, everything is not a reflection on me. Sometimes the things people say are more about them than they are about me.

I'm glad I spent some time by myself, just being. I still have to fight the urge to make myself busy doing something; anything to drown out the thoughts and emotions I'm not sure what to do with, but this time I simply let them all bubble to the surface. Yeah, there was a time I crawled into bed in the middle of the day, in an effort to hide from myself, and once or twice I cried until I was afraid I'd never be able to stop, but those passed and I'm still here. I'm starting to believe if I don't try to continuously keep a lid on my emotions, and simply deal with them in the moment, I may actually be better off in the long run.

-

"I forgot to ask you yesterday," Ryan says, when we're on our way to the second call of the day.

The first had been a fairly minor crash, and although one driver had a few scrapes, it didn't warrant a trip to the ER. Now we're on our way to a seniors' home to transfer one of the residents to the hospital. So far a quiet shift.

"What?"

"How are things with your FBI agent?"

JASPER

I watch as the door opens next to the two-story townhouse I've been staring at for the past hour. Surveillance sucks, but since I still haven't been able to link McMahan to Lipczyk with any concrete evidence, I've had to resort to the very basic of investigative tools, and that is observing.

Still, it beats staring at my ceiling obsessing over Bella, whom I haven't seen in a week. Fuck, I used to stay busy all the time, but these days I just can't bring myself to stir up interest in anything other than this particular case.

Our talk with the dispatcher, Trish, has indirectly netted the names of two more officers to look into. She was able to name the colleague who actually had taken the call from McMahan the night of Franklin Davis' shooting, who in turn was able to recall quite a bit of detail. Including the call number of the second unit that showed up at the scene. It wasn't hard to trace back the names of the officers.

I can't do much with those names, though, except keep an eye on them. If I question them, word will surely get back to the chief, and I don't want him to know we're looking into him. Not until there is something solid I can produce in evidence.

I followed McMahan coming out of his office tonight, but instead of turning right to go home to his family, as he'd done every other night, he turned left. He drove into a new residential area behind the hospital, turned onto a driveway, and got out to knock on the door. I wasn't able to get a good look at the person who let him in, so I've been waiting around, hoping to catch a glimpse.

This time I'm ready, and the moment the chief

comes out the door, I have my camera poised and start clicking.

—

"Get anything?"

Damian looks up when I walk past the open door to his office.

"Maybe. Our chief took an hour detour on his way home tonight. Give me ten and I'll show you."

The beauty of digital photography is that there is no time lapse for developing. It is instant, and the moment I download the images on my computer, I have the connection we've been looking for.

"You'll like this," I announce, walking into Damian's office and taking a seat across from his desk, tossing the printouts on his desk.

"Who is this?"

"The man walking away is McMahan, and the man who is standing in the lit doorway is none other than Eugene Lipczyk's son: Dr. Scott Lipczyk."

"Should I know him?"

"He happens to be an ER physician at Mercy and doesn't seem to have any qualms putting his hands on women without invitation, namely your sister."

"Are you shitting me?" I instantly feel the heat coming off Damian.

"Nope. And my guess is that if he got handsy with Bella, the likelihood is he's gotten handsy with others as well."

"Any record of that?"

"I haven't had a chance to look into it yet, but I will. Although with Lipczyk senior on the hospital board, any complaint against his son may have been squashed before it got anywhere."

"Unless they filed a complaint directly with the Durango PD," Damian observes, and I pick up on his train of thought.

"Which might not have gotten very far either, if McMahan got his hands on them."

"Damn. One hand washing the other. That might explain why Lipczyk was using that consortium trust fund to pay off the Davis family," he surmises. "Payback."

"Would be my guess."

"Okay. Get Luna up to speed tomorrow, ask her to see what she can find out at Mercy, fish around the ER without drawing attention. You work on police reports, see what dirt you can come up with. This is starting to make sense, we just have to find the right loose thread and start pulling."

"What about talking to Blackfoot? Who knows, he may have some insight."

"I'll talk to him tomorrow. We're meeting for breakfast at CJ's." Damian gets up, tucks his phone in his pocket, and grabs his keys off the desk. "I'm heading home. I suggest you do the same."

"I will soon."

Soon turns out to be almost one in the morning before I walk out to my truck. Too pumped to sleep, so I find myself driving in the opposite direction, up the mountain to Bella's house.

Her place is dark, quiet, but just sitting out here in my truck, like some creepy stalker, makes me feel more settled.

I recline my seat a little, so I can lay my head back, and mentally go over the bits and pieces I've uncovered, trying to put them in some kind of coherent order.

I found the reports. A whopping sixteen of them, dating back as far as eighteen years, when a girl at Lipczyk's high school had claimed Scott followed her into the women's bathroom and tried to force her to perform oral sex on him. The complaints vary from sexual harassment all the way to the statutory rape of a seventeen year old, only eight years ago. Scott had been almost thirty at the time.

Take one guess who was listed on all those cases as officer on record? Not sure how McMahan thought he'd be able to get away with that, except perhaps sheer arrogance.

I looked into Scott a little further and easily hacked his Facebook account. That's where I found several pictures that confirm the personal relationship between McMahan and the Lipczyk family. He appears in a photo taken at some kind of family barbecue, and again with his arm around Scott's shoulders at his graduation. In the description, McMahan is referred to as his godfather.

Slowly but surely, the puzzle pieces are starting to

add up, painting an unmistakable picture.

A knock on my window startles me, and the first thing I notice is it's starting to get a little lighter outside. A sleep-tousled Bella is standing barefoot in the dirt beside my truck.

"What are you doing out here?" I fire off at her the moment I open my door.

"I should be asking you," she counters, her hands on her hips as she steps back, giving me room to get out.

"At least I'm dressed. You're practically naked."

"I'm wearing a robe," she points out, but I happen to know what she has on under there is minimal to the point of nonexistent.

Without wasting any more words in this pointless conversation, I grab her hand and march her back inside.

"Coffee?" she asks, kicking the door shut and sauntering into the kitchen, as if I simply stopped by for a casual visit. At fucking four o'clock in the morning.

I'm pissed I fell asleep outside her door like some lovesick teenager, but I'm really ticked she caught me. Still, I answer, "Yes."

The little smirk of her mouth spells trouble, and it stares me in the face when she turns around, a steaming cup of coffee in her hand, and her robe undone. I was right; what is underneath does not constitute coverage of any kind. The only things not see-through are the lace straps of her top and on the edge of her panties.

She may as well be naked.

"Isabella…" I warn, when she walks over, her full breasts swaying with each careful step.

"I've been waking up every morning around this time, did you know that?" she asks, handing me my coffee, but making no effort to cover herself up. "I've tried going to sleep late, drinking a few glasses before I turn in, and I even bought a diffuser, hoping maybe aromatherapy would work, but nothing seems to keep me from waking up at the very crack of dawn. Why do you think that is?"

It doesn't sound like a question that requires an answer. Not from me anyway. Besides, I'm not sure I quite trust myself to speak yet, not until I can peel my eyes away from that body. I take a good swig of my coffee instead, burning my mouth in the process. *Jesus.*

"I miss you."

Those three words hit me hard. I focus on her liquid brown eyes that hold more than I deserve.

"Sweetheart, I don't—"

"It's funny," she continues, undeterred. "I've spent the past week working hard to feel solid ground beneath my feet again. To get real with myself. Trying to process what happened up in that cabin, instead of shoving it down—where I would normally shove feelings I don't want to examine too closely—only to have them blow up in my face at a later time. It's been good. It's been cathartic. A relief. Except for the one thing that has me wake up every morning between three and four, like some annoying internal alarm." I just swallow hard as she slowly closes the distance between us. "Seeing your truck out there this morning clued me in." She puts her hand in the middle of my chest, and I'm sure she can feel the heavy beat of my heart. "I miss you. I just wanted you to know that." She turns away and heads back to the Keurig, dropping in a fresh pod.

"Goddammit, Squirt," I grind out between clenched teeth, already moving close to her. I wrap my arms around her from behind, pulling her flush to my body as I drop my face in her tangled hair. "Are you sure you want this?" One hand slips under her flimsy top to cup her heavy breast, the other dives straight into her panties where I find her already wet for me.

The small gasp from between her parted lips as I roll the pad of my finger over her hard little clit, works like a red flag on a bull. I pull my hands free and strip down her robe before lifting hers to brace against the counter. I sink to my knees behind her and pull that flimsy piece of confection down her legs. The lush, dimpled cheeks of her butt are an invitation to put my teeth to. She jumps a little at my nip, but instantly lifts up on her toes and tilts her ass high enough for me to see the slick promise of her pussy.

"Yessss," she hisses when I spread her cheeks with my hands and lick her slit, front to back. There is nothing fucking sexier than a woman who knows how to take what she wants, and Bella knows. She rides my face with full abandon, and I almost come in my jeans when she throws her head back, brushing my face with her long hair, and moans out her release.

I don't know how fast to get to my feet, drop my pants, and tag my wallet to fish out the protection I'd started carrying around.

"Loose the top," I mumble, my lips on her shoulder as I try to focus on rolling the condom on. I whip my own shirt over my head, so I can feel her skin against mine as I curve around her. With one hand low on her belly, and the other bracing against the counter, I line my cock up to her entrance and slam balls deep into her wet heat.

—

"I think I could sleep a few more hours now," she says, twirling her fingers through the down on my chest.

We're lying on the kitchen floor, sticky but sated, and already I'm beating myself up.

"I'm not sure—" Her fingers come to press against my lips.

"I am. You're good for me, Jas," she whispers, pressing kisses to my chest. "I know you don't believe it, but give me a chance to prove it to you. That's all I ask."

I answer the only way possible.

"Come to bed, Squirt."

CHAPTER 23

BELLA

"Have you seen Joanne around?"

Ryan is waiting outside the women's locker room for me and pushes away from the wall when I come out.

"Not in the last few days. Why?"

"I've left a few messages already and I haven't heard back yet. Last time I saw her was the night she and I went out before our shift."

"Maybe she's on vacation?" he suggests, but I shake my head.

"No, I'm sure she would've mentioned something to me."

"If you're worried we can check with Brenda, I think she's working. If anyone would know, it's her." I follow Ryan into the ER where he easily locates her. "Hey, gorgeous," he flirts with the nurse who's old enough to be his mother. "Do you have a new haircut? Something is different about you."

Even the generally down-to-earth Brenda is not immune to his charms, but she gives as good as she gets, despite the faint tug of her lips. "Give it up, boy. Told you before and I'll tell you again; you ain't man enough to handle me."

"Breaking my heart, Brenda. Breaking my heart."

I shake my head at the silly banter, but can't help a smile. From the corner of my eye, I see Scott Lipczyk leaning an elbow on the nurses' station, looking in our direction.

"Have you seen Joanne around?" I ask, wanting to get out of here before LimpDick decides to come looking for another confrontation.

Brenda's eyes immediately swing around to the nurses' station. "Not here," she says under her breath. "I'll meet you at your rig. Give me five minutes."

She slips through the curtain into a cubicle, and Ryan motions for me to follow him out. Well, that doesn't do much for my peace of mind.

"What was that all about?" I wonder out loud, when we climb in the back of the rig to check it's all stocked up.

"We're about to find out." Ryan's eyes are focused over my shoulder, and I turn to see Brenda hurrying toward us.

"Didn't want open up that can of worms in there," she says by way of explanation. "I'm not sure exactly what happened, but Joanne called me, not last week but the week before, asking if I could take her shift that night. She said she wasn't feeling well, but I'd heard all about the showdown with *him*—" She tilts her head in the direction of the hospital. "—the night before. When I asked if it had anything to do with that, she didn't deny it, just said she might need to take some time off. That man is a snake. I suggest you be careful around him."

"Wait," I call out when she turns and starts back. "Will you tell me if you hear anything from her?"

She gives me a thumbs-up and keeps going. Just then the radio crackles with our first call of the day.

"I'm gonna call Jasper," I announce when Ryan pulls away from the hospital.

"You don't think it's a bit over the top to call in the FBI just because she hasn't called you back yet?" I swing my arm, hitting his shoulder. "Ouch. Didn't know you'd get violent."

"Don't be an ass. I was thinking maybe he could find out her husband's phone number so I could try that. He's good with stuff like that."

"Oh he is, is he?" Ryan teases. "So am I to deduce from that you two are back together?"

I smile, shrugging my shoulders. "It's complicated."

I don't tell him I kissed Jasper goodbye on my porch steps early this morning, or that he made it so I'll never be able to look at my Keurig again without smiling. The truth is, though, things aren't that simple. I'm sure there will be other roadblocks ahead, either thrown up by him, or even by me—but right now— I'm riding the high this morning left me on. Staying in the moment.

"Seems pretty simple from where I'm sitting."

JASPER

"That was Bella."

Everyone at the table turns their head toward me.

Damian had brought Blackfoot back to our office after their breakfast. CJ's diner being a favorite breakfast spot in town, the risk was too big they'd be overheard. We've been laying out what we've uncovered so far, and are in the process of planning out next steps.

"She hasn't been able to get hold of a friend of hers in well over a week and wants me to look up a number for the woman's husband."

"So look it up," is Damian's response.

"I will, but I thought it interesting that the friend also happens to be an ER nurse at Mercy, and she went AWOL right after a confrontation with the very man we were just talking about; Scott Lipczyk."

"What's her name?" Luna wants to know, already poised at her keyboard.

"Joanne Shredder."

"So what kind of confrontation?" This from Keith, who's been relatively quiet since walking in here.

"According to Bella, it was in the middle of the

hospital lobby; the guy was being a douche, her friend told him off and he threatened her job. Apparently the friend knew Lipczyk in high school."

"Joanne Thompson?" Damian asks, flipping through the sixteen archived reports I printed out this morning and pulling one from the bottom of the stack.

"Thompson is her maiden name," Luna pipes up. "Married Mark Shredder in 2010."

"This is her," Damian says, tapping his finger on the report. "Same Joanne who was accosted in the high school bathroom by this dirtbag. Report says she came into the station with her parents to file a complaint. She was brushed off as a..." he reads straight from the report, "...*jealous attention seeker. In contrast Scott was described coming across as an intelligent young man from an upstanding family.* Signed by Tom McMahan."

"Jesus." Keith lowers his head in his hands. "This makes me sick. Worked with this guy for twelve years, never liked him much, but this turns my stomach." He waves his hand at the pile of reports.

"Got a number for the husband," Luna says, handing me a piece of paper.

Via the husband, I'm able to get hold of Joanne Shredder, who according to him is visiting her sister in Pagosa Springs. The woman is more than a little apprehensive at first, but once I explain my call, she opens up. The same night of the incident in the lobby, Lipczyk followed her out into the parking lot after her shift. He shoved her against the car, had his hand around her throat, and threatened her. By the end of our conversation, I manage to convince her to talk to Keith Blackfoot, who takes the call in Damian's office.

"She didn't say anything to her husband, because she knew he'd insist she report the doctor, or worse, try to confront him. She just packed up her baby and left for her sister's."

"Don't blame her," Dylan comments. "Given her previous experience reporting the ass."

"Except she says she was planning to come back in a few days anyway," Keith interjects, walking into the room. "She needed some time to think, but had the foresight to have her sister take some pictures of the bruising around her neck. She wants to file an official complaint, she just wants to discuss it with her husband first. She will call to let me know when she's coming into the station, so I can make sure I'm there. We can kill two birds with one stone, if we play this right."

"You mean use the woman as bait?" Luna clearly does not like that idea.

"Her idea, not mine, Roosberg," Blackfoot fires back.

"It's a good one," I have to agree. "Filing an official report will provoke Lipczyk and prompt McMahan to try and intervene. We can be on top of it."

"Until then, I suggest we keep a lid on this investigation," Damian suggests. "Stick to gathering supporting background information, but no interviews. Nothing that might alert the chief or either of the Lipczyks. Only way this will work is if they're completely unaware we're digging."

"What about a warrant for phone records?" Luna asks. "Is there any way to get those without risking McMahan finding out?"

"I can get them," I offer, but Damian shakes his head.

"We're going to need to do this by the book. Let me call James in Denver, see what our options are."

"I'd get them anyway," Keith suggests. "We can still follow through with a warrant if we find something worthwhile.

Five minutes later, I'm outside in our parking lot that overlooks Durango, talking to Bella.

"I talked to her."

"Joanne? You did? How is she? Where is she?"

I chuckle at the flow of questions. "She's fine. She's at her sister's place. I told her you were worried and she said she'd call you tonight. Apologized for not calling you back, but she wasn't sure what she was ready to tell you yet."

"Ready to tell me? Why, what happened? Was it him?"

"Easy with the rapid-fire questions, Squirt. She really is fine. I can't have you going off half-cocked when I tell you, though. Any of this comes out, we lose a great opportunity to nail this case down."

"He attacked her," she concludes on her own, breathing fire. "The bastard attacked her, didn't he?"

"Bella…" I warn her. "This is exactly what I mean. He threatened her, yes, but she's fine. She's filing a report in the next few days, which is why you can't go off on a tangent. Keep it to yourself so we can do our job."

"Fine, all right, I'll suck it up but, Jas? Get this done with. I'd like to be able to go to work without having to look over my shoulder all the time. Maybe see what it feels like get back to a normal life, with you in it."

Fuck, I'd like that too. I never even got around to taking her on that first date. Given what we were up to this morning, perhaps a little like tying the horse behind the cart, but I still want to do this right.

I can't believe how easily I caved. She just has be near for me to forget all my reservations. My last attempt to walk away from this, when she was plastered against me on the kitchen floor this morning, was no more than a final scuffle in what I already knew was a losing battle.

Who the hell am I kidding? I've sensed since the first time I met her, she would burrow deep if I let her. I knew when I first kissed her, there'd be no turning back. Just like part of me was fully conscious sitting out there in her driveway, in the middle of the night, it would only take one glimpse of her, to have me throw in the towel.

"What are you doing tonight?" I ask, a smile on my face.

"Cooking you dinner."

"I like the sound of that. Better get back to work."

"Me too. I've got a drunk to deliver and puke to scrape off."

"In the middle of the day?"

"Apparently so. Yuck."

—

"So, you and my sister."

I look up to find Damian looming over my desk.

The rest of the office cleared out about half an hour ago, and I'd frankly forgotten about him locked away in his office. I'm just finishing up a few things before I was going to head over to Bella's.

I prop my legs up and lean back in my chair, crossing my arms over my chest. I was expecting this at some point. Now is as good a time as any.

"Looks that way."

He nods slowly and sits down on the edge of my desk. "So what changed since last week?" I look at the worn toes of my boots, trying to come up with the words, but Damian forges ahead. "Let me take a wild stab at this. You prefer to keep your world small, so it's easier to control and analyze, and even though my sister is much the same way, she comes with a whole truckload of issues, including a brother who happens to be your boss." He holds his hand up when I start to object. "Let me finish, I'm not done yet. You're feeling like a fish out of water and are scared you might not be the right person to give her the balance she needs in her life."

"Pretty much," I mumble, picking distractedly at a rip in my jeans. "I'm not worried about her, I'm worried about me. I'm the unpredictable factor in all of this. I'm the one flying by the seat of my pants. How am I supposed to know I won't fuck this up? If I do, I run the risk of hurting the person I care about most, and losing the only thing close to family I have: my team. I'm afraid I might do both."

"So what had you standing on her porch step at seven this morning, kissing her stupid?"

My eyes shoot up. "You were there?"
"Was gonna drop her off a coffee and Danish on my way to the diner, set her up for a good day. Came around the corner and saw you'd beaten me to it, so I turned around. But you haven't answered my question; what changed?"

This time I don't have to think at all.

"She trusts me, even though I don't trust myself."

CHAPTER 24

BELLA

I'm exhausted.

Last day of my week back at work before I can enjoy a proper weekend. It's been a long time since I've looked forward to a weekend like this.

Jasper told me this morning, when he was leaving my place, to get a good night's sleep tonight. He's working late and won't be over, like he has most of this week, but says he has plans for us this weekend. I couldn't get him to tell me more than to pack an overnight bag and make sure to bring easy shoes.

This first full week back sure has taken a chunk out of me, though. I'm sure the late nights spent with Jas haven't exactly helped either. It's like we've been trying to make up for not just a week's, but a year's worth of lost time.

Despite the fatigue, the slightly tender state of

some of my parts have me wearing a pleased little smile. I'm actually happy. Not that I have any illusions there won't be times when that is different, but as I promised myself during my time off, I am determined to stay in the moment. And this particular moment, I'm feeling pretty damn good.

"What do we have?" the attending asks, when we wheel our patient into the ER.

"Male, forty-four, presenting with chest pains and shortness of breath. Last BP eighty-five over fifty, heart rate one thirty-five and pulse ox is at eighty-six. He's had three hundred milligrams of aspirin en route," I rattle off, helping the man scoot onto the bed from his sitting position on the stretcher.

I step back to let the team do their work, immediately slapping electrodes to his chest and sticking a pulse ox meter on his finger. I lean in and give his shoulder a light squeeze. "They'll take good care of you, Mr. Viejo. You're in good hands."

Ryan is already standing at the counter, right next to the sliding doors of the ambulance bay, scribbling down details of this last call in a report.

"Makes you wonder, doesn't it?" Ryan comments when I join him. "The guy is about my age, looks in good shape, says he works out every day and lives healthy, which is more than I can say. Still, he ends up having a heart attack?"

"You can only control so much to lower your risk, but there's little you can do about a genetic predisposition. You heard the man; his father died of a heart attack at fifty-one. Out of the blue." I clap him on the shoulder. "I'm going to grab a coffee, do you want one?"

"Sure."

I leave Ryan to contemplate his mortality and pass by the cafeteria, where the coffee is just a tiny step up from sludge, and make for the small break room down the hall from the locker rooms. When Kerry and Damian bought me my new Keurig last Christmas, I donated my old one to the sparsely outfitted kitchenette in the small space. Nothing more than a set of couches, a kitchen table with four uncomfortable chairs, and an old TV. And as of six or so months ago, my old Keurig.

The thing takes almost as long as an order at Starbucks to brew one cup, but the results are at least drinkable, unlike what they serve next door.

I snap lids on the carry-out cups and make for the door, just as it swings in, knocking the cups from my hand and hot coffee all over me.

"*Sonofabitch*!" I curse loudly, making a beeline for the small sink where I run cold water over my hands and dab some onto my uniform shirt. That hurts.

"Here, let me see."

I don't have to turn around to know Scott is behind me. I freeze when his arms come around to hold my hands under the water, as he pushes his front to my rear. I almost puke when I feel the distinct outline of his erection pressing against my ass, and haul back with an elbow, catching him somewhere in his midsection. I don't wait around, but boot it out of there, down the hallway and into the locker room, locking the door behind me. With shaking hands, I pull out my phone and call Ryan, who answers on the first ring.

"Weren't you just here?"

"Can you come down to the locker rooms?"

"Why do you sound out of breath?" he asks, suspicion in his tone.

"Ryan, please. Just come?"

"Already on my way. Where are you?"

"Women's locker room."

"Be right there."

I lean my back against the door and wait to hear Ryan's footsteps. The moment he knocks and identifies himself, I have the door open and pull him inside.

"What the hell, Gomez? What happened to you?"

"Did you see Lipczyk out there?"

"Yeah, I passed the dirtbag down the hall, why? Did he do this?"

He takes in my front, dripping with coffee that has blessedly cooled off, as I tell him what happened.

"Take off your shirt and let me see," he orders, but my hands shake so hard, he has to undo my buttons. "Let's get some cold water on that." He grabs a towel from the shelf over the sink in the corner and soaks it. "Sit your ass down before you fall down."

"I'm not gonna fall down," I sputter, but sit down anyway.

"Woman, you're a magnet for trouble these days." He drapes the towel against my front, which instantly soothes the red skin of my chest and stomach, before sitting down beside me, pulling out his phone.

"What are you doing?"

"Getting ready to call the cops—what else?"

"Hang on one second," I plead, putting my hand over the phone in his. "I'll give Jasper a call when I get home."

"You *are* going to press charges, right?" he pushes, clearly confused.

"I will—I promise—but Jasper is in the middle of something that involves LimpDick as well. I need to talk to him first."

"Like what?" he wants to know, but at least he's putting his phone back in his pocket.

"Man, you're persistent. Let's just say I've already said too much. He made me promise not to breathe a word because it could hamper the investigation."

"Fine," Ryan gives in. "I won't put you on the spot, but I am going to call him tonight to follow up."

"Whatever." I roll my eyes with Gomez flair, making Ryan chuckle.

He ends up walking me to my car, after checking to confirm Scott's shift just started.

I'm tempted to stop at Walmart to pick up a few things, mainly Ben & Jerry's, but I change my mind when I see the store. Not the right day to tackle that particular hurdle. McDonald's is out too, which really sucks. My two favorite indulgences off the shelf. Who knows, this may be an opportunity to lose some weight, but I have a feeling a certain someone wouldn't be happy if I got rid of my soft padding. He really seems to be fan.

Just like that, without the aid of ice cream or French fries, I'm shaking off the encounter in the break room and smiling at the prospect of a weekend with Jasper.

I knew he was good for me.

JASPER

"Please come in."

I let Joanne go ahead into Blackfoot's office, and follow in behind her, closing the door.

Blackfoot called mid-afternoon to let me know Joanne had come home, and asked me to pick her up and bring her in. Her husband opened the door, a baby on his arm and worry on his face. The guy is scared for his wife, I get that, so I spent a few minutes reassuring him we won't let her out of our sight. The drive into the station is mostly quiet, but she does ask about Bella.

As agreed, I lead her right in through the main doors to the front lobby, where I ask to speak to Blackfoot. All for maximum exposure. Keith is hoping anyone walking into the station accompanied by an FBI agent, will at least pique interest. We need McMahan to see her complaint—take the bait.

"Have a seat, Mrs. Shredder."

"Joanne, please," she insists, sitting down.

I take the chair against the wall, so I have a decent view out of the large window that opens up to the hall. Blackfoot purposely left the blinds open halfway, slanted down just slightly. Anyone passing by would have to make an effort to see inside, but from where I'm sitting I can easily see outside.

"Before you start, let me tell you we've already read your report from the assault eighteen years ago. The statute of limitations has passed on that unfortunately, but it may be brought into evidence at some point. I just want you to be aware."

Joanne nods at Blackfoot, who seems to have a better bedside manner than I would've given him credit for. Over the course of this case, I've had to amend quite a few impressions I had of the man.

"So why don't you start from the beginning? This incident you mentioned on the phone, this was the first time since high school he's actually put his hands on you, correct?"

"Actually, no," she says, surprising us both. "There was one other time. I caught him pocketing medication in the ER dispensary and confronted him. He threatened my job then too." She looks up at Blackfoot and adds, a tad defensively, "Mark had just been laid off, and I couldn't take the risk."

"No judgement here, Joanne. Do you remember what he took?"

"I can't be a hundred-percent sure, but it may

have been propofol. I'd just inventoried at the start of my shift and one vial was missing. As far as I know, we didn't get any patients through that would've warranted the use of that type of sedative."

My eyes find Blackfoot's and I know at a glance he's thinking the same thing I am.

"Do you recall when that incident took place?" It had been on my lips to ask, but he beat me to it.

"Let me see, Mark got laid off maybe a month or so before Christmas. So it would have been toward the end of 2013."

While Blackfoot continues to get information from Joanne, I pull out my phone and start typing a message to Damian to move forward with a warrant to have Franklin Davis' wife exhumed right away, when I see something from the corner of my eye.

Standing to the side of the window, is none other than our own Chief of Police Tom McMahan, trying hard to peek into the office.

Gotcha.

Half an hour later, I lead Joanne right out the front door again. She's subdued when I drive her home, but when I pull into her driveway she turns to me.

"So what happens now?"

"See that car over there?" I turn in my seat and point at Dylan's black Bronco, parked along the curb across the street. "That's a teammate of mine, Agent Dylan Barnes. I would trust him with my life. He's one of the people who will be keeping an eye on you. You don't have to do anything. We'll start talking to some of the colleagues you mentioned, see if they'd be willing to file a police report as well. Sometimes all it takes is for one person to lead the way for the rest to follow. Especially in cases like this. We want to make sure to build a solid case against Lipczyk."

"What if I head back to my sister's to wait this out?"

"If you feel safer there, by all means. We'll be in touch with you as soon as we have some news."

"I'll see what Mark says."

I can't blame the woman for being afraid. Two weeks ago this dirtbag had his hand on her throat, and on top of that—she doesn't have much reason to trust law enforcement either—considering how things went for her the first time she filed a report on him.

I walk her inside, leave her with Dylan's cell phone number, and walk over to check in with him before heading back to the office.

Turning into Rock Point Drive, a call comes in and I pull over to the side.

"Hey, Sweetheart."

"Hey. Are you busy right now?"

"Just coming up to the office, why? Are you still at work?"

"No. I'm home…sitting in the car in the driveway if you want to get technical."

"Is everything okay?" I ask, alarmed when I notice a little wobble in her voice.

"Not really. Well, I was, but now I'm freaking out."

"Hang tight, I'll be right there."

I make a U-turn and head back out on the 160. Not five minutes later, I pull into the driveway beside her. I note she doesn't open the door until I get out of my truck, and she walks straight into my arms.

"What's going on?"

"I feel stupid now." She shakes her head lightly.

"Tell me anyway."

"Not here."

She takes my hand and leads me into the house, where I do my routine walk around, thinking it might help put her at ease. When I return to the kitchen, she's in the kitchen dropping a pod in her Keurig. I walk up behind her, wipe her hair to the side, and kiss her neck before leaning my chin on her shoulder.

"Ready to tell me yet?"

"Yes." She turns in my arms, holding on to them. "Scott followed me into the break room at the end of my shift. He knocked hot coffee out of my hands, all over me, when he swung open the door, but then he put his hands on me. I elbowed him and took off, shut myself in the locker room, and called Ryan." She rambles so fast, I have trouble catching all of it.

"Slow down." I lift my hands to her shoulders and lean down so we're almost eye level. "Why didn't you call me right away?"

"Because of your case. I was afraid you'd come barging into the hospital and maybe mess everything up."

She may have a point; my hands behind her back

are clenched into fists.

"Was he on his way out the door too? Is that why you were parked out front freaking out?"

"No. His shift just started. I just…I was fine driving home, I swear, but I pulled up here and I just couldn't bring myself to get out of the car."

"Monday we're going into the police station to file an official report. Did he leave any marks on you?"

"Not really. Just from the hot coffee."

When she pulls down the front of her shirt, showing angry red skin from the hollow of her throat running down between her breasts; I have to fight another wave of anger.

"We'll still take a few pictures. Take off your shirt," I grind out, fishing my phone from my pocket. Trying to stay impassive at the sight of the markings as far down as her belly button; I snap a few pictures when I notice her trembling.

Dropping my phone on the counter, I pull her back in my arms and she burrows her face in my shirt.

"Sweetheart, I have to go back into the office for at least a couple of hours, but I don't want to leave you here. Why don't you pack your bag now? I'll drive you to my place, set you up there, and go in to finish up what I need to do. I won't be too long, we'll get a good night's sleep, and tomorrow morning we head out."

She tilts back her head. "Where were we going again?"

"Nice try, smartass." I grin down at her. "Now get

packing. I'm gonna call Damian to let him know I'll be a few minutes late."

Half an hour later, Bella is set up on my couch, a pint of Ben & Jerry's I just stocked my freezer with in her hand, and a movie on TV.

I didn't tell her staying at my place this weekend had been the intent all along. My place is right downtown, with just about everything within walking distance. I'd planned for us to do all the things people do when they come to Durango. All Bella seems to have done since moving here is work.

When I had Damian on the phone earlier, I'd already filled him in on what happened, but he still grilled me when I walked into the office.

"*Fuck.* We're gonna need to put someone on her too. We may need to call in some more bodies, we're running short."

"No need," I assure him. "She'll stay with me at my place this weekend."

He glares at me, but then seems to shake it off.

"Fine. But I'm telling you, we better see some results soon. I'm about ready for another fucking vacation."

CHAPTER 25

BELLA

I wake up to the sound of muted voices.

It takes me a second to look around and get my bearings. Jasper's style is what you might call minimalistic, especially in the bedroom. Basically a large bed, two floating shelves on either side doing duty as nightstands, and one dresser that doesn't even have knobs on the drawers. The only things hanging on the wall are a flat-screen TV over said dresser and a large black and white print of a lone tree, standing on the edge of a cliff, over the bed.

It feels like waking up on a spaceship.

I discovered last night that Jas is very tidy. Not a cup or plate left in the sink nor a stray sock on the floor somewhere. No personal items left on the counter, no stack of mail, no take-out menus pinned to the fridge door. The apartment looks like one of those model units. Either the man rarely spends time here, or he's a little OCD.

For someone usually wearing ripped jeans, scuffed boots, and a mop of dirty blond hair that's probably better suited to a beach bum than an FBI agent, this place was not what I expected.

Swinging my legs out of bed, I notice the only thing out of place; my overnight bag in the middle of the floor, contents already spilling out everywhere. It seems almost symbolic of the chaos I seem to bring to his life.

I snag some leggings and an oversized tee from my bag and pad into the adjoining bathroom, where I left my toiletry bag on the counter last night. The plan was to have a shower, but that quickly changes when the scent of coffee hits my nostrils.

Last night I never saw or heard Jasper come in. By the time the movie was done, I was already half asleep. The only way I know he got in bed with me, at some point, is the imprint of his head on the pillow next to mine.

His head turns and eyes zoom in on me the moment I step out of the bedroom, a smile teasing the corners of his mouth as he stalks toward me. His hands cup my face and he leans in to kiss me sweetly.

"Morning," he mumbles against my lips.

"Morning," I echo.

"Morning."

I peek over Jasper's shoulder to find my brother leaning against the kitchen counter, coffee in hand

and eyes rolled to the ceiling.

Awkward.

Jasper doesn't seem fazed and tucks me under his arm, leading me to a stool at the kitchen island.

"Coffee?"

"Please. Hi," I direct at Damian. "You're out and about early?"

"It's a miracle I slept at all," he grumbles. "I spent most of the night going over cell phone records. Do you have any idea how fucking much time a chief of police spends on his phone? All on the tax payer's dime too."

"Find anything useful?"

My brother and Jasper exchange a look at my question.

"It's not like she hasn't already picked up enough to give her a good idea of the scope of this case," Jasper points out to Damian while handing me my coffee.

"I guess. Well, aside from the fact the man spends an uncomfortable amount of time calling one nine hundred lines, I managed to find a few interesting ones he made to Daddy Lipczyk. One or two just after the second shooting, but a whole cluster of them around the time we were looking for you."

"He was probably feeling the heat," Jasper suggests.

"Likely. Also noteworthy were the incoming calls he got from the doctor's cell phone. Those started two weeks ago, the day after he assaulted your friend in the parking lot. I'm guessing he was trying to get a jump on her, anticipating her to file a report."

"None of that would exactly be a surprise though, would it?"

"Not really," Jasper answers first. "But it helps pin down a timeframe, a sequence of events. We don't want to leave any stone unturned, not when we're trying to bring down the chief of police. This is the kind of tedious grunt work that goes to anchoring down our whole case against him."

"Well, I should get back to my grunt work," my brother announces, rinsing his cup and loading it the dishwasher. "My next stack of records is for 2013. I can't fucking wait." He rounds the island, puts his hand on my neck, and leans down to kiss top of my head. "Gonna have to get used to not being the top of your speed dial anymore, Sis. Knowing he took that spot," he says with a nod in Jasper's direction, "makes it a little easier."

"Stay in touch," Jas asks my brother as he walks him to the door.

"Will do. I hope you get to enjoy your weekend of leisure before the shit hits the fan. Show my sister a good time."

"I intend to."

He's off to a good start doing just that, not ten minutes after my brother leaves, in his nice oversized shower.

My back against the tiles, one leg up over his shoulder, my hand tangled in his hair, I'm having a really good time. As his eyes burn on mine from below, I realize he's all about my pleasure. All about the giving, about making sure I get what I need, and so far I've been greedily taking.

This relationship revolves entirely around me.

Jasper called me a princess once, shortly after we met, and I never realized how true that was until just now.

It's not that I feel entitled in any way, it's that I don't question it. I take things for granted, and if there's one thing I don't ever want to do, it's take this man for granted.

Perhaps it's not an appropriate time to think about your sex life as a metaphor for your relationship— while your boyfriend's mouth is between your legs— but now that the thought is there, I can't ignore it.

I lift my leg from his shoulder and push at his head. His eyes look up with concern as he lets me go.

"It's my turn," I announce softly but firmly. I reach down to help him to his feet and turn him so now his back is to the wall.

"You don't have to—" he starts, but I shut him up with finger to his mouth, before lifting up for a heady kiss that tastes like sin.

I slowly explore Jasper's body, memorizing every response when my lips or hands discover a sensitive spot. The taste of him, the sounds he makes, the sight of his slightly parted lips as he looks down on me. Even as I'm the one sitting on my knees at his feet, his eyes hold worship.

The moment my lips slide over the crown of his rigid cock, I watch his eyelids lower and his mouth drop open in surrender. I don't take my eyes off him as I test, taste, and tease using all my senses, until his knees start to buckle and his hot cum shoots down my throat.

JASPER

"You've got to be shitting me."

I grin at Bella's reaction when we pull into the parking lot of Mild to Wild Rafting on the north side of town.

"Come on." I get out, round the car, and open the passenger side where Bella is still staring openmouthed at the rows of paddles and life jackets. "Let's get you outfitted."

She turns to me with fire in her eyes. "You do realize I just spent half an hour doing my hair and putting on makeup, right?"

Oh, I know. Took everything out of me not to spoil the surprise and tell her not to bother.

After the best shower sex I have ever had in my whole fucking life, I fed her toasted bagels with cream cheese and smoked salmon, and told her to dress comfortably. Little did I know that even knee-long leggings and a slouchy shirt had to be paired with makeup and good hair. I don't even see the need; she's fucking beautiful first thing in the morning, nothing on her face and her hair a sexy mess.

"You'll have a blast," I promise her, ignoring her complaint.

"I'll look a mess," she grumbles, as she takes my offered hand and laces her fingers with mine.

It takes us fifteen minutes to fill out the disclaimer forms and get rigged up in wetsuits. An old school bus drives up and the small crowd waiting starts getting on.

"Us too, Squirt." I have to nudge Bella onto the bus. I'm starting to get worried I may have miscalculated this outing. So far she seems less than enthused.

When the bus stops at the edge of the Animas River and Bella spots the trailer with rafts already parked there, she turns to me.

"You really want me to do this?"

The question is not asked in a challenging way, but more like a gentle probing. Rafting is something I've taken up during the spring and summer since coming to Durango. A little bit of adventure for those days I need a break from the office. I was thinking it might be something we'd both enjoy.

"Try," I suggest. "If at any time you decide you've had enough, I'll get us to shore. Your call."

"Okay."

Her answer is firm and she doesn't hesitate getting off the bus. Even helps me unload a raft from the trailer—to the enjoyment of one of the rafting guides—who is a little too preoccupied with her ass for my liking. The moment we drop the raft on the river's edge, I stalk over to her, and with my hand on her ass I kiss her deeply, never taking my eyes off the little punk.

"What was that?" she asks when I release her lips.

"Just a thank you for trying this with me," I lie through my teeth.

I wait for the group to head out first, six to a raft, each with a guide to make seven.

"Aren't we going with them?" she asks with a little trepidation, as we watch the two rafts set off.

"I know this river like the back of my hand," I reassure her. "I often rent this smaller raft to go out by myself. It's just easier to hitch a ride on the shuttle. The bus will wait for us on the other side as well. You'll get a whole new perspective of the town from down on the river, and it's even better when you're not distracted by the other rafts."

I help Bella get in the raft and make sure her life vest is properly secured before I check my own.

"Do you want to paddle or just sit and enjoy? We can do both."

"Paddle," she says, finally showing a bit of a grin.

"That comes with a few basic rules," I tell her, handing her the shorter of the two. "You don't have to worry about steering. I'll look after most of that, all you have to do is paddle hard or easy when I tell you to. Hold your paddle like this." I show her with one hand on the knob and the other further down toward the end. "See those loops on the bottom of the raft? Those are your footholds. If things get bouncy, those will keep you in the raft instead of in the river. If you do fall out, make sure to flip on your back and turn so your feet are pointing downstream. That way you can see anything coming your way. Good to go?"

I get a tight little nod in response and I'm sure she's reconsidering, but I'm already pushing off into a relatively calm river. For now.

"Where do I sit?"

"If you're gonna paddle, you should come back here. Put your feet in the loops and hold on."

She seems to relax once we get into a little bit of a rhythm, but looks at me when she hears the sound of the first set of rapids around the next bend.

"Get ready," I warn her, right before we round the corner and immediately hit a sharp dip. "Hard! Three strokes."

A spray of water hits the raft full on, but a quick glance shows her working hard and not even noticing she's getting soaked in the process. She seems to hold her end of the raft, and by the time we coast out of those first rapids: her hair is in wet strands, her makeup is running, and she has a drop hanging off her nose, but her eyes are sharp down the river, and her smile is unmistakable.

"Can we go again?"

I grin when she throws her arms around my neck after we pull the raft up on shore.

"I'm gonna need some food first."

"Tomorrow?'

I laugh at her excitement; she's like a little kid.

"I suggest you first wait and see what tomorrow feels like after your first rafting trip, Squirt. I'm guessing you'll feel sore muscles where you never even knew you had any."

"Whatever." I get one of the patented eye rolls, but this one is playful. I like Bella playful.

When we get back to the parking lot, I grab the clothes we tossed in the back seat and direct her to the dressing rooms inside, while I get my phone from the glove compartment. Two missed messages. One from Blackfoot; *'Hook, line, and sinker.'* The other from Damian who is monitoring the wiretap we were able to get a warrant for last night on Scott Lipczyk's phone; *'Fucking gold mine.'*

Joanne's statement, specifically her recounting of the drug theft she witnessed, went a long way to convincing the judge, who hadn't been too pleased we bothered him on a Friday night. He wasn't convinced enough by our conspiracy theory to allow us a tap on McMahan's phone as well, which is why Damian was pulling apart those telephone records, but judging from his message, he's getting enough from Lipczyk's phone.

I quickly shoot off a thumbs-up to both, before stripping out of my own wetsuit.

"You're drawing a crowd." I turn my head as Bella comes up behind me, a big grin on her face.

"I'm in my bloody boxer briefs," I protest when I see a couple of people—fine, women—throwing curious glances. "I see guys at the public pool who run around in Speedos a third the coverage of these."

"Ewww. Not a good visual."

I quickly pull on cargo shorts and whip a shirt over my head, throwing a raised eyebrow in the direction of one particularly close observer.

"Don't be mean," Bella admonishes, as she steps in close and slips her hands under my shirt and over my abs. "Can't blame the girl; you make a pretty picture."

"Are you staking a claim right now?" I ask, barely holding back a grin as Bella almost climbs me.

"Do you object?" she asks coyly, leaning back so she can look at me.

"Not in the least," I freely admit. Hell, any time, any place this woman wants to lay claim on me like this, I'm game.

"Good, because if you can maul me in front of an audience just to show that guide I'm yours, then so can I."

Guess I wasn't as subtle as I thought I was.

CHAPTER 26

BELLA

My body aches from the top of my head to the tips of my toes.

The rafting Saturday morning was an absolute blast, although next time, I'll just pull my hair in a ponytail and go barefaced. We just roamed around town after that, did a little window shopping, visited a few galleries, and ended up on the rooftop patio at the Balcony Bar and Grill for a bite, some drinks, and live music.

I should've been satisfied with that, but I made the mistake of asking Jasper what the plans for the day were while we were having breakfast at the Strater on Sunday morning. I'm the one who told him I was sure I was up for another adventure when he asked me.

So we hiked a seven-mile trail up the Animas Mountain.

I even joked at the start, saying my arms and shoulders were sore from the day before, but there was nothing wrong with my legs. Those I didn't start feeling until we were halfway through the trail.

I've had the absolute best weekend, but this morning I can barely move.

"What happened to you?" Ryan says when I limp my way over to the rig.

"This is what a fun weekend looks like on me. Clearly I need practice," I grumble, and he starts laughing.

"Do I even want to know?"

"All I can say is, my enthusiasm far outreaches my fitness level—and we'll leave it at that."

Of course, just my luck, we start our Monday morning shift with a senior who likely broke his hip falling out of his bed. His bedroom is on the third floor of an old house, up two sets of very narrow stairs. He isn't a small man either. I'm pretty sure I threw my back just trying to stabilize him on a backboard.

Poor guy is in agony, and there's little I can do other than to keep him calm while Ryan directs the fire department we had to call in for help with the stairs.

It takes four hefty guys to carry him all the way down to where the stretcher is waiting.

One of the firefighters helps me load him in the back of the ambulance.

"Bella—right? I think we met a few months ago at a house fire on the north side of town?"

"That would be me," I answer, as I'm rechecking my patient's vitals. I can't for the life of me remember the guy's name, though.

"Look, a buddy of mine is having a party next Saturday night. Would you be interested in coming with me?"

"She's taken," Ryan shuts him down as he walks up, catching the invitation. Poor guy, the charming smile drops from his face as he looks back and forth between Ryan and me.

"I'm sorry, I didn't realize—"

"Not by me. I'm married," Ryan clarifies, wiggling his fingers to show off his ring. "Her boyfriend is a badass FBI agent. Possessive son of a bitch too."

"Ryan!" I scold him, holding back a chuckle at his teasing, but he already succeeded in chasing him off.

"Hey," Ryan says defensively. "I like your guy. I've got his back. Us brothers have to look out for each other." I just roll my eyes.

"While we're on the topic of your boyfriend, I never got around to calling him to check, but did you tell him about—"

"The incident in the break room? Yes, I did. He's taking me to file a report after work."

"You're filing charges? Good for you. I just suggest you watch your back after that."

"I have to watch my back regardless," I point out.

"Can we maybe get going?" the patient, in obvious discomfort, interjects.

"Of course," I mumble, slightly embarrassed as

Ryan quickly closes the doors. "I'm so sorry, Mr. Fielding."

"Not to worry," he waves me off, wincing. "If I weren't old enough to be your grandfather, and strapped down to a stretcher in the back of an ambulance, I might've tried making a play for you too." He tries for a self-deprecating smile that doesn't quite reach its potential. "But by the sounds of it, you're better off with a badass FBI boyfriend. You be careful, dear."

"I will, Mr. Fielding," I assure him, patting his hand. "I promise I will."

JASPER

"You should've seen his face." Blackfoot leans back in his chair, looking smug as all get out. "He couldn't believe I refused to leave the complaint up to him to look after. He tried to convince me he'd had dealings with Mrs. Shredder before, Ms. Thompson then, and she was less than reliable. When I let it drop that hers was not necessarily the only complaint, that I heard rumors there might be more coming, he slunk out of my office."

"He knows Scott Lipczyk is the weak link and can do some massive damage to his career," Damian observes.

We're in our office, laying out a plan of action. Luna is at Mercy getting some statements from ER staff, while at the same time rattling our subject's cage. Nervous people make mistakes.

"He's doing enough damage on his own," I point out, pulling up a recording Damian made this weekend of a telephone call made by McMahan to Lipczyk senior. "Listen to this."

The sound quality is not perfect, but good enough you can clearly hear the police chief talking.

"*...Your damn kid is gonna fucking bring us down. Get him the hell under control or ship his ass out of here. Blackfoot is close with the SAC, he's not gonna let up, Gene.*"

"*If I recall correctly you were all too eager to get Scott involved when that woman started running her mouth about her husband's death. He was mighty convenient then, wasn't he? Sticking out his neck to quiet her. It's your own damn fault we're in this predicament. Fucking fix it!*"

"*You're shitting me! I've been wiping your boy's ass since he was in fucking high school, and he had to force girls to suck his tiny micro dick to get any. Been cleaning up after him ever—*"

I stop the feed and look over at Blackfoot, who's grinning ear to ear.

"Did they just hang themselves?"

"Pretty much," Damian confirms.

"Why on fucking earth would they even discuss this over the phone?"

"They've been untouchable so far," I point out. "When you get away with something long enough, you start to believe it yourself. They're arrogant."

"Dylan also came up with some interesting intel this weekend. He talked to the two other officers, who were the first to arrive at the scene after McMahan shot Davis. One of them is still on the force and was only willing to say that he was unable to talk, but to try his former partner, who has since retired." Damian motions to Dylan to take it from there.

"Yeah, so Ben Chapman retired early, three years ago. He says he couldn't handle being under that sleazeball's thumb anymore—his words—not mine. He's been waiting for someone to do something about the shit that went down back then."

"Anyone but him," Damian interjects.

"Apparently," Dylan continues. "He says he and his partner arrived at the scene and found Sergeant McMahan on his knees, leaning in the driver's side of the pulled-over vehicle. The driver was slumped sideways, his upper body half over the center console, blood sprayed all over the inside of the window, the dash, and the passenger side. When McMahan saw them approach, he yelled at them to block traffic. Chapman recalls asking him if he already called it in and got his head chewed off. He wasn't about to question his sergeant and did as asked, but he did notice, at some point, McMahan rummaging in the trunk of his cruiser before returning to the stopped vehicle."

"*Christ*," Blackfoot hisses, running a hand over his face. "We've all been complicit. I know I'm not the only one who's had suspicions over the years, but no one ever did anything."

"Not sure you would've gotten anywhere at the time," I tell him. "McMahan may be an arrogant fuck, but don't mistake him for stupid. Connor was a contingency he simply couldn't have anticipated. Franklin Davis' kid was the first major crack in his veneer. If we play it right, Scott Lipczyk will be the one to break it open."

The plan is to see what Luna comes back with from ER staff, and add that to the report I'll take Bella to file in a bit. Once we have the complaints on record, we'll pick the doctor up and use the complaints as leverage to get him to spill on McMahan.

-

Just like I did with Joanne on Friday, I pick Bella up from home, drive her to the station, and lead her in the front door, asking for Blackfoot at the desk.

I do my best not to fly off the handle when she recounts not only the incident in the hospital's break room—where apparently that asshole did a little more than put his hands on her, he fucking rubbed his dick against her ass—but also events leading up to that last confrontation. Including an encounter in the parking lot, which landed her with that cut on her head. She never mentioned that.

I'm still fuming when we get to my truck.

"What the fucking hell was that?" I let rip when I get behind the wheel.

"Excuse me?" She comes right back, with attitude

flying, which at this particular moment, is not nearly as fucking cute as it can be.

"At any point, during all this time we've spent together, you never once fucking mentioned him coming after you in the parking lot. That was over a fucking month ago. Given everything that's happened during that time, you didn't think it might be something you'd wanna share with me? What the hell were you thinking?"

"I was handling it."

"Handling it? Really? So how was that working out for you when he was fucking dry-humping you against the counter last week? Jesus, woman! Every day you've gone into work you've played with fire. He's been lying in wait this whole time for an opportunity to get you alone, and like a clueless idiot, I've been kissing you goodbye and sending you off to work, right into his playground, every goddamn day in between. With all you've already been through, that fucking stubborn need to prove yourself could've really gotten you hurt."

I'm breathing hard, grinding my teeth together, and trying to reel my temper back in. I'd expected a returning salvo from Bella, but she is suspiciously quiet beside me all the way to her place.

I pull up beside her little red Dinky Toy and turn off the engine. I stare straight ahead for a moment, willing my blood pressure down, before turning to her. She's already looking at me, her face pale, and her body as far away from me as she can get in the confines of the truck's cab. Fuck.

"Look," I start, leaning over the center console.

"I'm sorry," she interrupts with a wavering voice. "I didn't…I just…with everything else going on, I kinda shoved it to the back of my mind. I wasn't trying to prove anything."

I hate it when a tear runs down her face, and reach out to wipe it away with a finger.

"Don't cry. Please. I shouldn't have yelled at you. I'm mostly mad at myself."

I slip a hand behind her neck and pull her closer, leaning my forehead against hers.

"I'm not crying," she lies, and lifts her face for a kiss.

"Are you hungry?" she asks when we walk into the house. "I pulled some of Ma's tamales from the freezer before I left this morning. Or are you still on the clock?"

"I have some time. We're waiting for Blackfoot to get a warrant signed for Lipczyk's arrest. Shouldn't be a problem after adding your charge to Joanne's, but it all depends on whether he can find a judge at this time of the day to sign off on it. Tamales sound good."

I accept the beer she offers me, and during dinner we manage to talk about things other than the persistent chaos surrounding us for a change.

It's been a bit of a learning experience for me; discovering I can have a wicked temper for one, but also that I apparently don't feel compelled to hold anything back with her. She's already shown me she's not easily scared off.

I get up to carry our plates to the kitchen when my phone starts buzzing in my pocket. It's Damian.

"I'll be there shortly," I tell him right away.

"He's in the wind."

"Sorry, what?"

"The doctor. I just got a call from Blackfoot, fifteen minutes ago; he was on his way to get the warrant signed. Then five minutes after that, Luna happened to intercept a call from McMahan to the older Lipczyk saying *'Get him gone—now,'* followed by an immediate hang-up. We checked in with Dylan at the hospital, and he said he just saw him going into X-ray with a patient. Except he never came out."

"Fuck."

"We lose this guy, we lose our case."

"That's not gonna happen," I bite off. "I'm on my way."

Bella's face shows concern when I turn to face her.

"Everything okay?"

"You still have your gun in your nightstand?"

"Yes, but what—"

I grab her shoulders to get her to focus. "It's loaded?"

"Yes, but why—"

"We lost eyes on the doctor. I have got to go, so I need you to lock the door behind me and go get the gun, Squirt. Now."

It takes her all of the thirty or so seconds to grab the weapon from her bedroom to work up a decent head of steam.

"No need to bark at me. I'm not your dog," she snaps, but can't quite hide the hint of fear in her voice.

I take a deep breath, take the gun out of her hand, and put it on the counter, before folding her in my arms. Hers wrap easily around my waist.

"Be careful?"

"I will be. Didn't mean to bark. I guess it comes with the unfamiliar territory, this macho protective instinct."

She leans back and looks at me quizzically. "What unfamiliar territory?"

I drop a kiss on her nose and give her a smile.

"Falling in love."

CHAPTER 27

Bella

It takes until well after I watch Jasper's truck disappear from the safety of my living room window for his words to sink in.

Falling in love.

He's falling for me.

I never had a chance to respond before he was out the door, demanding I lock it behind him. Not that I would've known how to respond. What does one say to that?

I'm wearing a stupid grin as I turn and head to the kitchen to clear away the dinner dishes. Then I strip my bed and start the laundry. It's when I'm on my knees in the bathroom, scrubbing the tub to keep busy while I nervously anticipate his return, that my phone rings in the living room.

"Hi, Ma."

"*Mi hija*, you sound happy."

"Because I am."

I realize as I'm saying, how true it is. Who would've suspected last year, when I had my harsh judgement ready for my brother's handsome teammate the moment I met him, I would get happy butterflies just at the thought of him.

"It's that boy, isn't it?"

"His name is Jasper, Ma, and he's hardly a boy. He's forty-one."

"Does he want babies?" I roll my eyes, something my mother has no way of seeing, but knows all the same. "And don't roll your eyes at me, young lady, it's a valid question. You're not getting any younger. If you're going to give me grandbabies, you're going to have to hurry."

"I've known him for maybe two months. Think you may be jumping the gun?"

"Don't get smart with me, Isabella. When you get to a certain age, you can't afford to play around."

"Ma, seriously, I thought you didn't like him, and now you want me to have his babies?" I pull a bottle of wine from the fridge, I officially need a little help keeping that happy feeling going.

"You're thirty-eight next month, did you know that? Almost forty. That's no joke, Bella. After forty everything goes south and your chances of finding a man will—"

"Isabella?" My father's voice is a welcome relief, even as I hear my mother's disgruntled sounds in the background. "Don't listen to your mother. You will be as beautiful when you're eighty as you are right now."

"Hi, Papa."

My mother has a way of rubbing my nose in reality until it bleeds, in just a few minutes, but my father can still make me feel special with only one line.

"So you and the young man, you're good?"

"Yes, Papa, we're good."

"I'm glad, *mi hija.* I like him for you."

"I like him for me too, but it's early yet."

My father is quiet for a while before he reacts. "Yes, it's new, but don't let that be an excuse not to grab a good thing with both hands, *preciosa.* Don't be afraid to believe in a future."

I realize after I end the call, what my mother tried to tell me in her blunt way, was not all that different from what Papa said. Both want me happy, the only difference is their presentation.

The beep of the dryer prompts me into action, and I quickly pull my sheets out. I never really bother folding them, they usually go straight from the dryer back on the bed. They don't get a chance to wrinkle that way. I'm just wrestling the last of my pillows in its pillowcase, when I hear a car door close outside. Instantly the smile is back on my face.

Jasper is back.

I quickly fluff the pillow, straighten the duvet, and hurry into the kitchen to get him a cold beer. I take the opener from the drawer and put it beside the bottle on the counter, before pouring myself a glass of wine.

Then I realize he should've been at the door already. Maybe I misheard.

Curious, I walk over to the front window and peek outside. There's no sign of Jasper's familiar truck, and his spot beside my Fiat is empty, but there's a car parked on the road. The light of my front porch doesn't quite reach that far, and I'm straining to see if I recognize it, when a face suddenly appears right outside the window.

Shaken, I rear back, stumbling over the coffee table and landing on my ass.

Outside my window, his finger pointed at me, is Scott Lipczyk.

JASPER

It's been a frustrating exercise in futility.

Dylan had his eye on the target the entire time, but wasn't able to follow the doctor into the X-ray room. What Dylan didn't know was that there was a second door, leading straight into the waiting room of the radiology department. From there it's an easy walk out to the parking lot from the hospital's main entrance.

In short, Dylan was made and the doc managed to give him the slip. Dylan isn't riled that easily but he's pretty pissed now.

Damian had already talked to Blackfoot, who ordered roadblocks put up heading out of town when

I got to the office. Police would monitor the 550 heading north, and the 160 on the south side. We'd hoped to keep him contained—there aren't that many routes out of town— but after hours of searching, we're coming up empty. I'm starting to wonder if he managed to slip through before the roadblocks were in place.

"Did you check his townhouse?" I ask, when Dylan walks into the office.

The only one still out there at this point is Luna, along with a small contingent of the Durango PD. The problem is, a massive manhunt is not really warranted for a couple of assault charges. There's only so long we can keep this search active, before someone is going to want to know exactly why we have such a hard-on for this guy.

If he gets away, the entire case we've been building could collapse like a house of cards.

"No one there. Talked to a few of the neighbors and he hasn't been seen since earlier today. I may have taken a peek inside. Doesn't look like he snuck in and packed a few things. His place looks like you'd expect when someone walks out with every intention of coming back."

"Shit. Well, Keith has a few guys on his parents' place, in case he shows up there," Damian says, a phone to his ear. "He also put a call in to the State Patrol, and they'll keep an eye out for the vehicle."

Lipczyk's car would be pretty hard to miss; he drives a navy 2017 Jaguar XJ.

I don't like this. The guy can't just walk out of the hospital, get into his fancy car, and disappear into thin air in a few minutes.

"Anyone keep an eye on McMahan?" I ask Damian.

"According to Keith, he's still in the office. Never left. Luna was gonna swing by his house to see if maybe Lipczyk showed up there, but since she hasn't called in, I'm assuming that's a no."

"What about his cell?" Dylan asks. "Any chance we can trace its location?"

"I'm on the line with Verizon." Damian says. "They're working on it."

I'm already pulling up a map of cell phone towers in the area on my computer, when Damian tosses his phone on the desk.

"*Fuck!* Son of a bitch. Last ping they got off his phone was hours ago. He must've disabled it."

"Let me take a wild guess, you don't have good news either," Luna comments as she walks in the door and drops down in the nearest chair. "I've got bupkus. Nada."

"This doesn't make sense," I voice my thoughts. "The guy may be a doctor, but he is cocky and arrogant to the point of stupid. All he knows is who to call when he fucks up. He's done it his whole damn life. There's no way all of a sudden he's savvy enough to disappear. No way in hell."

"True," Luna agrees. "He has no finesse. He's a bully who thrives on intimidation."

Suddenly the hair on my neck stands on end as her words hit home.

"Anyone check the Shredder place?" I throw out there, getting out of my chair and tucking my phone in my pocket. "You might want to. Luna makes a good point; intimidation is what he's good at."

"I'll go," Dylan says.

"Where are you off to?"

The moment I meet Damian's eyes, I see realization dawn on his face.

"Checking on Bella."

I'm halfway down the stairs when I hear the heavy fall of his footsteps behind me.

"Try her cell," I suggest when Damian climbs in the passenger side of my truck.

"No answer."

"Keep fucking trying."

BELLA

I'm jerked into action when I faintly hear the familiar ring of my phone.

Scrambling to my feet, I turn away from the window to look for it. Last place I recall having it was right here in the living room when my mother called. I frantically pull pillows from the couch, thinking maybe it slipped between, but find nothing other than a stray tissue. I try not to think about what could be happening behind me as I rush into the kitchen, spotting the gun on the counter. I grab it, just as I hear a bang against my front door.

The ringing stops, only to start up again immediately, and this time I get a bead on where it's coming from. Another bang on the door, this time with the sound of wood splintering and I throw a quick peek over my shoulder. The frame is cracked but the door is holding.

Diving into the laundry room, I snatch my phone off the washer where I must've left it earlier while pulling the sheets from the dryer. My hands are shaking so bad, I have a hard time answering, when a loud crash startles me and I drop it on the floor. One quick glance up shows my front door hanging off its hinges and just as I see him push it open all the way, I quickly shut the door, closing myself in the laundry room and hoping he didn't see me.

Except there's no lock on this door.

The only thing close enough to block the door with is the dryer. There's enough space between it and the wall to wedge myself in and I sink to the floor. With my back against the wall and feet braced against the base of the dryer, I push with all my might. I manage to move it halfway in front of the door.

I'm sure he knows where I am now, so I ignore my phone, which starts ringing for the third time, and with every ounce of strength I have I push the heavy appliance the rest of the way. Only then do I dive for my phone, scramble back behind the dryer, train the gun I'm still clutching in my hand on the door, and answer the call.

"*He's here,*" I whisper.

"Is he inside?" my brother's deep voice has an instant calming effect on me.

"*Yes.*"

"Where are you?"

"*Laundry room.*"

Just then the door shakes with a loud pounding and I scream, drop the phone, and use both hands to hold my gun as steady as I can.

"*We're here,*" I can faintly hear my brother say.

JASPER

Damian is out the door before I can even slam the truck in park.

My heart is beating in my throat after hearing Damian's end of the conversation.

I'm close behind as he steps over the remnants of the front door, his gun already trained on Lipczyk, who is in the kitchen, kicking the door to the laundry room. The idiot is making such a ruckus, he doesn't even hear us come in.

"FBI! Get your fucking hands up and step away from the door. Step away from the goddamn door!" Damian bellows as we approach cautiously.

"Get down on the floor! On the floor and spread your arms!"

Like the coward he is, the moment Lipczyk

whips his head around to see two guns pointed in his direction, he folds like a cheap suit.

I take great satisfaction from his pained yelp when I plant my knee on his neck with a little extra force, while Damian cuffs and quickly checks him for weapons.

While he pulls the douchebag to his feet, I focus on the laundry room door.

"Bella? I'm coming in. Stand clear of the door."

I brace my back against the door, and with my legs use steady force to push it open far enough for me to squeeze through. I'm almost knocked off my feet when a shadow comes flying and wraps around me like a monkey.

"It's all good, Squirt," I mumble, my hands under her ass to hold her up as her face burrows in my neck. "You did good, sweetheart."

"Everything okay in there?" Damian calls out.

"Took you long enough," Bella suddenly yells back at her brother, more feisty than her trembling body feels in my arms.

She drops her legs to get down, and I reluctantly let her go, stepping back so I can see her face. It's clear she's trying to pull herself together before facing her brother, and I help by brushing a few tears from her cheeks. She grabs my forearms and raises her eyebrows in question.

"You look fine. Tough. Cool as a cucumber."

I'm rewarded with a small grin before she flings her hair back and steps around me and through the partially opened door. I follow her out, and am just in time to see her walk up to where Damian is holding Scott Lipczyk in handcuffs, and haul back and kick him square in the nuts.

I look at Damian over her head, both of us grinning wide.

CHAPTER 28

JASPER

The only thing worse than a crooked cop is a corrupt chief of police.

That's why the last twenty-four hour period will be going down as one of the best memories of my law enforcement career.

"You have a right to an attorney present, but you realize then you'll be going down for much more than those assault charges, right?"

It had been gratifying to see the panicked look on that son of a bitch's face.

"What? You can't pin anything on me." Lipczyk tried for defiance but failed miserably.

"No?" Damian prompted, leaning over the table between them. "How does first-degree murder sound?" He casually checked his watch before sitting back in his seat. "In less than two hours from now, the body of one Margaret Elizabeth Davis will be on the medical examiner's slab in Farmington, New Mexico. They're digging up her body as we speak."

"I had nothing to do with her murder. All I did was get him the propofol," the coward sputtered, easily rolling over with his own ass on the line, much as expected.

"Who's *him*?"

He glanced nervously at the one-sided mirror, likely afraid the man he referred to was on the other side, but he was at the police station, under close watch by Luna and Dylan. The only people on the other side of that mirror in the small interrogation room, in the basement of the FBI field office on Rock Point Drive, were Keith Blackfoot, our mayor, and myself.

Finally he turned back to Damian and nailed not only the chief of police to the cross, but his own father as well.

"My dad told me, Tom McMahan needed it. McMahan killed her."

That was yesterday, and right now I'm crowded into a similar small closet-sized space on the other side of a one-way mirror, but at the Durango police station. This time I'm in the company of my team, while Blackfoot has the privilege of informing McMahan of his rights and the charges against him. U.S. Marshals are waiting outside the door to transport McMahan to New Mexico, where he'll be answering to the murder charge first.

McMahan knows he's done for and just glares at

Keith, who looks like he might actually be smiling. He doesn't utter a single word when the Marshals come in and cuff him, but turns his eyes to the ground in front of his feet, as he is led through a dead silent station house under the condemning scrutiny of his entire department.

Shackled and waiting in the transport truck outside is Eugene Lipczyk, ready to be handed over to the authorities in New Mexico to face charges of bribery, and conspiracy to murder.

The drive to Farmington will be an interesting one. I'd love to be a fly on the wall.

"Where are you off to?" Damian asks, when we step out of the police station.

"Picking up your sister from work. I dropped her off this morning."

I chuckle when he winces.

"Grateful you're looking after my baby sister, but for fuck's sake, do you have to remind me she's in your bed every night? This shit is awkward enough."

"Better get over it," Luna pipes up as she passes by. "Our Jasper looks like he might like to keep her there indefinitely."

"Ah, Christ. You serious?"

I clap Damian on the shoulder and grin at his scowl.

"Better fuckin' believe it. Shouldn't you be welcoming me to the family, Bro?" I tease.

"That's fucking *Boss* to you, Greene."

I laugh all the way to my truck.

Bella is waiting for me outside, talking to Joanne, when I drive up.

"Hey, honey."

I smile at her endearment when she pulls open the passenger door. "Squirt."

"Joanne wants a chance to thank you."

"Sure thing."

I'm barely out of my seat when I have Joanne hanging off my neck, with Bella grinning in the background. I hug the woman back before setting her firmly back on her feet.

"I just wanted to thank you, and everyone else who helped bring him in." She smiles shyly. "I was this close to giving up my job here and moving."

"Team effort and we wouldn't have had a case against him if you hadn't been courageous enough to file charges."

"And I wouldn't have done that if you hadn't convinced me. So thank you, and one of these days, I'd love to have Bella and you over for dinner."

"That sounds good to me. I'll leave the planning up to Bella, I have a feeling she'll be in charge of our social calendar."

I grin when I get back in the truck, realizing how true that statement probably is. I've never had a social calendar to begin with. I watch as the two women hug and seem to share a moment of levity before Bella climbs in the passenger seat.

"What was that all about?" I ask, as I drive off the parking lot and Bella starts to giggle.

"It's a girl thing. She was telling me earlier she had no idea you were such a hunk until you picked her up the other day, but she was too nervous to enjoy the view. So I told her if she hung around until you got here, she could get her fill."

"You think I'm a hunk?" I grin, looking at her sideways, as she rolls her eyes.

"I never said that. Joanne does, though." The little minx is laughing at me.

"Right. So you thought you'd invite her to feel me up?"

"Shut up, she did not feel you up," she mocks, smacking my arm. A moment later she adds, "Did she?"

Now it's my turn to laugh.

"Hey, where are we going?"

Instead of heading to my apartment, where she's been staying the past couple of nights, I continue on the 160 to her place.

"What? How did you get that done so fast? I was going to send the landlord an email first." She's looking at the new frame and front door, I had put in this morning.

"One of my neighbors is a handyman. I ran into him yesterday and he had time today."

"It's gorgeous. How much is that gonna set me

back?"

"Shouldn't set you back anything. Your insurance should take care of it." I hand her the keys I picked up at my apartment earlier, along with her things I have tossed in the back seat. "Head on inside, he fixed the door to the laundry room as well."

I grin as she almost skips to the front door and lets herself in. I snag both her bag and my small overnight from the back and follow her inside.

"These are solid wood," she says. She's busy inspecting the laundry door, but turns when she hears me come in. "I don't know if the insurance…" She stops mid-sentence when she notices her bag in my hands. "I'm staying here tonight?"

"We both are." I show her my overnight stuff too.

"Phew—for a minute I thought you were trying to get rid of me."

I drop the bags and walk over to her, lifting her on the counter so we can be eye to eye, and take her face in my hands.

"Just so we're clear—there is not a chance in hell of that ever happening."

Her face softens and those pretty brown eyes of hers turn to liquid heat.

"Never?"

"Not. Fucking Ever."

BELLA

I've been on cloud nine since Jasper's declaration. Of sorts.

Despite the fact, once again, I just couldn't find the words for an appropriate response, I'm in a celebratory mood.

So I'm making enchiladas and refried beans, occasionally taking a sip of my wine, while Jasper sits on a stool at the counter and gives me the details of his day, nursing his cold beer. It feels very domestic, and I can readily imagine this being a daily routine. One that would take no effort at all to get used to.

"So when do your parents get here?"

"Sometime Saturday afternoon, they're staying at the Best Western, although they could've bought a condo by now with all the money they've been wasting this past year alone."

Of course my folks found out about the latest drama in my life and called yesterday to announce they were coming to Durango to see for themselves that I survived. *Again.*

"I'm sure they don't see it as a waste, but I was thinking…wouldn't make sense for them to stay at my apartment? It could sleep four—the couch is a pullout—and six if you throw a couple of air mattresses on the floor. It's big enough."

"You mean stay with you?"

My face must've conveyed my puzzlement because Jasper starts laughing.

"Not exactly, Squirt. Since I'll be staying here with you."

"Not that I'm complaining, but are you sure you'll be okay here? I mean, I couldn't help but notice how very tidy your apartment is—everything in it's place, a little stark and austere—and my place is…well… *not*."

He throws his head back and howls. A little peeved, I forcefully shove the enchiladas in the oven, put my fist on my cocked hip, take a few sips of my wine, and wait for him to be done.

"Come here." He tries to charm me when he notices my stance, beckoning me with both his hands, but I stand firm. "Isabella…I need you to come here so I can explain something."

It's on my lips to tell him I'm not a dog, but instead I raise an eyebrow. Finally he gets up, walks over to me, takes the glass from my hand, and folds me in his arms. Mine are down by my side, but already I feel myself melting. He doesn't play fair. Won't even let me hold on to a good snit.

"My apartment has no personality. It's a place to roll into bed at night, and eat an occasional meal, if I'm lucky. It's bare, because it's not a home." He lifts my chin with a finger so I have to look at him. One side of his mouth is pulled up in a swoon-worthy grin, and his blue eyes sparkle. "That's why I like it here. Your house is warm, inviting—like you. It feels like home because I look forward to coming here—to you."

"Gah!" I stomp my foot in frustration. "Every time you do this to me."

"What did I do?"

"You say these really sweet things that make me feel all mushy inside, and I want to say something sweet back, but every time I'm at a loss for words. It's frustrating."

He slips his hands around my neck and dips his head to kiss me sweetly.

"You don't need to say anything," he murmurs against my lips.

"But then how are you supposed to know I like coming home to you too? And that you're not the only one falling? In fact, I'm pretty sure I'm already in love with you."

"I already know, because I'm a master of observation. It's all in the eyes."

Right. Whatever. I instantly roll them heavenward; let him read *that*.

"I'm not kidding," he insists. "Here, try it. What do you see?"

Slowly I focus on the laugh lines framing his eyes, the crystal clear of his blue, and finally the message they hold.

"You're in love with me too."

I'm rewarded with a warm smile and a soft brush of his thumb along my bottom lip.

"That I am, Squirt."

CHAPTER 29

JASPER

"Are you ready? They're expecting us in twenty minutes!"

"Squirt, I've been ready for the past twenty."

I scroll through my emails, just killing time when she comes rushing out of the bedroom, dives into the bottom of the small wardrobe closet by the front door, and starts tossing shoes into the living area.

"I can't fucking find my red sandals!"

"Did you check your walk-in closet?"

She pulls her head from the closet and throws me a scathing look. "Of course I did. I looked there first. We're going to be late." She looks me up and down. "Is that what you're wearing?"

"That was the plan," I mumble, looking down at myself and wondering what's wrong with the best pair of jeans I own and the shirt I wore to her brother's wedding. Granted, it's hanging loose over a white T-shirt with the sleeves rolled up, but still.

"It's fine," she says, waving her hand and diving back into the closet.

Dismissed, I head into her bedroom and pull open the closet. Looks like she did search here before, judging from the piles on the floor. My eyes immediately zoom in on her red sandals; the only pair of shoes in the specially designed cubbyholes. I grab them and walk back into the living room.

"Is this them?"

She backs out of the closet and her mouth falls open when she sees them dangling from my fingers.

"Where'd you find those?" She snatches them from my hand, grabs my arm, and hops on one foot while she tries to get a sandal on the other.

"In your closet."

"They weren't in there, I looked." She switches feet and puts the other sandal on.

"Not sure what to tell you, sweetheart. They were right there in the shoe rack."

"Well, who put them there?"

I take it as a rhetorical question as she scoots past me on her way to the kitchen. I presume to get the elaborate dessert she spent yesterday slaving over.

I've been staying with Bella all week, and I'm starting to see that if chaos doesn't find her, she creates her own—and to my surprise—I enjoy it. Even this mini crisis. It says to me she is comfortable enough to be herself around me, and that means something.

"Are you coming?" she asks, even as she's passing me out the door.

"Right behind you." I grin as I watch her skip down the front steps, the ends of her shiny long hair bouncing on the swell of her round ass.

Life will not be boring with Bella, that's for damn sure.

With her dessert secure on the back seat, I turn to her and grab her hand.

"What are you doing? We're late."

"I know, and we'll be a few minutes later. Hush," I silence her when she opens her mouth to protest. "I need you to listen to me." I lean in a little closer to make sure I have her full attention. "You look beautiful, you're amazing, you smell delicious, and your dessert is worthy of a center spread in a foodie magazine. So tell me, why are you so nervous? This is just a family dinner."

She turns her eyes out the front window and bites her bottom lip. "But it's not," she finally says. "Ma called earlier and said the girls are all coming down."

"Your sisters?"

"Yes." She says it like she's not impressed at all. "It's your first official dinner as my boyfriend, and they're going to make it uncomfortable."

"So what? That doesn't bother me."

"How can you say that? Last time you—"

"Last time I had my head up my ass. That's not the case anymore."

"Are you sure?"

I tag her by the neck, lean in, and kiss the uncertainty from her face.

"Positive. Now can we go?"

"Yes, and step on it. We're already late."

This time *my* eyes roll to the ceiling.

We clearly are the last ones to arrive at Damian and Kerry's, and I'm surprised to see not just Bella's sisters, but a couple of guys I assume are husbands and a couple of kids running around the backyard. It looks like the entire Gomez clan has landed.

Bella's father—Ignacio, I'm firmly told when I call him Mr. Gomez—takes care of introductions, clearly proud of his sizable family, while Bella is whisked off to the kitchen.

"Beer?" One of the brothers-in-law, Brent I think his name is, offers me a cold one from the large cooler on the deck.

I only hesitate for a moment, it's still pretty early but the older guy nudges me with the bottle.

"Okay, sure," I give in.

"Smart man. Any little buzz helps with these shindigs."

"Shindigs?"

"Yeah, family gatherings." He holds up his bottle. "This is the only way to get through them. Be prepared to hand in your balls at the front door, and if you're lucky you get them back after." I chuckle at his description. "Luckily these family get-togethers don't happen all the time."

"Are you telling lies already?" Chrissy walks up and hooks her arm in Brent's.

"Nothing but the truth, baby."

"How are you, Jasper?" She dismisses her husband with a raised eyebrow and turns to me.

"I'm well, thanks. You?" I haven't forgotten my previous encounter with this particular sister and brace myself.

"Good. Although, I think I might owe you an apology," she says a tad sheepishly.

Her husband apparently finds this amusing and chuckles. "Better take note," he directs to me, "those words don't pass her lips very often." That earns him an elbow in the ribs.

"No apologies needed," I assure Chrissy. No point in pretending I don't know what she's referring to.

"You guys, food's on the table." Bella comes up beside me, nervously darting her eyes between her sister and me. I tug her to my side and drop a kiss on the top of her head to ease her.

From the spread laid out on the kitchen counter, I can see why they'd start eating in the middle of the afternoon. This family is apparently all about the food.

At the oversized dinner table, conversation luckily revolves mostly around Kerry, whose pregnant belly seems to have popped in the past few weeks.

"How far along?" Bella's sister, Fran, the quieter one of the bunch, asks.

"Twenty-six weeks," Carmella answers for Kerry before turning to her. "And you should probably stay away from those chile rellenos. Too spicy for your baby."

"Ma," Damian intervenes. "Kerry has a stomach of steel, leave her be."

"I'm just looking out for my grandbaby," Bella's mom says with feigned innocence, which no one at the table really seems to buy. "And talking about grandbabies…" Damian groans out loud when she turns her attention on me. "I hope you want children. My Bella will make a wonderful mother, but she doesn't have much time."

"Ma!"

"Carmella, we talked about this," Ignacio interrupts.

"I'm just asking. It doesn't seem unreasonable, seeing as they're living together now."

"Ma, we're not living together," Bella says beside me. "He's staying with me so you can have his apartment."

"Why not?"

"Because we haven't really discussed it, and I don't even know if my landlord would allow it."

"So call him and ask." I'll grant her that, Carmella is persistent.

On the other side of the table, Damian sounds like he's choking on something, and I throw him a dirty look. The rest of the table appears to be following along in the exchange while enjoying their meal—

like some kind of dinner theatre. They're probably relieved they're not the ones in the hot seat. The only one who knows it's really my ass in that hot seat is my boss.

"Ma, enough. They can figure it out for themselves, and they don't need to do that in public. Leave them be."

"I'm trying to help," she responds defensively. "And we're not in public, we're among family."

Fortunately the subject is dropped, until I give Bella a hand in the kitchen getting coffee and her dessert ready.

"Sorry about earlier," she says, wrapping her arms around me from behind. "I warned you about my family."

"Nothing to be sorry about. Your mom is just trying to look out for you." I turn in her arms and drop a hard kiss on her lips. "Besides, maybe it is a discussion we should have. I already told you I like coming home to you. I like waking up with you even better, so I'd be happy making our current arrangement permanent."

"But my landlord—"

"I have a feeling he's not going to mind, Bella." Of course, Damian would choose *that* particular moment to walk into the kitchen.

"But—"

"Ask him," Damian pushes, a mischievous look on his face as he winks at me. The snake, warning off his mother only so he could throw me under the bus himself.

“I don’t have his number.”

“You don’t need a number. For shit’s sake, Bella. The man is standing right in front of you.”

BELLA

The fuck?

We’re on our way back to my place—well, apparently *his* place—and my mind is still reeling. My brother’s words hadn’t quite sunk in until I saw the guilty look on Jasper’s face.

I never got a chance to question him, because of course, right at that moment—my mother came in— looking to see what happened to coffee and dessert. I simply pushed out of his arms, grabbed my dessert, and took it to the dining room.

The one benefit of my rambunctious and crazy family is that they don’t really notice when one of us is quiet. They didn’t, but Kerry did. She raised her eyebrows questioningly when I removed Jasper’s hand from my knee for the third time.

“Are you going to let me explain?” Jasper asks when we pull up in the driveway, ignoring my palm in his face, after trying to talk to me a few times during the long and loaded drive home.

“Nope.” I pop my P loudly and get out of the truck.

I have the door open before he can catch up to me, dive for my bottle of wine in the fridge, and lock myself in the bathroom.

With bubbles up to my chin and the bottle of wine dangling from my hand over the side of the tub, I close my eyes and try to sort through my feelings. There are plenty, but I don't get much of a chance to get them in line before there's a knock at the door.

"Go away. I'm not ready."

I hear his footsteps retreat and, to my shock, the front door close only seconds later.

Shit.

All I want is a little space, but not that much. Of course my mind immediately aims for the worst-case scenario, and I almost have myself in tears, when the front door closes again. Footsteps stop outside the bathroom, followed by rustling and scratching noises from the other side of the door.

Suddenly, the doorknob falls with a clang to the tile floor and the door swings open, revealing a buck naked Jasper. Momentarily distracted with the view, I forget to protest, and before I know what's happening, he's wedging himself behind me in the tub.

"What are you doing?" I finally manage, inadvertently scooting forward so he can stretch his legs around me.

"Seems like the only way to get you to listen. Any of that wine left?" he asks, grabbing the bottle from my hand and taking a deep swig before he hands it back. "Now—I'm happy to give you time alone when you need it, but not without you having all the facts, and not when I know it'll just be festering inside until you get it out. That's not how we do things, so let it out."

Not needing much of a prompt, I start venting. "You lied to me and involved my brother, which really pisses me off. You guys manipulated me, which is nothing less than what Ma tries to do. I don't know what to believe anymore. You tell me I'm the reason you like being here, but now I discover you like being here because you fucking own this place. Why? Why would you keep that to yourself? Why not just tell me? It's not like there's not been plenty of opportunities. Jesus, I feel stupid. And that's what makes me maddest of all!"

"Are you done?" he asks, when I suck much needed air into my lungs after my rant, but doesn't wait for an answer. "I lied by omission. Technically, your brother knew before you even moved in here—before I even knew you—since he's the one who alerted me to the fact the owner planned to sell once Kerry's lease was up. Then you came along, needed a place, and since I wasn't in any rush, I was happy to have you live here."

"But why not just tell me?"

"Because, Squirt," he says, tightening his arms under my breasts and kissing the side of my head. "You didn't particularly like me back then, if you recall, and I'm pretty sure you would've balked at having me as your landlord."

"Probably," I grudgingly admit. "But you could've said something since we started seeing each other."

"Yes, I could've, but we've both had other things

on our minds, and besides, I didn't want to make things potentially awkward. As for manipulating you? I don't see it that way. Is it such a bad thing for your brother to want you safe? Or for me to want to make sure the woman I love is well looked after?"

"You weren't in love with me then." My protest is feeble and I know it. Call it a final spasm in a battle already lost.

"Not in love, maybe, but if you remember correctly, I was pretty smitten with you right from the start. You're the one who shut me down ruthlessly." I feel his chest move as he chuckles in my hair.

"That's true. You did make a move that first time." I turn and slide my body up his until we're nose to nose. "I probably should apologize for that."

"No need," he says, grinning. He slides his hands over my ass to the backs of my legs, encouraging me to pull my knees up until I sit astride him, my core poised over the crown of his engorged cock. "You were more than worth the wait."

I straighten up, put my hands along his jaw, and lean in, my tongue tasting his lips before slipping between.

"I love you, BCHoldings at gmail dot com." With my eyes on his, I slowly sink down his length.

—

"So what does BC stand for?" I ask when we finally make it into bed.

His eyebrow shoots up. "You have to ask? I thought that would be clear after making you come for the second time in the past hour."

I'm drawing a blank, I have no idea what he's talking about.

"I'm sorry, I've got nothing."

"Wrong, Squirt," he whispers, grabbing my hand and sliding it down to his crotch where I find him hard again. "It's all yours."

It takes me a second.

EPILOGUE

BELLA

"Bella! Get your butt up here, I need your help!"

It's the fear in my brother's voice that has me running up the stairs, two at a time.

Jasper and I stopped in at Damian and Kerry's place on our way back home after a relaxing weekend in the Ouray hot springs. Well, the springs were relaxing, but my body was still a bit sore from the hike he dragged me on.

It was worth it though. He convinced me by pointing out that with the dropping temperatures since October hit, this would likely be our last hike for the season. Every weekend since he moved in this past July, we've managed to fit in at least one mini-adventure. Mostly hikes around Durango, but Jasper insisted we visit Ouray before winter hit.

Cascade Falls was beautiful. With daytime

temperatures still shy of freezing, we were virtually alone on the trail and had perfect conditions climbing up to the falls. I guess I could've guessed something was up when he picked out a rock for us to sit on, and pulled a full picnic from his backpack, complete with two small bottles of champagne.

I certainly didn't expect the small velvet box that appeared in his hand or the simple two-word proposal that followed. I didn't need words. Every day Jasper shows me how much I mean to him, so it took me no time at all to throw myself around his neck, and tell him yes. About twenty times, before he shut me up with a kiss I still feel on my lips.

We spent a frosty night lounging in the hot springs, which went a long way to soothing my muscles. And a hot night in our hotel room after.

This morning, after we'd had breakfast and were packed and ready to head home, I was primed to share the news with someone.

My brother and his wife were beyond excited, but shortly after we got here Kerry said she wasn't feeling great and was going to have a bath. The past month has been pretty tough on her physically, to the point Damian insisted she hand over all responsibilities for her bookstore over to her assistant, Marya.

She's been home the past week, and from conversations we've had on the phone, she can't wait for the final almost three weeks to be over.

I knock on the bathroom door, which is immediately opened by an alarmed looking Damian.

Kerry is in the tub, her head back and her eyes closed, a telltale blush high on her cheeks and her forehead.

"What's going on?"

"She's having fucking contractions, and won't come out of the damn tub," my brother growls.

"That's okay," I assure him. "Why don't you run downstairs and get my kit out of Jasper's truck? I just need a pair of gloves," I quickly add when I see the panic on his face.

The moment he runs out of the bathroom, I crouch down next to Kerry and put my hand on her forehead. She blinks open an eye.

"Hey." I smile gently. "Looks like maybe junior has had enough of waiting too?"

"Looks like," she says, trying to smile but that immediately turns into a grimace when the next contraction hits. These are doozies, I can see her stomach tighten in a way that tells me she's in active labor. From a general not feeling well to this means things are moving at lightning speed.

Damian comes charging back up the stairs, this time with Jasper following, but he stops in his tracks when he sees Kerry is in the tub and stays discreetly outside.

"Was that another one?" Damian asks, as I move aside to open my bag and he sits down beside her head.

"Yup." I quickly locate the box of gloves and pull on a pair. I shoot Jasper a quick glance, before turning back to Kerry, trusting he read my message correctly.

"Honey, before your next contraction, I'm just going to quickly check you, is that okay? I have a feeling things are moving fast."

"Jesus! We should be in the hospital."

I give my brother a sharp look. "Would you like to stay?" I ask him with my eyebrow raised.

"Fuck yes."

"Excellent, then since your wife is cool as a cucumber, and perfectly relaxed, I suggest you take your cues from her." I get a sharp nod and an irritated look in response. Whatever. "Kerry, can you put your heels together, pull them as close as you can to your bum, and drop your knees to the side? Yes, just like that."

It takes me two seconds to confirm what I suspected. There's no way we'll be able to get her in a car and to the hospital.

I wait for the next contraction to pass before I address Kerry. "From what I could feel, you barely have any cervix left, but your bag of water is bulging ahead of the baby's head. Now you can stay in the tub if you really want, but it's a little difficult to move around you, so I think if there's any way you can, I'd much prefer you in bed or on the floor."

"If I can get her to come out of the tub, we're going straight to the hospital," Damian states.

"And then your wife is likely to have her baby on the side of the road. Is that what you want?"

"I'll try the bed." Kerry's eyes are closed but her hand searches for my brother's, and I get a little choked up when she whispers, "It'll be okay, Bella knows what to do."

"Can you toss me that towel?" I point at the towel hanging behind Damian, and drape it over Kerry, so at least she's half decent. "Did you put the old shower curtain under the sheet like I suggested last week?"

"It's still sitting on the dresser."

I turn to Jasper, who is back in the doorway, giving me a little nod before disappearing again. Apparently he doesn't need many words either.

"As soon as Jas is back and this contraction is done, the two of you are going to have to help her out of the tub." Catching on, my brother just nods affirmatively.

JASPER

I quickly toss the pillows on the floor, pull the comforter off the bed, and slip the plastic between the mattress and the fitted sheet. It takes no more than a minute before I'm back in the doorway.

"Jas?"

I quickly move past Bella and help Damian get his wife to her feet. With Kerry mostly held up between us, we barely get her out of the tub, before she threatens to go to her knees with another contraction.

"Her water just broke," Bella says, but I think Kerry is beyond hearing.

Between us, we manage to get her in bed, and I'm

about to slip out of the room, when Bella calls me back.

"I need all the clean towels and sheets you can find. Linen closet is the narrow door next to the bathroom."

"Is there anything you want me to boil?" I ask when I hand over a stack of linens. Bella actually chuckles at that.

"No thanks. Anything else I need I have in my bag. But I think you can get a stiff drink ready for Damian, he's gonna need it. And before you come back up, could you unlock the door so the EMTs can get in?"

I love that she blindly trusts I understood her earlier message and followed through. No words necessary.

Instead of just pouring Damian a drink, I grab three tumblers and the bottle. I have a feeling we could all use one after.

I open the door a crack and head back upstairs, where I sit down on the floor in the hallway and listen to Bella's calm and confident voice guide Kerry.

Barely twenty minutes after Damian first called her upstairs, I hear the first tentative cries of a newborn, and I take a head start and pour myself a stiff one to celebrate.

"Ma? Congratulations."

Damian hasn't stopped grinning.

The EMTs arrived about ten minutes too late. They came in, offered to take mother and child to Mercy for aftercare, but Kerry adamantly refused. So instead, they stayed to look the baby over and make sure Kerry was all right, before heading back to Durango with an empty rig.

We're all sitting around the bed, Kerry is nursing the little one, and the three of us are nursing a scotch, when Damian calls his family on speakerphone.

"What? Already? Is it a girl? Like I said?"

"It's a boy," Bella says, smiling at her brother.

"It's a boy!" we hear her muffled yell, presumably to Ignacio, before she gets on the phone again. "What time are visiting hours over?"

"We're not in the hospital, Ma. Kerry delivered at home," Damian says, looking at his wife with pride.

"What? What do you mean she delivered at home?"

"Things went so fast. We were lucky Bella happened to be here." Now it's my turn to look proudly at my wife-to-be, as I put my arm around her and she snuggles into my side.

"Bella?"

"You should've seen her, Ma. She was an absolute rock. I don't know what we would've done without her."

At his heartfelt words, I feel Bella turn to hide her face in my chest.

"Best weekend ever."

"You can say that again," I tell her, my face buried in her hair.

I tighten my arm around her, and pull her even closer to my front, as her fingers play through the hair on my arm.

"Dante Ignacio Gomez. Did you see Papa's face when they told him?"

"Sure did," I mumble.

I almost had to drag her away from Kerry and baby Dante. Her parents showed up just two and half hours after Damian called them with the news, and after another hour or two of celebrating both Dante's birth and our engagement, she finally conceded. Unfortunately, she is clearly too wired to sleep. Not even the orgasm I gave her tired her out. We've been in bed for near two hours already and clearly her mind hasn't topped spinning yet.

"Jas?"

"Mmmm."

"Did today scare you?"

"No. Why do you say that?"

"I was just wondering. With Damian freaking out at first, I thought maybe you'd think twice about having kids."

"Is that what you've been mulling over?"

"Maybe."

I press my lips to the soft skin behind her ear.

"I can't think of anything better than to have babies with you. I've only ever dreamed of a family of my own."

For a minute, I think perhaps she's finally fallen asleep, but then she turns with tears in her eyes but a cheeky smile on her lips.

"Wanna start now?"

THE END

ACKNOWLEDGMENTS

This time I want to start with the blogging community. If ever there was an underappreciated breed of people, bloggers would be it. These women (and men) who give tirelessly of their time, without any compensation for the hours they put in promoting the work of others, are often forgotten, and the reality is, we wouldn't get our books seen if it wasn't for their continued efforts. Thank you, from the bottom of my heart, for sharing, promoting, reading and reviewing my books.

My Barks & Bites group of friends always look out for me. They have one thing in common: love for my books. There are no words to thank them enough.

Deb, Debbie, Pam, Sam and Nancy: thank you so much for picking apart my manuscript. You are imperative in making Cabin 12 the best it can be.

Two women who have become indispensable to me are my fabulous editor, Karen Hrdlicka, and my amazing proofreader, Joanne Thompson, who are much, much more than those titles suggest. They are co-plotters, critique partners, mood stabilizers, voices of reason, cheering squad, and most importantly they are my friends, and I truly would not know what to do without them.

My agent, Stephanie Phillips of SBR Media, should actually be added to that list above. In our daily talks she listens to my rants and insecurities, before smoothing my feathers or boosting my confidence. Stephanie is my guru and I'm blessed she was willing to take me under her wing.

A new addition to my team in recent months is Buoni Amici Press, or Debra and Drue—the double Ds as I call them. In the short time we've worked together they have taught me so much about marketing and advertising, and I have no trouble putting myself in their more than capable hands.

I also want to thank Ena and Amanda of Enticing Journey for their incredible professionalism and their ongoing support in promoting my stories. You guys are amazing.

Last but certainly not least my readers—thank you for the kind words of appreciation, the warm hugs of friendship, and the fabulous shows of support. Without you there would be no point.Love you all.

ABOUT THE AUTHOR

Freya Barker inspires with her stories about 'real' people, perhaps less than perfect, each struggling to find their own slice of happy, but just as deserving of romance, thrills and chills, and some hot, sizzling sex in their lives.

Recipient of the RomCon "Reader's Choice" Award for best first book, "Slim To None," Freya has hit the ground running. She loves nothing more than to meet and mingle with her readers, whether it be online or in person at one of the signings she attends.

Freya spins story after story with an endless supply of bruised and dented characters, vying for attention!

CONTACT FREYA @
freyabarker.writes@gmail.com